# Praise for the novels of Heather Graham

"An incredible storyteller."
—*Los Angeles Daily News*

"Graham wields a deftly sexy and convincing pen."
—*Publishers Weekly*

"A fast-paced and suspenseful read
that will give readers chills while keeping them
guessing until the end."
—*RT Book Reviews* on *Ghost Moon*

"If you like mixing a bit of the creepy
with a dash of sinister and spine-chilling reading with
your romance, be sure to read Heather Graham's
latest…Graham does a great job of blending
just a bit of paranormal with real, human evil."
—*Miami Herald* on *Unhallowed Ground*

"Eerie and atmospheric, this is not late-night reading
for the squeamish or sensitive."
—*RT Book Reviews* on *Unhallowed Ground*

"The paranormal elements are integral to the
unrelentingly suspenseful plot, the characters are
likable, the romance convincing, and, in the wake of
Hurricane Katrina, Graham's atmospheric depiction of
a lost city is especially poignant."
—*Booklist* on *Ghost Walk*

"Graham's rich, balanced thriller sizzles with
equal parts suspense, romance and the paranormal—
all of it nail-biting."
—*Publishers Weekly* on *The Vision*

"Heather Graham will keep you in suspense
until the very end."
—*Literary Times*

"Mystery, se
What's
—*Kirkus* or

D0965189

## Also by HEATHER GRAHAM

\* \* \* \* \*

Look for the next *Krewe of Hunters* novel,
*Sacred Evil* by Heather Graham.
Available from MIRA Books
wherever books are sold.

# HEATHER GRAHAM

## HEART OF EVIL

WITHDRAWN

MIRA®

**MIRA®**

Recycling programs
for this product may
not exist in your area.

ISBN-13: 978-0-7783-2998-5

HEART OF EVIL

Copyright © 2011 by Heather Graham Pozzessere

# Prologue

Blood.

She could see it, smell it.

*Hear* it.

Drip...drip...drip...

The air was heavy with black powder, and the brilliant red color of the blood seemed to form a mist with the powder, and she was surrounded by a haze, a miasma of gray-tinged crimson. The day was dying, becoming red, red like the color of the blood seeping to the ground, making that terrible, distinctive noise. Drip, drip, drip...

Ashley Donegal was there. She wasn't even sure where *there* was, but she knew that she didn't want to be there.

Suddenly, the mist seemed to swirl in a violent gust, and then settle softly, closer to the ground. It parted as she walked through. She could see her surroundings, and, at that moment, she knew. She was in the cemetery. She had played here so often as a child—respectfully, of course. Her grandfather never would have had it any other way. Those elegant tombs, all constructed with such love, and an eye to the priorities of the day. The finest craftsmen had been hired, artists and artisans, and the place was truly beautiful. Angels and archangels graced the various tombs, winged cherubs, saints and crosses. She had never been afraid.

But now...

From a distance, she could hear shouts. Soldiers. Ridiculous. Grown men playing as soldiers. But they did it so well. She might almost have been back in time. The powder came from the howitzer and the Enfield rifles. The shouts sounded as the men played out their roles, edging from the river road to the outbuildings and then the stables, to the final confrontation on the lawn and in the cemetery. The blood would come from stage packets within their uniforms, of course, but...

This was *real* blood. She knew because it had a distinctive odor, and because, yes, damn it, she could *smell* it. Nothing smelled like real blood.

She looked at the ground, and she could see the puddle where the blood was falling, but she was afraid to look up. If she looked up, she would see a dead man.

But she did so anyway. She saw him. There was a hat pulled low over his face, but soon he would lift his head.

He did. And she saw a man in his prime, handsome, with strength of purpose in the sculpture of his face. But there was weariness in his eyes.

Weariness and death. Yet they were just playacting; that past was so, so long ago now....

She didn't speak. Neither did he. Because his face began to rot. It blackened, and while she watched, the scabrous decaying flesh began to peel away. Soon she was staring into the empty eye sockets of a skull.

She started to scream.

Above that sound, she could hear someone calling to her. Someone calling her name. The sound was deep, rich and masculine, and she knew it....

*It was Jake!* He would help.... Surely he would help.

But she could only stare at the skeletal mask in front of her.

Smell the blood.

And scream.

A strange sound in the middle of the night awoke Ashley. She sat up with a start and realized she was doing the screaming. She clamped her own hand quickly over her mouth, embarrassed and praying that she hadn't roused the household. She waited in silence; nope, no one.

That was pretty pathetic. It must have been a horrifically pathetic scream. If she ever really needed to scream, she'd probably be out of luck.

Lord, that had been some nightmare.

She didn't *have* nightmares. She was the most grounded human being she knew; hell, she had grown up next to a bayou full of alligators and cottonmouths, and she had lived in a downtrodden area of New York City near Chinatown in order to afford NYU. She knew all about *real* monsters—ghosts were creations to reel tourists in.

So...

With a groan, she threw her head back on her pillow and glanced at the clock. She needed to sleep. In a week's time, they'd be celebrating Donegal Plantation's biggest annual event: the reenactment of the skirmish here that had cost her ancestor his life.

Ah, yes, and she had been dreaming about the skirmish—or the reenactment?

That was it, she thought, grinning. She was dreaming about the events at Donegal Plantation because they were preparing for the day.

History was always alive at Donegal. The plantation house was furnished with antiques, most of which had been in the family forever. There was an attic room that contained more artifacts from the Civil War than many a museum, down to letters, mess kits, knapsacks, pistols, rifles and bayonets. Still, the reenactment remained a major undertaking.

But they'd been running it since before she had even been born. It was rote by now. All the same, there was still plenty of bustle and confusion, along with everything that had to happen before the event could take place, including a mound of paperwork on her desk that had to do with the "sutler's tent," the pop-up shop where period clothing and curios and other paraphernalia, such as weapons and antiques, were sold. Which meant registrations and taxes. Then there was the insurance they needed for the day, and the officers to direct traffic and so on.

That was it. She just had a lot on her mind.

And the reenactment always reminded her of Jake. He'd never been a soldier, North or South. But he'd dressed up, and he'd played his guitar and sang music from the era. And sometimes she had played with him, and he'd always known how to make it just right, to bring back the past, with the light of truth.

She eased down in her covers, determined to forget both her anxiety and Jake.

Not so easy, even though it had been a long time since Jake had been in her life.

Finally, she started to drift again. She was comfortable; she loved her bed and her room, even if she had lived here her whole life other than college. Though she loved to learn about new people and new places, she also loved to be home.

She started again, certain that she had felt a touch; something soft and gentle, smoothing her hair, stroking her cheek.

She sat up. Moonlight streamed into the room, and there was no one else here; with so many guests around, she had locked her bedroom door. She looked at her pillow and decided that she had merely rubbed against a side of the pillowcase.

As she did so, she glanced at her dresser.

There was something different about it. She studied it for a moment, wondering what it was.

Then she knew.

She kept a picture of her parents there, on her dresser. It had been taken almost twenty years ago. They were together, holding her between them, when she had been five. It had been developed in sepia tone, and they'd had it done when one of the guests at a reenactment had found a way of making nice money by pretending to be Matthew Brady, the famed Civil War photographer. Throughout the day, he had answered historical questions about photography and its place in the Civil War.

As was the custom of the day, none of them was smiling, but there was still something exceptionally charming about the picture. There was a light in her father's eyes, and just the hint of a curl at her mother's lips. Her father's arm was around her, his hand coming to rest tenderly on her mother's shoulder. She was sandwiched close between them, and in her mind, the picture had been filled with love. It had become an even greater treasure when she had lost them.

It usually faced at a slight angle toward her bed.

The picture was turned away, as if someone had been looking at it from a different angle. It was such a little thing, but…

Maybe someone had wandered into her room. Cliff ran the property and she ran the house, but they employed extra housekeepers in the main house when they had guests. They hadn't had guests *in* the house in the last few weeks, but the house was usually open, and her grandfather loved to walk anyone staying on the property through it. Depending on his mood, a tour could get long.

And the picture…

She turned over, groaning. It was just the angle of the picture.

Jake Mallory should have slept well, with a hard case finally settled.

But he didn't.

The odd thing about his nightmares was that they were a recent phenomenon. When he had begun to realize and make use of this gift or curse—those things he somehow *knew*—there had been no dreams.

During the summer of the storms, during Katrina and the flooding, they had all been so busy. While it had been happening, he'd never explained to his co-workers that he was so good at finding the remains of the deceased because they called out to him; they spoke to him. It was heartbreaking; it was agony. But the dead needed their loved ones to know, and so he listened. And he didn't dream those nights.

Later, the dreams had come, and they were always the same.

He was alone in his small, flat-bottomed boat, though he'd never been alone during any of the searches.

He was alone, and the heat of the day had cranked down to the lesser heat of the night, and he was searching specifically for someone, though he didn't know who. As the boat moved through the water that should have been a street, he began to see people on the rooftops, clinging to branches here and there, and even floating in the water.

They saw him; they reached out to him. And he felt like weeping. They weren't living people. They were those who had lost the fight.

As he drifted along, he looked back at them all, men and women, old and young, black and white and all colors in between. He wanted to ease their suffering, but he could no longer save them. Their faces had an ashen cast, and the bone structure was sucked in and hollow; they didn't seem to know that there was nothing he could do for them anymore. In the dream, he knew that he, like many law-enforcement officers, scent dogs and volunteers, would be called upon to find the dead in the future.

But now he was seeking the living.

They called out to him; they were trying to tell him something. Bit by bit, he saw they were trying to show him the way. He thought that there should have been sound, but there was none. He didn't hear his passage through the water, and nothing emitted from the mouths of the corpses he passed.

Then he saw the figure on the roof far ahead. He thought it was a woman. She seemed to be in something flowing, which was not unusual. Many victims, living and dead, had been found in nightgowns or boxers or flannel pajamas. What was strange was that she seemed to be the only one alive. She was in tremendous peril as the water rose all around her. He felt that there was something familiar about her, but he didn't understand what it was that seemed to touch him. The light of the full moon turned her hair golden and gleaming, her white gown flowed in the breeze. Amidst the destruction, she was a beautiful survivor.

He tried to get closer.

The watery road grew more clogged and congested. Downed tree branches and appliances floated by. A soaked teddy bear with big black button eyes stared at him sightlessly as it drifted. He ached inside; it was an agony to fight the river, but it was also something he knew he had to do. Especially when *she* waited; when he could save her. He just had to reach her before the water level rose higher and higher, and swept her away.

He grew close…

And that was when he felt the darkness at his back.

He tried to turn, but he could not. The wind had picked up, and the effort was too much. No matter how he strained, he couldn't see what evil thing seemed to be tracking him.

There was suddenly sound. The woman. She was calling out to him.

She called him by name.

But he could feel the thing behind him gaining on him. He could almost reach out for her, but he had to turn, had to find out what seemed to be breathing fetid air down his back....

She called out again.

*Jake!*

If they were to survive, to outrun whatever horror was behind him, they would have to do so together.

*Jake!*

Her voice rang out almost as clearly as if she were next to him in the boat.

But the darkness was on him, so close....

He could feel it then, enveloping him, crushing the sound of her voice as it did.

And he woke with a jerk.

Jake sat up in bed, deeply disturbed by the reappearance of his frequent dream. For the first time, he knew who he had seen on the roof of the house, about to be swallowed up by the floodwaters.

It was Ashley. Ashley Donegal.

He stood and stretched, irritated. The clock on his mantel indicated it was still early.

He swore and got dressed. He knew why he'd had the dream—and made Ashley the woman on the rooftop. He knew the date. The reenactment was coming. Donegal Plantation would be busy and alive; Ashley would still hurt from the fact that her dad had passed away and would no longer be playing Marshall Donegal, his ancestor. But she'd never show it. She'd be the grand mistress of the ceremonies, beautiful and regal in her Civil War attire.

He wondered if he would ever fall out of love with her. And then he wondered if the dream had meant something more. Angela—who seemed to have the best sixth sense in what the FBI called their special unit—had told him that dreams could open many doors. In REM sleep, the mind was at the stage where dreams came, and those dreams could easily focus on what the conscious mind rejected. When she was trying to reach memories of the past, she often used sleep.

If that were the guide, he could easily convince himself to think that Ashley now wanted him. Needed him. And that this was the sign.

Of course, that was just Angela's way of seeking the ghosts of the past—even in their own group, they weren't sure about all the rules of seeking out the help of ghosts.

He wasn't sure if he wanted to laugh at himself or not.

Their team was legitimate; they were on-the-books federal agents. They had just spent days at the local training facility, improving their weapons skills, computer literacy and understanding of the mission policy.

But they were a one-of-a-kind unit, and their true designation wasn't written down anywhere. Among themselves, they were the Krewe of Hunters; on paper, they were Adam Harrison's Special Unit. In bizarre situations, they were supposed to smoke out the fakers—and find what might really be remnants of the past.

The world was filled with ghost hunters and would-be ghost hunters. The problem that most people didn't see was the fact that few ghosts would really appear for a television crew. Some ghost lore did seem to be true. There were the residual hauntings—ghosts that played out a situation, such as a battle scene at Gettysburg, over and over again. And there were intelligent hauntings: ghosts that lingered for some reason. Ghosts didn't seem to have rules. Some could find certain individuals who saw them as clearly as day; they could carry on long conversations, appear and disappear, and interact. Sometimes ghosts were frightened of the living, and they hid, and only someone with a real ability to suspend disbelief could coax them out. It was complicated; he was still learning. Sometimes ghosts tried to warn those they cared about when something evil was about to occur, and ghosts often entered into the REM sleep of those they hadn't managed yet to really touch in the conscious world.

So the dream meant that Ashley needed him....

Or he wanted the dream to mean that Ashley needed him.

He stood up and walked over to his hotel window and looked out over the dark streets of the French Quarter. There was so much history here. So many lives had been lived; so much drama had taken place. Sometimes it was impossible to believe that the energy of the past *didn't* remain. Ghosts didn't have to be old; he knew that himself, though he hadn't wanted to accept the truth until he had met Adam Harrison and become a part of the unit Adam had started for the FBI. He had been glad of his ability to *feel* where people were; to imagine that he heard them telling him to come, please. Sometimes he had even been able to find the living. And sometimes he had heard the voices of the dead, when he hadn't known that they were dead.

His "gift" had cost him Ashley.

So why now, all these years later, was he seeing her, adrift, about to be engulfed, and yet reaching for him, even as he reached for her?

# 1

"Ah, dammit! I don't want to be a Yankee," Charles Osgood said.

It was there; it had finally come, and Ashley was grateful.

And the semi-drama going on here surely meant her mind had been trying to warn her that the day was not going to come without its share of trouble, because it was already proving to be one hell of an afternoon.

Morning had brought the business of breakfast, visitors pouring onto the property to spend time at the campsites. Now they were coming close to the main event of the day, the reenactment of the battle that had taken place at Donegal Plantation.

She'd never expected the real trouble to come over the sad situation of an ailing faux-Yankee.

"Dammit!" Charles exclaimed again.

Ashley thought that the man sounded like a petulant teenager, though she knew that he didn't really want to argue. Not on a day like today. He flushed as the words came out of his mouth, and cast her a quick glance of dismay. She wasn't even the one handing out the assignments, though she was the only Donegal among them now. The relish the group was taking in telling Charles his new role unsettled her a bit. Charles Osgood was the newest in the "cavalry unit" of reenactors, which meant that he got the assignment to play for the other side. Yet this seemed to be turning into a college hazing; they were all friends, and they were usually courteous to one another.

"Charlie, come on! Being a Yankee will be fun. Okay, so they were jerks—well, the ones here—who couldn't spy on a neon sign, couldn't hunt, couldn't shoot.... But come on! Being a Yank will be fun!" Griffin Grant teased.

Ashley shook her head; how could grown men be so immature?

In *her* mind, although she truly loved the living history that took place at the plantation, she thought the units clinging to so-called glory were nothing more than inane. The event had ended with the *death* of one her ancestors—not a party.

"Hey, hey, all of you!" Ashley said, addressing the men around her and using the voice she would utilize when working with one of the school groups—the grade-school groups. "I know you all like to cling to the magical illusion that the antebellum South was a place of beauty, grace and honor—where men were men. Real men, hunting, riding, brawling—but honorable. Yes, we reenact what was. But this is now, and that was then! None of you would seriously want to go back to the Civil War, and no one here is prejudiced. The slavery of any person was a horrendous way of life."

"Ashley—you're making it sound like being a real man is bad thing!" Cliff Boudreaux commented, laughing. Cliff, horse master at Donegal, was clearly amused and having a good time.

"Well, of course, Ashley, it's not like we take this too seriously," Griffin Grant said, staring back at her as if she was the one who didn't understand the question. Griffin was a striking man in his early thirties, sleek and slick, a CEO for a cable company in New Orleans, though his ancestors had lived out here, two hours down the road from the big city. "We know reality—and like it. But this is important playacting!"

She groaned softly.

They were good guys, really.

It was playacting, and for the playacting they were able to believe truly with their whole hearts that it had been about nothing other than states' rights. Ashley knew all the statistics about the fighting men— most of the men who fought and died for the South during the war couldn't have begun to have afforded a slave—and war was seldom caused by one issue. But her parents and her grandfather had never been the types to overlook the plantation's complicated history. Cliff was part of that with his gold-green eyes, bronze-colored skin and dark tawny hair. She knew that half their visitors were immediately enthralled with him. He was one of the reenactors on the Southern side because of the Donegal blood that ran in his veins. Early on, a Donegal widower had fallen in love with a slave, creating the first racial mix in his background. In the 1920s, his great-grandfather had married a Donegal cousin, something that caused a serious scandal at that time in history, but which now gave both halves of the family a sense of pleasure and pride. She wasn't sure how to count second and third or twice-removed relatives, so she considered Cliff to be her cousin.

History was history. Donegal was steeped in it, good and bad, and they didn't hide any of it.

"Charles, they're right. It's a performance, you know," Ashley said. "It's a show, maybe even an important show in its small way. It's where people can see the weapons of the day, the uniforms that were worn. And, actually, remember, this particular fight started because men had a bar brawl—and then an excuse to fight because the war was getting under-way. You're all examples of keeping history alive, and I'm so grateful to all of you."

Charles stared back at her blankly; the other men were smirking.

Why didn't they all get it? They were actors in a show, hopefully teaching American history, with several perspectives, along the way. But some things died really slowly here, in plantation country. Family was still everything. Loyalty to hearth and home, kin, parish and state. They'd been wrong; they'd been beaten, and they knew it, but still, only one side of the cast of players was considered to be elite. And the reenactors could be incredibly snobbish.

That made Charles Osgood the odd man out.

Toby Keaton cleared his throat and then said softly, "Charles—come on. You're lucky to be in with the 27th Bayou Militia Cavalry Unit. Most of the time, the fellows taking part in the reenactments here are direct descendants of those who fought before. You've got to see the truth of this thing. You claim your place in the ranks through marriage—your stepfather was an O'Reilly, and I know he raised you, but, you know, in other old Southern units, that wouldn't count." Toby was forty-four, and Ashley's next-door neighbor at Beaumont, his Creole plantation, though they both had acres and acres of land. Toby grinned as if to cut the harshness of his words. "Newcomer—odd man out. You're a Yankee if I've ever seen one!"

"Great! So now I'm a newcomer—and that makes me an outsider?" Charles asked, staring around the room. "Come on, guys, you've just got to understand. This will really make it look as if I don't belong here at all!"

He gave his appeal to the others gathered at the horse master's office in the old barn at Donegal Plantation that day—Cliff Boudreaux, Griffin Grant, Toby Keaton, Ramsay Clayton, Hank Trebly, all still with property in the general area, John Ashton, tour director from New Orleans, and Ashley herself. The

"Yankees" were gathering in the old smokehouse—
a separate building, and now a small apartment.
Charles would be joining them soon; all of the reenactors gathered together for their roundtable discus-
sions on the war, but each side met separately first on
the day of the reenactment to make sure that every
member knew the character he was playing. Later,
they'd all meet back here to make sure that everyone
was apprised of all the safety factors involved.

One, Charles, so it seemed, would have to play a
Yankee, and go join the group in the apartment. They
were short a Yankee, and that's the way it was. All of
them belonged to Civil War roundtables, and these
days, none of them really cared about sides—they
just liked to discuss tactics and procedure. They often
met in the dining room at Donegal; Ashley loved to
listen, because they also knew their history, and they
spoke about events in the lives of many of the key
players in the war, and the fact that the generals had
often been best friends before they had been forced
to choose sides in the bloody conflict. They knew
about weapons, uniforms, sad stories about treason
and resisters, draft riots, food, clothing, trade and so
much more.

"Charles," Cliff Boudreaux said patiently. "We're
all just teasing you here, really. We're short on Yankees today, on account of Barton Waverly being sick
with the flu. We're pretty desperate. And that's the
rule; newcomers play Yankees when our brothers
from up North ask for help. Hell, remember that year

when half of us were laid up with the croup? Three of them Yankees had to come play Southern boys. We're not doing anything bad to you—really."

Ramsay Clayton was seated across the table from Cliff. Ramsay looked like an artist; he was tall, with a wiry muscle structure, long dark hair and classical features. He owned a small place down the road, but he spent a lot of time in New Orleans, where he sometimes showed his work at Jackson Square and sometimes had showings at the galleries. He grinned at Charles. "Yeah, and don't forget, the Yankees won. Hell, come to think about it, where were all the Southern boys when we were losing this thing?" he asked lightly. "Ah, well. Born in our day and age, it's easy to look back at the South's part in the Civil War and wonder, 'What the hell were we thinking?'"

Ashley smiled. She liked Ramsay. He was a good guy.

"Well, I wish I could just step up to the plate, but I can't. I can't play a Yankee—I just can't," Toby Keaton said. "Hell, my great-great-great-whatever grandfather was the first one to answer Marshall Donegal's call for volunteers. He was one of his best friends. I think he'd roll in his grave if I played a Yankee. Good God! I own a plantation! Wouldn't be fitting for me to play a Yankee. Lord knows, it could be bad for business."

Hank Trebly grinned. "Well, I'm just big sugar. I don't really give a whit. I see the war as over, over, over, and that's the way it is. Lord A-mighty! The damn thing ended in 1865." Hank owned the property next to Donegal, and his ancestors had owned it forever. The old plantation had been replaced by a sugar refinery years ago. He was a small man, in his early forties, and his business meant everything to him.

John Ashton shrugged. "My family might have been here, but I don't care," he said. "The Civil War means my income these days—tourists love to go back. But I love 'em all. Yankees, rebels, Brits, Brazilians! Bring them on. They all spend money and take tours."

"And what happened here was in 1861, for God's sake, before the thing had really even gotten going," Griffin said, shaking his head. "Come on, now! My ancestor went on to die at the Second Battle of Manassas—now, that's a damned big battle. We're here to teach, and to remember everything that happened in the past—and how it made us what we are today. Let's have fun, folks. C'mon—I come out here to forget the office and programming and statistics, computers and red tape. I don't care who plays what. It's just for a good time."

"I spend most of my time in New Orleans, art on the square and all that—you can call me a doughboy for all I care. It's the spirit of this thing," Ramsay said. "And Lord knows, what happened here couldn't even be called a battle. My ancestor and most of the Southern boys except for Marshall survived, but, as we've all pointed out now—the

North won. We are living the United States of America. This wasn't even really a battle."

He was right. What had taken place late in 1861 hadn't even been a battle. Drinking downriver, toward New Orleans, two Yankee spies had heard about Donegal's then-owner—Marshall Donegal—preparing a major summons to area troops to prepare them for an invasion of New Orleans. In trying to draw Marshall Donegal's men out further on the subject, they had all gotten into a fistfight when one made a ridiculous statement about Northerners being chickens. The two Confederates suspected the men of being spies, and had run back to Donegal. The spies went back to their headquarters, but they were *spies,* and thus their numbers were small. On each side, six men were mustered—and, rather than be executed as spies if they were caught, the Union men donned their uniforms.

The fighting had ranged from the stables to the porch of the main house and out to the chapel and cemetery—ending when Captain Marshall Donegal had died of a bayonet wound in his own family graveyard. The enemy had "skedaddled," according to the Southern side; the rebels had been left in utter defeat, according to their Northern counterparts.

Now, the "battle" was something that taught history, and, largely due to its small size—and the fact that the current owner of the plantation, Ashley's grandfather, Frazier Donegal, was a history buff and glad to welcome the units on his property—it was a popular event. "Living history" took place frequently at Donegal, as often as once a week, but an actual reenactment was done only once a year. Sometimes the actors doing the reenactments were involved in other locations. Some belonged not just to Civil War units, but Revolutionary War units, and it just depended on where the biggest shindig was going on. Luckily, most of the men who could claim to have had ancestors in the brawl loved the plantation and the nearly exact-to-the-past-moment location of the place, and they usually made this reenactment a priority.

Donegal House was surely one of the prettiest places left on the river road, with memories of the antebellum era held in place. The great house still maintained a gorgeous front. It had been built with magnificent Greek columns and wraparound porches, and elegant tree-shaded entries stretched forever before the front and back doors. The currently used stables, housing only six horses, were next to the house, while the larger stables needed in a bygone era were far back from the house, to the left, riverside, and offered three apartments for those who wanted to stay for the night. The old smokehouse and servants' quarters were available for rent as well, and sometimes they even rented out five of the rooms in the main house. With Beth there, Ashley's extraordinarily talented friend and chef, and the efforts they were making with the restaurant and the crazy business that came along with the reenactment, they had chosen this year just to let rooms in the outbuildings.

All this—living history and their bed-and-breakfast rentals—was done to survive into the twenty-first century. But the Donegal family had been letting the place out for nearly thirty years now. And the living history and the reenactments were the true highlights to be found here, distinguishing it from other great plantations along the river.

"Okay, sure. You all are right," Charles said. "It's over. Long over. Hell, the Yankees did win the war."

Cliff laughed. "Still hard to convince my mama and a few other folks I know that it's true. But thanks, Charles, that's great. The Yanks are good guys. Man, it's sad to think back, though, huh? We would have wound up being enemies."

"Who knows what our feelings would have been back then?" Ashley asked. "We might have chosen to fight for the North."

"It was a different time, a different lifestyle," Griffin pointed out. "You're all indignant now about injustice, but you didn't live back then. You didn't grow up in an economy of cotton and sugar."

"Rich men wanted to stay rich," Ramsay agreed dryly.

"Who's being Marshall Donegal today?" Charles asked.

"That would be me," Ramsay said. "I've done it the past five years." He was quiet a minute; he had done it since Ashley's father had passed away. "Ashley could don a uniform herself, but she thinks we boys should just be boys. So I get the honor."

Ramsay was trying to move quickly past the mention of her father, Ashley knew. He had been gone five years now; he had died shortly after her mother. She had accepted their loss—and she knew as well that there would still be a little core of pain when she thought about them, even if she lived to be one hundred. Inwardly, she winced. She hadn't just lost her father that day; that had been the end of her and Jake. Her fault, her call, and she still wasn't sure why. He had frightened her, she thought. It seemed he had scratched the surface of something, and she didn't want to know what was beneath. And still, to this day, she knew that although she had closed the door, she missed Jake. And missing Jake had colored everything else in her life.

"He died," Charles reminded him. "Marshall Donegal was killed, you know," he added quickly.

"Well, as we've said, the war is long over, so I guess they're all dead now anyway," Ramsay pointed out.

"Gentlemen," Ashley said, speaking at last, "I want you all to know that you are greatly appreciated. You're all such wonderful actors, taking on whatever role is needed, whenever it's needed! Charles, the Yankees are great guys. Michael Bonaventure lives in town, and his ancestors lived there as well, right in the heart of the French Quarter. His family left when the war started, because Bonaventure's ancestor was fighting for the Union. Hadley Mason is from Lafayette, but his ancestors agreed with the Northern cause as well. It will be fun for you to be a Yankee. It's acting, just like when we act out the encampments. And I truly appreciate you taking on the role."

"It's really amazing," Griffin said. "We do get all tied up in what *was*. The way the past still has so much to do with the present! Charles, come on, you're a *stepchild*. We all really had ancestors back then who were involved with this thing. You're welcome among us—totally welcome. But, hey, if I had come in on this recently, I'd be happy just to be a part of it all."

Charles Osgood offered Ashley a weak smile. "Sure. You know me—I'm just happy to be here."

To Ashley's surprise, Ramsay Clayton suddenly spoke up again. "Charles, I have an idea. Some of those guys really are my friends. My good friends. I'll be a Yankee today. You be Marshall Donegal."

Charles opened his mouth, stunned, and stared at Ramsay. "Oh! Oh, no. I couldn't take that honor away from you!"

"You get killed, you know," Ramsay reminded him.

"Oh, like you said, they're all dead now. I just couldn't—I really couldn't."

"Hey, I think I want to be a Yankee for once," Ramsay said. "It's cool. You be Marshall Donegal, and I'll be a Yankee. No arguments—it's decided. I'll be a winner for a change!"

"I don't know what to say!" Charles told him.

"Say thanks, and let's get on with it. We have to finish planning this thing," Ramsay said.

"I'm going to be Marshall Donegal!" Charles said, still awed.

Ashley lowered her head, hiding her laughter. These guys really were like children when it came to the reenactment. They were so dedicated. But it was really good, she reminded herself. They kept history alive. It had been on a trip to Europe with her parents when she had seen the quote that meant so much to her: "Those who cannot remember the past are condemned to repeat it." It was the philosopher George Santayana who had written those words, and she had seen them above the gates of a concentration camp. So, whether history was sterling or not—pitting man at his best and his worst—it was necessary to remember.

The reenactors did a fantastic job. Although there had been only a small encampment at Donegal Plantation at the time, they recreated a larger one, complete with a medical tent, where surgeries were acted out, officers' quarters and tents for enlisted men.

"This is a right nice place to meet, but we need to get to business," Griffin said, winking at Ashley.

"Yeah, Ramsay, looks like you need to skedaddle!" Cliff teased.

"I'm out of here!" Ramsay said, rising. He looked

around. "Sadly, I do like Cliff's digs better than being cramped up in an apartment!"

Griffin was right: they *were* in a nice place to meet. The office/living quarters in the stables were extremely pleasant; there was no heavy smell of hay, horses or droppings in any way, since the office had long ago been fitted out with air-conditioning and an air purifier to boot. There were a number of trophies along with books on horses, horse care, tack and maps on the shelves around the old massive desk with its iMac and printer. It was the horse master's realm. No matter the state of riches or poverty the Donegal Plantation might be in, there was always a horse master. These days, the horse master did more than look after the six horses that remained. He was a tour guide, overseer—though they didn't grow anything other than a few flowers now and then and a tomato plant or two—and general man about the house.

Ashley stood and gave him a shove. "Our apartments are beautiful. Get on out of here, and get this all moving!" She spoke with teasing force. "I'm going out to check on the camp setup and see that everything is running smoothly, then get ready. I'll leave you gentlemen to agree on the final assignments and action. The day is moving on. We need to be prepared to start with the battle at sundown."

"Hell, I hope they got a uniform that will fit me!" He winked. Ramsay was a good guy. He had a small house that had once been a working plantation, but his land had been eaten up over the years.

Plantation actually meant farm, and Ramsay had no farmland left at all. He spent most of his time in the city, where he actually was a working artist making a nice income.

"I'm off to join the Yankees!"

"Thanks!" Charles Osgood lifted a hand to Ramsay, and then to Ashley, looking dazed. He was getting the prime role for the day, and he still seemed to be surprised.

It didn't mean as much to Ramsay, Ashley thought, watching him as he walked from the stables to the old barn. He was from here; he'd been born a part of it all. He'd played soldiers over and over again, and though it had been magnanimous of him to hand over the role, she wasn't sure that Ramsay hadn't decided that being a Yankee might not be that bad a thing for the day. After all, they ended the day with the Pledge of Allegiance and the "Battle Hymn of the Republic." Even if they did begin it with a rousing chorus of "Dixie"!

She left Cliff's to make a quick check of the horses. "Thank God you darlings don't care if you're Yankees or rebels!" she said affectionately, pausing to rub Abe's ears. She saw that the tack for the Northern cavalry was ready for each of the mounts, saddles and saddle blankets set on sawhorses and the bridles with their insignias hanging from hooks right outside the stalls. Abe, Jeff, Varina, Tigger, Nellie and Bobby were all groomed and sleekly beautiful, ready to play their parts. She paused to give Varina a pat; she loved all the horses, but Varina was her special mare, the horse she always chose to ride.

Leaving the stables, Ashley paused for a moment to look across the expanse of acreage to the left, where the tents of the living encampment had been set up. She could see the sutler's stretch of canvas, and she walked over to see who was working that day. Tourists—parked way down the river road—were milling around the goods for sale. She heard children squealing with delight as they discovered toys from the mid-nineteenth century, just as she heard women ooh and aah over some of the corsets and clothing. She saw that a crowd had gathered around the medical tent where reenactors were doing a spectacular job of performing an amputation. The patient let out a horrific scream, and then passed out. Dr. Ben Austin—playing his ancestor, also Dr. Ben Austin—stood in an apron covered in stage blood and explained the procedure. Ben would later be part of the battle reenactment, but for now, he was explaining medicine. Ashley reached him in time to capture part of his spiel.

"Amputation was frequently the only choice for a Civil War surgeon, and field surgeons could perform an amputation in as little as ten minutes," Ben told the crowd. "Chloroform existed, but it was scarce. The South had alcohol. When the surgeon could, he would do everything in his power to make the traumatic operation easier for his patient, but at major battles, the pile of amputated limbs could easily grow to be five feet tall. There was no real understanding of germs, and more men died from disease than from wounds or bullets. To carry that further, more men died in the Civil War than in any other American war, and more men died at Sharpsburg, or Antietam, as those of you from the North might know it, than died during the D-Day invasion."

Ben saw Ashley watching him and lifted a bloody hand. Well, it was covered in faux blood from the faux surgery. Ben knew how to be dramatic. She smiled and waved in return and went on, stopping to chat with some of the women who were cooking, darning or sewing at the living-encampment tents. There were soldiers around as well, explaining Enfield rifles to little boys, whittling, playing harmonicas or engaging in other period activities. One laundress was hanging shirts and long johns out to dry—a nice touch, Ashley thought.

"When the war started, the North already had a commissary department—and the South didn't," Matty, the sutler's wife, was explaining to a group who stood around the campfire she had nurtured throughout the day. "Hardtack—dried biscuits, really—molasses, coffee, sugar, salted beef or pork and whatever they could scrounge off the land was what fed the soldiers, and the South had to scramble to feed the troops. Didn't matter how rich you were—you were pretty much stuck with what could be gotten. There were points, especially at the beginning of the war, during which the Southern soldiers were doing all right. They were on Southern soil. But war can strip the land. What I'm doing here is boiling salted beef and trying to come up with something like a gravy to soften up the hardtack. With a few precious spices, salt and sugar, it won't be too bad. A few people can taste, if they like! Of course, I've made sure that our hardtack has no boll weevils. The soldiers were fighting every kind of varmint, big and small, to keep their own food."

Everything seemed to be in perfect order; Ashley's dreams had been for nothing.

Except, of course, that the reenactment always made her think about Jake.

They were due to leave soon, within the next few days, but since Adam Harrison's group was still in New Orleans, they finished with the training they were doing there, and waiting for the move, Jake had agreed to go wandering around the French Quarter with his fellow newly minted agent, Whitney Tremont.

"I must admit, I'm going to be sorry to leave New Orleans," Whitney said. She stared out toward Jackson Square. "There was so much paperwork after the Holloway case, it felt like we were picking up the pieces for days at first. But it's been nice to have this bit of time to get ready for our move, since we're all taking up residence in the D.C. area. Though, I'm excited—I mean, we're going to have *offices*, Jake. Like really cool offices, in a building in Alexandria—with help! A forensics lab! State-of-the-art equipment."

Jake grinned. "Yes, it's going to be interesting to get settled in."

Whitney grinned back. Her skin was like the café au lait that sat before them. He knew that the others had thought the two of them might wind up together, but what they had formed instead was a friendship, deep and binding.

"But it was good, I think—just being thrown together as freelancers of a sort for our first case. Don't you think?" she asked. "But federal positions… though I don't think we really get to stay in those fancy buildings that often, do you?"

"We're like any other team or unit for the FBI, I believe. The cases come in, and I'm assuming that Adam Harrison and Jackson Crow decide what looks like something we should take on. We'll get to discuss the situation then. And make the plans."

"Do you think that any of us could put a case forward?" she asked.

"Sure." He smiled. "Let's face it, Whitney, we are an experiment in paranormal investigations. We're unique, and I'm sure there are those who will make fun of the 'Krewe of Hunters' unit."

"Not anymore. Not after the Holloway case," she said proudly.

"We have to keep proving that we're good at what we do," Jake said. The name "Krewe" they'd given themselves had begun as a joke, but they'd become a real crew through their passion for the work.

"Hmm," Whitney said, twirling her straw in her iced café au lait. "It's here somewhere."

"Here? What's here? Sometimes you make no sense."

That made her laugh. "Only sometimes? I think that our new case is going to be here. Somewhere in Louisiana."

"We're about to move to Alexandria," he pointed out.

"I don't know…I just have a feeling. I don't think we'll be going yet. You wait and see."

"What makes you think that?" Jake asked. Whitney's prowess was with film, sound and video. But she also seemed to have amazing intuition. Of course, they had all been gathered into the group because of their intuition, their ability to solve problems where others could not, but where Angela Hawkins was quiet, finding what she found without much ado, and Jackson would always be the skeptic, Whitney went in wide-eyed, eager for whatever might not be considered *normal*.

"Feelings and logic, that's kind of the Krewe of Hunters motto, right?" she asked.

He laughed, but something was knotting in the pit of his stomach. "I think it's supposed to be *logic—and then feelings*," he told her. He gazed idly across the street. The mule-drawn carriages were starting to arrive in front of Jackson Square. An early-morning tour group was forming on Decatur Street. One of the history tours, he thought.

"Well, of course, good old Jackson, he's still swearing solving cases is all logic, and we all know that he knows best," Whitney said.

Jake wasn't really paying attention. He had seen the tour-group leader come out—he wasn't sure where she had come from. Of course, there were a number of restaurants and bars in the area, and some had been open forever. It was New Orleans. No one frowned if you discovered you were dying for that 8:00 a.m. drink.

The tour guide was a blonde woman dressed in Civil War attire. Her bonnet hid her face, but she was tall and statuesque, and he had a feeling that she was going to be an attractive woman before he saw her face. Assured, probably in her mid to late thirties, she moved among the chattering crowd as they waited.

She was coming toward the sidewalk, politely excusing herself as she did so, but people didn't seem to notice as she made her way through them, which said a lot for the good nature of the group, since she was wearing a respectable day dress with large hoops.

She paused when she reached the sidewalk.

Jake started. She was staring straight at him, and she smiled, but her smile seemed to be very sad. Her mouth moved. He squinted. He wasn't all that much at reading lips, but it was almost as if he could hear her.

*"We're waiting, we need you. Hurry,"* he thought
she said.

"Jake?"

"Huh?" He turned back to look at Whitney.

"Want to move on?" she asked.

"Yes, sure," he agreed. He stood and left a tip on
the table, having already paid the waiter.

When he glanced up again, the tour had moved on
down toward the cathedral. He didn't see the woman,
but they would be walking in the same direction.

"Whitney," he asked as they did so, "did you understand what that woman was trying to say?"

"What woman?"

"She was the guide for that group that's ahead of
us. She looked right over at us and said something,"
Jake told her.

Whitney arched a delicately formed brow. "First,
I didn't see the woman, but I wasn't looking. And
second, if she'd spoken from across the street, unless
she'd been yelling, how could I have heard anything
she had to say?"

He shrugged. "Good point."

They walked up St. Ann Street, took a pedestrian
thruway as they passed by the square, then turned in
right in front of the cathedral, where the tour group
had now paused.

The woman wasn't with them. There was a man
in a top hat and frock coat leading the tour.

Jake stopped short.

"Hey! Hey there, remember me?" Whitney said, nudging him.

"Just a second," Jake said. He knew that the man would finish his spiel about St. Louis Cathedral, and then allow the group to take pictures.

This guide, however, apparently liked to hear himself speak. He added in several personal anecdotes regarding the cathedral, before allowing his group to disperse for pictures.

When the group finally thinned, Jake approached him. The fellow, in his mid-twenties, saw them coming.

"The tour offices are actually on Decatur, sir, if you're interested in any of our offerings. We do history tours, ghost tours, vampire tours, plantation tours—"

"Actually, we're locals and could do the tours," Jake said, interrupting him with a pleasant tone. "I'm just curious—why did you all change tour guides at the last minute?"

The man frowned. "We didn't. I've been scheduled for over a week to do this tour."

Jake frowned. "I saw a woman with your group. She was dressed in antebellum clothing, bonnet and all."

"Oh, she was probably heading for Le Petit Theatre," the tour guide said. "They're doing several performances of *Our American Cousin.* She's a bit early to be in costume for the matinee, but I imagine you saw one of the actresses."

"Oh, well, thanks," Jake said.

"Why?"

"Oh, I just thought she was trying to tell me something," Jake said.

"If she was trying to tell you something, wouldn't she have just done so?" the man asked.

Jake was irritated by the tone; frankly, he hadn't liked the man since he'd heard him giving his own life's history along with the tour.

He felt Whitney's hand on his arm.

He forced a smile. "Thanks, thanks for the help," he said.

Whitney pulled him along. "Jerk," she said.

"Ass," Jake agreed.

"I meant you," Whitney teased. "No, sorry—he was a jerk. But come on now! We don't have any reason to go to the theater."

"But we're going to pass it!" Jake protested.

"Let it go, Jake. You saw an actress, and you thought she had something to say. Without sounding just as jerky as that jerk, it's true—if she'd really wanted to talk to you, she would have come on over. I don't want to help you stalk a woman, Jake."

"I don't want to stalk her. I want to know who she is," Jake said.

But they did pass right by Le Petit Theatre. He couldn't help but stop to read the playbill and look at the pictures of the actors in the show.

"She's not here," he said.

"Well, God knows, this is New Orleans. Maybe

she's just a kook who likes to dress up in Southern belle attire, though God knows why, the heat can be a bitch. Forget it, Jake."

Jake agreed. He didn't know why it was bothering him so much that he'd seen the woman and hadn't been able to talk to her.

That wasn't true. He did know. There had been something vaguely familiar about her, although he couldn't quite put his finger on what it was.

"Jake? Are you okay?" Whitney asked.

"Fine."

"No, you're not."

"It's nothing, really. Hey, nothing that car bombs tonight after dinner with the group won't cure, right?" he said, setting an arm around her shoulders as he led her down the street.

Car bombs weren't going to fix anything. He was truly disturbed by the woman.

Why was she so familiar? Was she real, or was she in his imagination? Had he brought his dream world to the surface, and did he want her to be from Donegal?

It was absurd, even for a ghost hunter, to believe that someone from the past was calling out to him, trying to reach him.

Logic—and then feelings. That was Jackson Crow's motto. It was only logical that he think about Ashley now, and logical that even after all these years, he wanted her to need him.

Logic...

Somehow, it just wasn't working. *Feelings* were taking over. And thoughts of Ashley and Donegal Plantation.

# 2

Ashley surveyed the expanse of the property one last time; everything was going extremely well. Children were playing and laughing, the camp looked wonderful and there were activities going on everywhere.

She headed for the house. It was time for her to become Emma Donegal and get ready for the evening's battle.

But as she walked toward the house, she slowed, paused and looked over at the cemetery. The gate was locked.

Still, a creeping feeling of unease swept over her.

She shrugged it off; a dream was a dream. Good God, she'd dreamed once that she'd kissed Vance Thibault in high school one day, and she loathed him! She hurried on toward the house, trying to forget her unease.

Her grandfather, Frazier Donegal, was sitting on the back porch. She grinned; he looked spectacular, she thought. Frazier was eighty-three, but he showed little sign of slowing down. Today he was dressed in a frock coat, pinstripe breeches and high riding boots—a pure gentleman of the age with his full head of snow-white, a Colonel Sanders mustache and goatee, and bright blue eyes. She worried about him constantly; his health was good, but he *was* eighty-three.

He was really in the mood today, though, she thought. He was sipping a mint julep. He didn't even like mint juleps.

"There you are!" he said. "I was starting to wonder."

Ashley sat in one of the wicker rockers across from him. "Last-minute details in the stables," she told him. "Charles Osgood didn't want to be a Yankee."

Frazier rolled his eyes and shook his head. "It works, you know, for the property, it works. But why on earth everyone always wants to be on the losing side, I'll just never know. Did he finally accept his assignment?"

"He did—but Ramsay Clayton stepped in at the last minute to let him play Marshall Donegal," Ashley said.

"Oh?"

"I don't think Ramsay cares. It's all play to him," she said.

"Ramsay is a good fellow. You think he was trying to appear magnanimous in front of you?" Frazier asked.

Ashley shook her head. "There's never going to

be anything between Ramsay and me, Grampa, there just isn't."

He lifted his hands. "I was just asking about his motives."

Ramsay had asked Ashley out the previous year; she had always liked him. He was a good artist, and a handsome man, but she had never felt the least bit of chemistry with him. He had accepted her wish that they just maintain a good friendship. Ramsay had been on the rebound, having broken up with his longtime lover. She wondered if she was still on the rebound—even if she had been the one who had run from Jake.

"I honestly believe Ramsay just doesn't care," Ashley said. "I think he'll have fun saying, 'Oh, Lord! I had to be a Yankee.' No, Ramsay isn't trying to impress me. Griffin even asked me to be his friendly companion for a dinner he had—and I said no. They all understand that the friendships we have are too important."

"Well, then, good for Ramsay. And you—you better get dressed," Frazier told her.

"Yep, I'm on it."

She rose and walked into the house from the riverside.

The original architects had taken advantage of the river and bayou breezes when they had built the house. It hadn't been changed much since the day it had been built. One long hallway stretched from the front of the house to the back, and before the advent of air-conditioning, the double doors on each end had often been kept open. The house had one unique feature: double winding staircases to a second-floor landing that led to the six bedrooms, three on each side of the house on that floor. The stairway to the third floor, or attic, where there were still two rooms that could be guest rooms or let out to renters, was on the second floor, bayou side, of the house.

Beth Reardon was in Ashley's room, sitting at the foot of the bed and drawing laces through her corset.

Her skin was pure ebony; she was tall, regal and beautifully built. But she had chosen to get into the action. She was wearing a cotton skirt and cotton blouse and her hair was wrapped up in a bandana. She gazed over at Ashley. "Hey! Time is a-wasting, girl. Where have you been?"

"Settling an argument over who had to be a Yankee," Ashley told her.

"Yankee. That's the North, right?" Beth asked. Beth was from New York, and before that, her family had lived in Jamaica. Her accent, however, was all American, and none of her ancestors had been in the United States during the Civil War.

Ashley frowned.

Beth laughed. "Just kidding! Come on, I took history classes."

"Sorry!" Ashley said.

"You should be. Let's get you in this ridiculous contraption. So, people really churned butter in these things? No, wait—your relatives sat around looking pretty while the slaves and servants churned the butter, right?"

"Actually, in our family, everyone worked. And I think that everyone had to sweat when churning butter. Most of the time, the plantation mistress had to work really hard."

"Supervising?"

"And making soap and doing laundry and all the rest," Ashley said. "Well, maybe if you were really, really, really rich you just sat around. We were rich, but not that rich, and if we're ever going to be rich again, it's up to you, since I can barely boil water." Beth had come to work at Donegal as the chef less than a year ago, determined to make the restaurant one of the most important in the South.

"Anyone can boil water," Beth assured her. "And you cook okay. You're not great, but, then, you are one hell of a storyteller. Step into the skirts already, I'm dying to see this show."

Arranging the layers of clothing that constituted the formal dress of a Southern plantation mistress took some time. They both laughed over the absurdity of the apparel that had been required in Louisiana despite the heat and the humidity. Ashley told Beth, "It's worse for the guys. The authentic uniforms are wool—those poor little puppies just die out there."

"Well, honey, I think I'm glad that I'm the unpaid help for this shindig, then," Beth told her, grinning.

"Cotton like this—it's nothing. And I do love the bandana! Poor Emma."

"Yes, it really was poor Emma," Ashley told her. "Lots of the soldiers left journals about what happened at the battle. It was only *after* the war that the rumors about Emma having killed her husband got started. It's as if someone wanted to sully her name. Of course, nothing that we can find was written about her having been charged with the crime."

"But it was a different time. Maybe she did the unthinkable. Maybe she took a lover. Maybe even, God forbid, he was a Yankee or a carpetbagger!"

"Maybe," Ashley agreed. "From all the family lore, she loved her husband, she was devastated when he died, and she managed to hold on to the property and raise her children here, even though the South lost and carpetbaggers did sweep down on the South. Carpetbaggers were even more despised than Yanks," she explained. "They were the people who weren't fighting for a cause—their cause was just to prey off the vanquished and get rich."

A few minutes later, Ashley was ready, and they headed back to the porch that faced the river. A crowd had already gathered, since the schedule for the day was printed out on brochures that attendees could pick up at the entrance to the property. A high-school student, seeking extra credit in history, was usually given that job.

Ashley came out to stand next to her grandfather, looking out over the property as she could see it from the back porch. Bright tape in blue and gray cordoned off the areas where the reenactors would move during the events, though they no longer went into the cemetery for the moment of Marshall Donegal's death and the tactical retreat of the two surviving Union soldiers.

She found herself staring at the cemetery off to her left again. An odd tremor washed over her, but she quickly forgot it and looked at Frazier.

"Nice crowd today," he said quietly. Ashley squeezed his hand.

The small band—posing as the military band that had been part of Marshall Donegal's cavalry unit—launched into the haunting strains of "Dixie."

Frazier Donegal began to speak midway through, giving an excellent history lesson. He didn't shy away from the slavery question, admitting that cotton was king in the South, and sugarcane, and both needed workers. The citizens of the South had not invented slavery; many had clung to it whether, in their hearts, they accepted the injustice or not. Few men like to admit they were wrong or cruel to their fellow human beings. And they had hardly been magnanimous when it meant they would also lose their livelihood. It wasn't an excuse, but it was history. Then as now, prejudice was not something with which a man was born—it was something that was taught. He spoke with passion, conviction and sincerity, and a thunderous round of applause greeted his words; he would have been a great politician, Ashley thought. Except that he had never cared about politics; he had always cared about people.

The first roar of close fire sounded from the stables area, and people screamed and jumped. It was all sound and black powder. There was no live ammunition at the reenactment.

The Yankees, mounted on their horses, rode in hard from the east, dismounting at the stables to use the buildings as defensive positions as they began their attack.

Ashley went on to introduce herself as Emma Donegal. She told about the beginning of the war, and how her husband, Marshall Donegal, famed for his exploits in the Mexican-American War more than ten years earlier, had returned to the military, raising a cavalry unit for the Louisiana militia that would be ready to join the Confederate army at any time. But federal forces were always spying in Louisiana. It would be the Union naval leader, David Farragut, a seasoned sailor, who would assault New Orleans and take the city in 1862, but before that time, Union forces snuck down regularly to survey the situation and report back on the Confederate forces guarding the city. The battle at Donegal Plantation began when the federal spies who had participated in the bar brawl rode swiftly to the plantation in uniform, hoping to engage the Confederates before they could summon more men. At Donegal Plantation, however, four of the spies died at the hands of the small Confederate force to be found there, and the only Confederate casualty was Marshall Donegal himself, who had succumbed to the onslaught of the federals, killing three before falling in a pool of his own blood. She explained that history longed to blame her—Emma Donegal—but she was innocent. Truly, she was innocent! The world hadn't changed that much; people loved to talk, and everyone wanted there to be more to the story. There simply wasn't. She and her husband had been married thirteen years; they had four children they were raising happily together. She was heartsick at her husband's death and survived her grief only because she had to keep food on the table for her children.

Of course, she knew the story like the back of her hand. She told it well and was greeted with wild applause when she pointed across the yard. "There! It all begins!"

And thus began the round of shots that made the expanse of land between the stables and the house rich and ripe with black powder. The federals had been traveling with a small, easily maneuvered six-pound howitzer, and in their attempts to seize the property, they sent their bronze cannon balls sailing for the house and ground. In fact, they had missed. At the time, their attempts to use the small cannon had done little but rip up great chunks of the earth. Today, it caused the air to become heavy with black powder.

"The Confederates had to stop the attack before the barn, stables and outbuildings could be set afire,"

Frazier Donegal announced from the porch, with a microphone, his voice rich and deep and rising well above the screams and shouting.

Though there was no live ammunition, the small fight clearly taught onlookers just how horrendous it must have been for men in major battles. As the Confederates and federals fought here with guerilla tactics, Ashley asked the crowd to imagine thousands of men marching forward side by side, some of them able to reload three times in a minute. The carnage was terrible. The Civil War was considered to be the last of the ancient wars—and the first of the modern wars.

The defenders split, most of the men rushing the stables from the front. But the Yankees had come around the other side, and in their maneuvering they escaped the body of men they had been determined to fight. One of the attackers was killed at the stables; the others made it around to the cemetery, attempting to use the old vaults as shields. But Marshall Donegal had come around the other side, and while his men were held up, he met up with the attackers at the cemetery.

The fighting originally ended *inside* the cemetery, but now they ended it just outside, the only difference from that day to this. First, the crowd wouldn't be able to see any of the action if it occurred there, and, with that many people tramping through, historic funerary art could be destroyed. And so, Charles Osgood, as Marshall, brought down several of the enemy and perished, brutally stabbed to death by bayonets, in front of the gates. The two surviving federal men—Justin Binder and Ramsay—raced toward the stables, whistling for their mounts. They leapt atop their horses and tore for the river road.

Frazier announced, "And thus did the fighting at Donegal Plantation come to an end."

They said the Pledge of Allegiance, and then the band played "Dixie" and then "The Battle Hymn of the Republic." After the burst of applause that followed the last song, people began to surround the actors—who had remained in the battle positions where they had fallen—as they came to their feet, and they all seemed to disappear into the crowd as they were congratulated, questioned and requested for picture-taking opportunities. Then, at last, the crowd began to melt away, and the sutler began to close down his shop.

Darkness was falling in earnest.

It had been a tremendous success; standing on the porch and watching the crowd ebb, Ashley told herself that she'd been an idiot, letting a dream get to her.

But, as she looked out, it seemed that the plantation was covered in a mist again.

It was the remnants of the black powder from the guns, she told herself.

The mist bore a reddish color. Bloodred.

The sun had set in the west; it was due to the dying of the day.

Whatever the explanation, the entire scene was eerie.

A breeze lifted, and she had the odd feeling that somehow everything had gone askew and changed, and she had somehow entered into a world of mist and shadow herself.

"Well, old girl," Frazier said quietly, smiling as he set a hand on Ashley's shoulder. "Another wonderful day. Thank you for all your hard work on this."

Ashley smiled. Her grandfather was happy. She adored Frazier, and she was always glad when he was happy. She worried about him constantly—driving him crazy, she knew. He had always been somewhat bony—though dignified! But now he seemed thinner, his cheeks hollow. He was old; but a man's life span could be long, and she wanted him with her for many more years. Now he was smiling, basking in the pleasant glow of the day's success.

"Come on. Let's head into the parlor," Frazier said. "I think we should probably be there to toast our actors and friends, eh?"

The family and some friends—including the soldiers for the day—traditionally retired to the riverside parlor for drinks and unwinding.

"You go on," Ashley said. "I'll be right there, I promise. I just want to see that everyone is really moving on."

Her grandfather gave her a kiss on the cheek. "I'm sure Beth has already put out all manner of delicious little snacks, despite the fact we told her that chips would do. I'll go supervise my liquor cabinet," he said, wiggling his white brows.

She grinned. "You'd better do that. Ramsay will say that he deserves your hundred-year-old Scotch for being so generous!"

Frazier pantomimed real fear and then walked on into the house. Ashley was exhausted and ready for a fine glass of hundred-year-old Scotch herself.

But she left the porch to walk around to the front for one last look. Jerry Blake, one of the off-duty officers they hired for traffic and crowd control, was still out by the road, waving at the last of the cars to get them safely on their way. She lifted a hand to him and shouted, "You coming in, Jerry?"

He waved back at her and shouted in return, "No, thanks! I'm on my way home. I have an early patrol shift tomorrow. See you, Ashley!"

A minute later, she saw him check that the day visitors' cars were all gone. Then he headed for his own car.

The buzz of chatter from inside filled the new silence. She followed the sound to the front parlor, where the reenactors were gathering. Looking around, she had the same strange sense of time encapsulated that she had felt before; none of the soldiers had changed out of their uniforms yet, and she was still in her Emma Donegal attire. Even Beth, who had seemed to get a tremendous sense of entertainment out of the day, was still in her 1860s garb. Some of the men had cigars, and they were allowed to smoke them in the house that night. Only the beer bottle in the hand of Matty Martin, the sutler's wife, provided a modern note.

Matty came over and gave her a kiss on the cheek. "Why, Mrs. Emma Donegal, you do create a mighty fine party, a mighty fine party! What a day!"

"Why, thank you, Mrs. Martin," Ashley said, inclining her head regally as a plantation mistress of the day might have done.

Matty dropped the act for a minute. "Oh, Ashley, we sold so much! And I can't tell you how many people ordered custom uniforms. I'll be sewing my fingers to the bone for the next months, but what a great day we had."

"I'm so glad," Ashley told her. She walked for the buffet with its crocheted doily and poured herself a Scotch whiskey—it wasn't a hundred years old, but it would do. Others came up to her and she responded—so many friends, and everyone involved in the reenactment. The men bowed and kissed her hand, still playing elite gentlemen of the era.

Ramsay grinned when he was near her. "I'd say ninety percent of the fighting men never tasted a good brandy, so I'm sure glad we get to be the rich of the past."

She smiled, and agreed. "Wouldn't it be something if we could have Lee and Grant, and Davis and Lincoln, and show them all that the war created the country we have now?"

Griffin walked over to them, lifting his glass.

"Grant was an alcoholic. A functional one, but an alcoholic. No relation, of course. My Grant family was Southern to the core. Cheers!"

"You're a cynic, Mr. Grant," Ashley said, inclining her head.

Griffin laughed. "Not at all. We strive for an understanding of history around here, right?"

"We do," Ashley agreed. "And, historically, many of them were truly honorable people. Can you imagine being Mrs. Robert E. Lee—and losing a historic family home, built by George Washington's stepgrandson and filled with objects that had belonged to George and Martha? Remember, Arlington was a home long before it became a national cemetery!"

"Cheers to that, I suppose," Griffin said. "Whiskey, Mrs. Donegal? Why, my dear woman, you should be sipping sherry with the other wives!"

"I need a whiskey tonight!"

Ramsay and Griffin laughed, and she joined them while she listened to her guests chatting. Some of the other men argued history, too—and she saw that everyone involved in the actual reenactment had shown up. Cliff, Ramsay, Hank, Griffin, Toby and John—and the Yankees, Michael Bonaventure, Hadley Mason, Justin Binder, Tom Dixon and Victor Quibbly, along with John Martin, of course, and Dr. Ben Austin.

Everyone but Charles Osgood. She couldn't imagine that he wasn't there. He must have been thrilled to death with the day.

"Hey, where's Charles?" Ashley asked, interrupting a rousing discussion of Farragut's naval prowess.

A few of those close to her quit talking to look around.

"I haven't seen him since he very dramatically died of his wounds," Ramsay said. "I 'skedaddled' right after and rode out with Justin, before we rode back to take our fair share of the applause."

"Cliff?" Ashley asked.

Cliff shook his head. "No, I was with the soldiers who came rushing in too late when Charles was being besieged by the enemy. I thought he just stood up and bowed when everyone was clapping. I don't remember seeing him when you and Frazier started talking…or when the band played."

"He's probably outside somewhere. I'll call his cell," Ramsay said. He pulled out his phone and hit a number of buttons.

Ashley watched him. She realized the others had already turned away and were becoming involved in their conversations again.

Ramsay shook his head at her. "No answer."

Cliff cleared his throat. "Not to be disrespectful in any way, but maybe he met a girl and—got lucky."

"Yeah for Charles!" Justin Binder said, lifting his glass. He was somewhat tipsy—if not drunk—Ashley thought. Good thing he was staying on the property.

The others were all still playacting; they were entrenched in the past.

They didn't want to look for someone they obviously believed was just off enjoying his own star turn. But...

"He would have wanted to be here tonight," Ashley said stubbornly. "He was so thrilled to be taking the part of Marshall Donegal. I'm going out to see if his car is still here."

Ramsay lifted a hand. "Sorry, don't bother, Ashley. He didn't drive. He came with me. I told him that I couldn't give him a ride back since I was going to stay at the house out here for a while, but he told me he'd hitch a ride back in with someone. Said he didn't have to be back to work until Tuesday morning and for me not to worry."

"Gentlemen, perhaps a search is in order," Frazier said. "A Civil War parlor game of sorts."

They all stared at him blankly.

"Exactly," Ashley said, relief coloring her tone. "Find the lost rebel. Beth will create a five-star private meal for a party of four, payable to the man—or woman—who finds Charles!"

"I will?" Beth said. She looked at Ashley. "Um, it will be—sumptuous!"

"It's a lot of property to cover," Ramsay murmured.

"We need to organize, then," Griffin said. "It will be fun. Yankees take the cemetery side, and rebels search out the bayou side."

"Is that fair?" Griffin asked. "If he's still around, old Charlie would be by the cemetery, don't you think?"

"I pick scouting detail!" Justin said.

"Yes! Let's find Charles!" Toby said.

"I'll check out the area around the oaks out front," Matty Martin offered. She was watching Ashley and seemed to realize that Ashley was seriously worried. "John, you can come with me. It's mighty dark out there, even with all the lights from the house and the property floodlights."

"Of course, my dear," John told her. "They should have let women fight the war," he muttered, following her out.

Hank laughed. "Yeah, imagine, mud wrestling at its best."

"Hank!" Cliff admonished. "War is always a serious affair."

"Well, of course it is," Griffin said. "War is very serious—but we're not at war. We're playing a game. We're looking for old Charles. Hey, Ashley, if no one wins…"

"Well, at some point, we'll just all have dinner," she told them.

"Great!" Beth muttered to her. "Now I get to cook for all of them!"

"It's good that I've got the bayou side!" Toby Keaton said. "Borders my property."

"I'll take the cemetery," Frazier said.

"You will not. It's dark and dangerous in there," Ashley told him.

"Not for me, dear. It's memories for me," he said softly, and quickly turned away. Neither of them wanted to think about Ashley's parents, entombed in the majestic family vault.

"Grampa, please—you need to be here as everyone returns," Ashley said.

"I'll take the cemetery," Ben offered. "I'm really familiar with the living and the dead," he added and winked. "Just give me one of the big old flashlights at the back door. I'll be fine."

Ben would be fine. He was a big, strapping man in his mid-forties. Besides, he'd attended funerals for both her parents and knew the cemetery well.

Ashley wanted to take the cemetery herself; that dream had to have been a sign.

No, that would be insane. Ben knew what he was doing. She wasn't going to let a dream dictate what she did in her life.

"Okay, so where are we going?" Beth asked Ashley.

"The stables?" Ashley suggested.

"I'll come with you and stand there, but I'm not going near the horses!"

An hour later, they had finished the actual search as best they could in the night.

Ramsay went to speak with the guests who were staying in the rooms that had been the old stables, and the Yankee contingent spoke with those in the other outbuildings. Cliff went to his office, wondering if Charles might have slipped in there to rest.

They all searched, from the river to the road, from the sugar fields to the bayou, but there was no sign of Charles Osgood. By midnight, all the searchers were back at the house.

"Ashley, really, he must be out somewhere else," Cliff told her.

She looked at Ben. "You searched everywhere in the cemetery? There are so many paths, little roads between all the vaults."

Ben sighed. "Ashley, I searched. But we can all take another look."

She nodded.

"That was actually not a suggestion," Ben said.

"It's all right. I'll go myself," Ashley said.

"We'll help," Ramsay said, tugging at Cliff's sleeve.

"I've still got the key, so I'll come, too," Ben said.

Ashley led the way, wondering why she thought that she'd really find Charles in the cemetery, just because she'd had a dream.

But she was determined.

Ben opened the lock on the gate, though, of course, they could have all crawled over the stone wall.

Ashley headed straight for her family tomb. The real Marshall Donegal had died there.

The last interment had been her father's. The usual little pain in her heart sparked—it always came when she thought about him, and her mother. And tonight, especially, she missed Jake.

There was no sign of Charles there, and no sign that he had been there.

She almost fell, she was so relieved.

The tomb glowed white beneath the gentle touch of the moon, dignified in its decaying majesty. She heard the three men calling to one another from different sections of the graveyard, and she followed a voice to reach Cliff. He looked at her. "Ashley, Charles left. Whether he was spirited away by aliens or not, I don't know. But he isn't here. This isn't any parlor game, is it? You're really worried."

"I am. Did you go in the chapel?" she asked.

"You think that Charles is hiding in the chapel? Or kneeling down, still thanking the good Lord for the chance to be Marshall Donegal?" Cliff asked dryly.

"Please, Cliff?"

He groaned. He walked around the ell that would lead them to the chapel, in the far corner near the embankment of the river. The chapel had carved oak double doors, which creaked when he opened them. He fumbled for the light switch, and light flared in the lovely little place with its stained-glass windows, marble altar and old mahogany podium.

The place was empty.

"Happy?" Cliff asked her.

"No. I can't help it—I'm worried," she told him.

He just shook his head. "Come on. Let's just go."

They walked back to the house, where the others were still milling on the back porch—many of them having retrieved their drinks.

"So, the bastard did get lucky!" Ramsay said, laughing. "Hell, if I had foreseen that, I'd have had him play Marshall Donegal a couple of years ago!"

"I'm going to call the police," Ashley said, looking at her grandfather.

"He's been missing just a few hours," Beth pointed out. "He might have thought that he said good-night to everyone. There's so much confusion going on when the fighting ends. I mean, I thought it was amazing—it really was living history. But it's mass confusion. I can only imagine a Gettysburg reenactment."

Ashley realized that everyone was staring at her—skeptically. They had searched and searched, and grown bored and tired. But she couldn't help her feelings of unease, even while they all stood silent, just staring at her.

The river breeze brought the chirp of the chickadees—her senses were so attuned to her home area that somewhere, distantly, down the bayou, she thought she could hear an alligator slip into the water. This was her home; she knew these sounds.

They were normal; they were natural. But the sounds of the darkness weren't reassuring to her now.

"Grampa, I think we need to report this to the police," she repeated.

"Great. He's probably at some bar in the big city,

bragging about the fact that he got to play Marshall Donegal today," Ramsay said. "And they'll drag him out and he'll act like a two-year-old again."

Frazier stared at Ashley and nodded. If she wanted to call the police, they would do so.

The parish police were called, and Officer Drew Montague, a nice-enough man whom Ashley had met a few times over the years, took all the information.

"You say you all saw him just a few hours ago?" he asked. Montague had a thick head of dark hair and eyebrows that met in the middle.

"Yes," she said.

"What makes you think that he's actually missing? Perhaps there's a woman involved. Is he married? Look, Miss Donegal, you know that we appreciate everything that you do for the area, but…we're talking about a grown man who has been gone just a few hours," the officer said.

"He was proud of the role he was playing. He would have stayed," Ashley insisted.

Officer Montague shifted his weight. "Look, I've taken the report, and I'll put out a local bulletin to be on the lookout for him, but he's an adult. An adult really needs to be gone for forty-eight hours before he is officially missing."

Frazier spoke before Ashley could. "Anything you can do will be greatly appreciated. We're always proud that the parish is about people, and not just red tape and rules."

Montague nodded. "Right. Well, I'll get this moving, then. We'll all be on the lookout for Mr. Osgood."

Ashley thanked him. The others had remained behind, politely and patiently waiting. Now it was really late, and once again there were a number of weary men and women—all still in Civil War–era attire—staring at her.

Officer Montague left, mollified by Frazier Donegal over the fact that he had been called out on a ridiculous mission.

"I'm sorry," Ashley said to the others. The evening had started out as a party and turned into a search committee.

"Hey," Cliff said, grinning, "I don't have far to go home."

"We're staying in the stables anyway, kid," Justin Binder told her. He had played a Yankee, and happily. His family hailed from Pennsylvania.

Griffin laughed and gave her an affectionate hug. "You made me sober up, which is good. I am driving."

"Me, too," John Ashton said. He held her shoulders and kissed her cheek. "Charles is just fine. I'm sure of it."

She thanked them all and said good-night, and they drifted away, some to the old outbuildings where they were staying, and some to their cars, parked in the lot out front and down the road.

She stood on the porch with Beth and her grandfather. She couldn't tell whether they thought she was being ridiculous or not, they were both so patient.

Beth gave her a kiss on the cheek and said, "We still have about sixteen guests, and the household. I've got to get up early to whip up our spectacular plantation breakfast."

Ashley bid her good-night. It was down to her grandfather and herself, and Frazier was going to wait for her to be ready to head off to bed.

"Something is wrong. I can feel it, Grampa," she said.

He set an arm around her shoulder. "You know...I have an old friend. I've been meaning to call him for a long time—tonight seems a good time to have a chat with him. If Charles really is gone, he may be able to help us. His name is Adam Harrison. I don't know if you remember meeting him—I see him up in Virginia and D.C. sometimes. He worked for private concerns for many years, finding the right investigators for strange situations. Then the government started calling him, and his projects were all kind of combined for a while, civilian and federal. But he's got a special unit now, and he's got federal power behind him on it. His people are a select group from the Behavioral Analysis Unit of the FBI. I'll give him a call. We'll get someone out here to help by tomorrow. And if Charles turns up, no harm done."

She lowered her head. Adam Harrison. She knew the name. His unit had been involved in solving the death of Regina Holloway—it had been all over the media because she was a senator's wife. And she knew, too, that Jake Mallory was part of that unit. She might not be a part of his world, but she hadn't been able to miss it when she'd seen his name in the papers. She had broken off something that had been real with Jake, because he had terrified her...because he was certain that he had spoken with her father, after he had died. And now....

Now Frazier was going to call Adam. Of course, it could come to nothing. She was panicking over a missing man because of an equally irrational dream.

She looked out on the beautiful expanse of their property. The river rolling by. The moon high over the clouds. The vaults in the cemetery silent and ghostly and opalescent in the pale glow of night.

*Jake, I'm so...scared.*

Something was wrong. It was the oddest thing; she felt that she really understood the expression *I feel it in my bones*. Something wasn't right about Charles's disappearance, and she knew it.

It was almost as if the past had truly merged into this eerie and haunting reality, and the collision of time here was not going to go away.

# *Interlude*

*He'd known for a long time what he'd had to do. The voice had been telling him for years.*

*At first, of course, he had ignored it. The vision he'd seen of the past hadn't been real. But then he'd known. He'd known who he was, and he'd come to know that the voice wouldn't go away until he'd done what needed to be done. And he'd carefully planned it all out, though things had gone a bit strangely today. Didn't matter, though, who was playing Marshall Donegal. It didn't matter at all. Because, of course, an actor was just an actor.*

*It was Donegal Plantation itself that needed to repay the old debt. That old debt could only be repaid one way.*

*With blood.*

*God bless a crowd. There was nothing in the world like mayhem, nothing like hundreds of witnesses to pull off an escapade such as he had planned, and to do it perfectly.*

*There had been a horde surrounding them. One particular brunette was the right age, exceptionally pretty and with a Massachusetts accent. When she spoke, there was an r on the name Linda, and there was no r on the car she had "pahked" down the river road.*

*She had giggled when she spoke to Charles, so it was easy to whisper in the man's ear in his moment of greatest achievement and convince him that the girl was waiting to meet him.*

*And in the madness surrounding everyone engaged in the action then, it was easy enough to meld into the crowd himself, and to swiftly disappear, and hurry to the river road.*

*And there was Charles.*

*He'd approached Charles with a smile.*

*And, of course, Charles was smiling as well. At least he would go in a state of sheer happiness. It might even be a kindness. How many people got to die that happy?*

*Poor, dumb Charles—he never suspected a thing. After the initial whack, he never even felt the prick of the needle.*

*He'd thought it all out, exactly where he'd send Charles, because it all had to be done in plain sight. In plain sight, people never really knew what they saw.*

*There were tourists heading to their cars. But they'd never notice two fellows in uniform chatting by a car. Not at an event like this. People liked to dress up.*

*Maybe everyone wanted to be someone else, someone they weren't.*

*But to them, it would just appear that they were two cronies, faces covered by their broad-brimmed hats, leaning against one another as they chatted and laughed over a joke.*

*Then...hide the body. Or if he had been seen, "help" an inebriated friend into a car.*

*He would need more time for the pièce de résistance. Initially, it had taken him less than twenty minutes to stash Charles and rejoin all those rejoicing over the day.*

*He had never felt more victorious. The difficult part, of course, would be to hide his anticipation for all that was destined to follow.*

*It didn't seem that anything could go so impossibly well.*

*Ashley, damn her, though. Leave it to Ashley to be worried about Charles! Still and all, it did make the entire plan more exciting. Now, with the evening at a close, he was feeling elated.*

*The place had settled down; though everyone had been willing to look for Charles, only Ashley had been really concerned. He had played with the idea of actually disposing of poor old Charles immediately, but now he was satisfied that he had decided he should make it something more dramatic—and allow time between the reenactment and the beginning of the end.*

*Oh, he had worked with the others. He had searched so hard. There might have been just a few minutes when he feared someone would actually search the cars, but Charles hadn't driven.*

*It had almost been as if he'd been part of the plan.*

*Now he sat next to good old Charles.*

*This was necessary. The voice had said that it had to be done, and his ancestor made him know that nothing could be right until then.*

*He'd never realized that he'd enjoy it all so much.*

*He patted him on the back. Charles didn't move. The drug was holding, but he'd administer more. He didn't want the big lug waking up.*

*He needed him alive until the time was right.*

*Every time he'd been at Donegal recently, he'd felt as if he were being pushed harder and harder. The past was the past—so they all said. But it wasn't. The past created the present, and he knew now that he had to use the present to set the past right. It wasn't crazy; he'd heard the voices in his head. A collective consciousness that seemed to scream through history.*

*Now, maybe, the voices would stop.*

# 3

Car bombs didn't exactly do it for him, but Jake indulged in a few anyway.

"Cheers!" Jenna said, dropping her shot glass into her Guinness, and swallowing down the mixture.

"Cheat!" Will said to Whitney. "You poured your shot in—you just drink the whole thing."

"Hey, you drink it your way, and I'll drink it mine!" Whitney protested.

"You're not doing it the Irish way," Will said, looking to Jenna for help.

"Drink it however you like!" Jenna said, smiling sweetly at Will.

There was a small room in the back of the bar, and Jake, Will Chan, Jenna Duffy and Whitney Tremont had it to themselves that night, so it was nice. Jackson Crow was back at the hotel with Angela Hawkins. They'd all just met for the first time on the Holloway case, and Jackson, the skeptic, had quickly fallen in love with Angela—despite their different approaches to their work. Go figure. The entire team respected and admired them both, and they were glad that the two were indulging in some quality time together.

And for Jake, it felt good to be in the bar with his coworkers.

During the Holloway case, they had gotten to know one another. Will and Whitney were excellent with cameras and sound systems; Jenna was a registered nurse, something that could always come in handy when traipsing through strange landscapes and old buildings. His own expertise was computers—and computer hacking. He could usually find any piece of information on any site, public, private or even heavily coded. Yet they'd all had certain unusual experiences in life that had led them to being excellent investigators—and, together, able to discern deeper, darker undercurrents to the event they researched. Now, they also had badges. After the Holloway case, it had been deemed that they would continue to work together, and they would do so with all proper credentials as FBI agents.

"Now, quit whining over the way a woman drinks her drink," Jenna said and turned, leaning an elbow on their table, to talk to Whitney. She had brilliant green eyes and red hair, and a smile that could melt ice. "I want to know what else I've missed. The World War II museum, the Civil War museum, plantations, the zoo…"

"Shall we have another drink?" Whitney asked.

But before Jenna could answer, they all heard their phones buzz.

"Text from Jackson," Whitney murmured.

"Meeting in the morning," Jenna said, the slight Irish lilt in her voice grave.

"Hmm. Do you think that means that we're not heading to Alexandria?" Will asked.

"It means something is up," Whitney said, looking at Jake.

"I'll pay the bill," Jake told them.

They walked back to their hotel slowly and silently, each wondering what they'd discover in the morning. After they parted, Jake sat up a very long time.

It became morning at last. Ashley didn't feel as if she'd slept at all. The dreams continued to plague her, only now she *was* Emma Donegal, leaving the house in the aftermath of the battle to find the bloody body of her husband. And when she woke herself from the dream, she could have sworn that deceased Confederate soldier was sitting in the wingback chair by the doors to the second-story wraparound porch. She was more tired from being in bed than she was from being awake.

A shower helped revive her a little. Dressed and ready for the day, she headed down to the kitchen. Once it had been a gentleman's den, and then it had been an office, and then, when it was no longer deemed necessary to have the main kitchen in an outbuilding, it had become a wonderful, bright kitchen. The walls were a pale yellow. There was a center

granite worktable with stools around it, and sus-
pended racks that held several dozen shining copper
cooking utensils. A breakfast nook held a table that
sat eight.

Beth was just pouring milk from a carton into
serving pitchers. "Coffee is on. None of the guests
have made it in yet," she said cheerfully.

"What's for breakfast?" Ashley asked.

"Down-home comfort food this morning," Beth
said. "Corn bread, blueberry muffins, bacon and
cheese omelets, and country cheese grits. Want to
grab a plate and eat before it starts getting crazy?"

"Sure," Ashley said. She watched as her beautiful friend made art out of an omelet and shook her
head as Beth handed her the plate full of light, fluffy
eggs.

"Grits are in the bowl, corn bread is sliced and in
those baskets," Beth said.

Ashley helped herself. "I'm going to waddle across
the lawn soon," Ashley told her.

Beth grinned. "I doubt it. You're too fond of those
awful creatures out in the stables. You get plenty of
exercise." She shivered.

"I can't believe that you're afraid of horses."
Ashley laughed.

"I told you—one of the bastards bit me when I
was a child!" Beth said.

"Well, ours won't bite you. You should try riding
Tigger. She's a twenty-year-old sweetie. She moves
like an old woman."

"Then she may be crotchety as one, too," Beth said. "No, honey, you stick to your horses, and I'll stick to cooking."

Ashley dutifully bit into her omelet, and it was delicious. As she was finishing, guests began to stream by her, heading in for breakfast or stopping to clear their tabs. They'd be down to eight guests that night; the reenactment had taken place on a Sunday, and many of those who came for the reenactment managed to take off the Monday if they had a regular workweek. By Monday night, they were usually down to just a few guests.

She heard Frazier speaking with people on the other side of the stairway, his tone rich and filled with humor as he told old family tales and pointed out certain portraits on the walls.

Ashley took her place at the desk to fill out the registry and books—by hand; people actually signed her guest book, and she wrote personal thank-yous— and then could have sworn that someone had approached her. She looked up, but she was alone. For a moment, her brows knit in consternation, but people milled throughout the lower level of the house now and any one of them might have stopped nearby. She gave her concentration back to the project at hand.

She heard a throat being cleared then, and looked up—this time, someone *was* there. Justin.

He sat in the one of the period wingback chairs that faced the desk.

She frowned. "Are you checking out? I thought you were staying a few days."

"I am staying another few days, Ashley. I just stopped to see how you're doing," he told her.

She liked Justin. At forty, he was a widower, though years before, he had brought his wife with him, and she had played at being a camp follower—with great relish. They had been married for years before he had lost her to cancer. But Justin still came.

"I'm fine, thanks. Nancy's got the girls?" His mother-in-law, Nancy, now came along to help Justin with his ten-year-old twin girls. Hard to be a "fighting federal" and keep an eye on twins.

"Yes. Any word on Charles?"

She set her pen down. "No. But I haven't tried calling anyone this morning. Everyone on that search party last night is weary of me torturing them, so... If he's been found, I'll be called right away."

He reached across the desk and put his hand on hers, giving a comforting squeeze.

"Ashley, you are part of the charm of this place. You really care. None of us thinks you were torturing us. I was thinking of taking the family for a horse ride later, and I know that Cliff does a lot of the riding tours, but I thought you and I could make another search of it, too."

She was surprised. "Sure! And thank you."

"Jeanine and Meg don't ride well. They don't get

a chance to go riding often enough. You still have two horses calm as the Dead Sea, right?"

"Nellie is our sweetest. And Tigger is a good old girl if I've ever known one. Nellie loves him, so they're great on a ride together. They'll be perfect for the twins."

Justin grinned and stood. "Nancy's bringing the crew in for breakfast. Say an hour or two?"

"Two hours will work for me."

Justin thanked her. She finished with paperwork and realized she was constantly looking up, certain that she was going to see a Confederate soldier staring at her.

"I don't believe in ghosts," she reminded herself. But saying the words out loud sounded defensive. "I don't. I really don't!" she said to the empty room.

Irritated with herself, she went out to the stables. Justin's family would be out soon.

Ashley saddled Varina and stroked her mane. The farmer they had bought her from when Ashley had been a teen had been an avid fan of Varina Davis, the one and only first lady of the Confederate States of America. Because she had been named Varina, they named Nellie's last colt Jeff, for Jefferson Davis, the one and only President of the Confederate States. That morning, she and Justin chose Varina and Jeff as their mounts, while she assigned Nellie to the younger, slightly more timid of Justin's twin girls, and Tigger to the other, while Nancy, Justin's mother-in-law, was on the slightly more spirited Abraham.

Ashley took the girls around the paddock a few times, just going over the basics. Justin had been right about their experience, but they were smart little girls with common sense, and Ashley thought they would do well.

Ashley gave her attention to the girls as they rode around the outbuildings and then toward Beaumont, the Creole plantation "next door." The girls were delighted by the ride, waving to everyone they passed while traversing the house and outbuildings area and then concentrating on their father's and grandmother's admonitions to be on the lookout for wildlife.

"Are there alligators?" Meg, the bolder of the twins, demanded.

"Yes, by the bayou. But they'll leave you alone if you leave them alone. We won't dismount anywhere near the bayou. Now, you don't want to bring a small-sized dog or even a medium-sized dog out there. *They* look like dinnertime to the alligators," Ashley told them. She was listening to the girls; she was looking everywhere. They had searched last night, but it had been dark. Now it was daylight, and, hopefully, if Charles Osgood had come out here and fallen, hurt himself or had some other trial, they might find him now.

"We don't have a dog," Jeanine, Meg's sister, younger by five minutes, said.

"Can we get a puppy, Dad?" Meg asked.

"Soon enough," Nancy said, grinning at Ashley.

"Why not now?" Meg asked.

"Because Daddy is busy," Nancy answered. Nancy was one of those women who had gone to a beautiful shade of silver-white naturally.

"Watch for animals, girls," Ashley interceded. "We'll be close enough to see the alligators basking in the sun. These woods aren't that dense, but with all this land, every once in a while a black bear or a cougar wanders across the road. I know that you see nutria—"

"What are nutria?" Meg interrupted.

"They're the largest rat, essentially," Justin said.

"Ugh!" Jeanine said.

"The buggers were brought over years ago, in the 1930s, and they've multiplied into the millions," Ashley explained. "There's actually a bounty on them, because they can be so destructive. But they don't hurt people. The animal that you do have to be careful of in these parts is the cottonmouth snake. But it likes water, too, and we're not going in the water. Animals usually leave you alone as long as you leave them alone."

"Watch for herons!" Justin said.

"I wouldn't mind seeing a cougar," Meg announced.

"They're shy, too. But we'll see what we see," Ashley assured them.

They counted seven herons, two raccoons, an armadillo and three owls up in the trees. When they came to the bayou, Ashley pointed out two alligators sunning on the opposite bank. As she did so, she saw that staff members at Beaumont were engaged in their work already. A man dressed in a droop hat, cutoff denim and a dotted cotton shirt was standing by a wagon that showed freshly hewn sugarcane. Another, dressed more like an early nineteenth-century Louisiana French businessman, was giving a tour.

She looked up toward the second story of the plantation house, where the family had lived. A man was standing there, dressed in a Confederate uniform frock coat.

Ashley blinked against the light. He looked like…

Like her ancestor, Marshall Donegal.

The man lifted a hand to her.

Yet when she blinked again, he was gone. Her imagination at work again. Of course, she was still concerned about Charles Osgood. But he was due back to work the next morning. If he didn't turn up by then, the police would have to get involved at a serious level.

She realized that Justin was watching her.

"Are you okay, Ashley?" he asked.

"I'm fine. The light is playing tricks, that's all. I thought I saw a Confederate soldier at the window. Toby Keaton does workshops and tours on the real workings of a sugar plantation over there. We do the Civil War—keeps me sending tourists to him, and him sending them to Donegal Plantation," she said. Would she have told the truth if Jake were here? Jake, who seemed to know what the dead were saying.

"You have Charles Osgood on your mind," Justin said.

"I do. I can't help it."

They rode along the bayou for a while, and then Ashley led them around the second trail to head back to the house. The girls chattered the whole time.

Justin nudged Jeff and the horse trotted up next to Ashley again. "I know you were hoping to find Charles," he said.

"I am worried, Justin, really worried," she said.

"He'll show up. But let him know how worried you were. That will make him feel good," Justin told her.

Ashley offered him a smile. "Sure, thanks."

Back at the stable, Ashley tried to keep her mind busy, letting the girls help her with the saddles and bridle and tack. She taught them how to groom their horses.

As she put away the last of the brushes, Justin strode over to her. "Great. Now Jeanine doesn't want a puppy anymore. She wants a horse."

Ashley laughed. "Maybe you better look into the puppy thing, fast. Of course, there's always kittens, you know."

Restless, she returned to the house, showered again and went down to join Beth, who was planning the offerings for the restaurant's evening meal.

Jackson Crow was nothing if not a man of incredible thought and organization; there were six folders on the table awaiting them all.

Jake and Whitney were precisely on time, but he was the last to slide into his seat at Le Café, the Hotel Monteleone's bright and charming dining facility for breakfast and lunch. There were other diners about, but they'd been given a table in the far corner, near the windows to Royal Street, and they were certainly far enough from others to carry on a meeting in normal tones.

Jackson, ever the gentleman, had risen while Whitney took her seat, which meant that Will did, too. They were both tall, and the kind of men who drew attention. Jackson had the rugged, square-jawed history of Native Americans in his face, while Will's Trinidadian mix of English, Indian, Chinese and African ancestry gave him a fascinating appeal.

"Thank you all for being on time," Jackson said. "Though I want you all to know that we're not in an emergency situation."

"What is our situation?" Will asked.

"As you know, we'd been due to leave here and set up shop in our headquarters in Alexandria. But instead we're going to stay here, in the area, a few more days," Jackson said.

Whitney kicked Jake under the table. He scowled at her.

Jackson continued, "This may be absolutely nothing, but since we were already in the vicinity, we've been asked to check out a disappearance."

"Oh, no, not a child?" Jenna asked softly.

"No, no, a man named Charles Osgood, thirty-eight years old," Jackson said. "As you may or may not know, Adam Harrison is quite the philanthropist, and he's friends with a Louisiana legend with whom he's worked on many committees to improve education in the Southern states, housing reform, storm relief and so on. Apparently, although the local police aren't terribly concerned, Osgood disappeared right after a battle reenactment."

Jake knew; he already knew. There had been the dreams; there had been the woman he had seen when he'd been out with Whitney.

There had been those images of Ashley calling to him.

He knew, damn it, knew….

"A what?" Jenna asked.

Jackson glanced at her, remembered she had spent most of her own school years in Ireland, and explained. "A Civil War reenactment. We do tons of them in this country. Many battlefields are now national parks, and many of those that aren't are owned by people who don't mind reliving the Revolutionary War and the Civil War. It's 'living history,' and a good thing, in my opinion. We learn from our mistakes."

"True, or else you'll die," Jenna said. She looked around and shrugged. "Survival of the fittest. But, yes, they do reenactments everywhere, of course."

The others smiled at her tone. Jake felt the unease sweeping through him. Déjà vu.

"How long has he been missing?" Whitney asked.

"Not even twenty-four hours," Jackson said.

"Are we even sure he's missing?" Jenna asked.

"No," Jackson said. "But we're going to hang in a bit—wait here in New Orleans. You have a day entirely to yourselves. If he's still missing after this evening, we'll become involved with the search. Adam is making sure that we're officially invited in. I have folders regarding Osgood's situation—when he was last seen, the location and why the people at Donegal are so concerned."

*Donegal.*

Jake picked up his folder, his fingers feeling oddly numb and too big. When he flipped the page, he felt a sweep of old emotion.

Donegal. The computer printout offered a beautiful shot of a large and majestic plantation house, complete with sweeping oaks, pine forest, outbuildings, horses in a paddock and the low wall and gates of an historic family cemetery.

He didn't need the computer printout. He could see the plantation clearly in his mind's eye at any time.

He looked up.

Jackson was staring at him.

"Adam mentioned that Frazier Donegal told him that one of the team members had a history with the family and the plantation. That's not a problem for you in any way, is it, Jake?"

"No," Jake said.

Jackson was still staring at him.

"No," he repeated quietly. "Our families are old friends, that's all. But I haven't been out there in ages," he explained. "Ashley Donegal and I spent a lot of time together when we were kids. I saw her at her father's funeral, and I stayed on a few days after. She was pretty devastated when he died. She'd lost her mom just a few years earlier."

*We were more than friends.* Somehow, he kept his gaze steady as he met Jackson's eyes.

Every word he had said was absolutely the truth.

"Then, be advised, we're officially on hold," Jackson said. "If this fellow turns up at work tomorrow, green from celebratory alcohol, we'll be clear to head up to Alexandria. If not, we'll start working on the disappearance. Take your folders and read up—we'll need to be ready either way."

The official part of the meeting was over. They all chatted casually and ordered breakfast as the restaurant was about to close for the break before lunch. Jake joined in. But he opted not to go to the World War II museum with Will, Jenna and Whitney, or join Angela and Jackson on a trip to the aquarium with a hop over to the casino. He shrugged off both groups, saying that he had woken early and thought he'd get in some sleep, just in case they were on call.

He didn't take a nap.

Hell, he'd never sleep. He didn't want to sleep.

He wandered the city, looking for the woman in the historic costume.

No, he knew exactly who he was looking for: Emma Donegal.

He didn't find her, but he hadn't expected to.

Ghosts never seemed to appear when they were needed. It was aggravating. They reached out—and then stepped back and disappeared, assuming that they had gotten the living working on whatever it was that they wanted them working on.

"You know, you could be helpful," he said out loud, standing on Jackson Square near the spot he had first seen her. All he received for his effort was a worried glance from a woman passing by. She gripped her husband's arm tighter.

It really wasn't prudent to attempt speaking to ghosts when others were near. They just thought you were crazy or worse—dangerous.

Had Ashley thought that he was dangerous?

He stopped for coffee at C.C.'s, then returned to his room, where he did lie down.

Ashley. Donegal Plantation. The light was fading; night had come.

He couldn't stand it. He would be crawling the walls by morning. He stood up and looked around at his room. Packing up would take him all of ten minutes.

He picked up his phone and dialed Jackson. When Jackson answered, he said, "I'm heading out tonight, if that's all right. If this fellow shows up in the morning, I'll come right back. Frazier Donegal is not a spring chicken. If they're worried, I'd just like to be there."

"You read your folder?"

"I'm doing so right now. I'll pack up and be out of

this room in another few hours. I'll get to the plantation really late, but I'll give Frazier a call and tell him I'm coming in."

"Fine. Just be careful, Jake. If you have a personal stake in this..."

"It may be nothing," Jake reminded him.

"If it's not, wait for the team before rushing into danger."

"Of course."

He hung up and finished packing, the same two words running through his mind over and over again.

Ashley. Donegal. Ashley. Donegal.

Ashley....

# Interlude

*Nighttime—the haunting time...*

*When all the earth was still.*

*And old Charles, while still breathing, was getting a little ripe.*

*Unconscious now for over twenty-four hours, he had a certain... Well, honestly, there was a stink about him. The man was still dressed in wool, for God's sake, and since he'd never had a chance to regain consciousness, he hadn't managed to handle personal hygiene, and, well...*

*But that was all right. He didn't blame poor old Charles for the way he smelled.*

*With any luck, no one would see him. He'd sail through this, and it would be easy, as easy as luring the man to his car, as easy as that first solid blow against his head, as easy as the injection of the needle into his flesh. Not long now...*

*He anticipated the horror when others found the body.*

*Of course, when they found the body, he'd be as horrified, stunned and confused as all the others.*

*He grunted, picking him up. Damned Charles—the man was no lightweight.*

*He didn't go through the gate, and crawling over the wall with his victim's dead weight was no easy feat.*

*"You should have laid off the andouille,*

*fried chicken and Cajun rice, buddy!" he whispered aloud, struggling. He was careful, of course. His shoes were encased in plastic shower caps, and he wore thin latex hospital gloves. Now, well, hell, if someone caught him now...*

*"I was by the water, searching for a buckle I lost, and I couldn't just stick my hands in the muck...."*

*That one didn't fly. Not at all. Not even to him. Didn't matter. He was near the end.*

*He found the right place. Now he needed all his strength and the aid of the broken stone marker he'd made note of earlier. He heard himself grunting with exertion and paused, making sure that he wasn't sweating—it was all no good if someone could pull sweat off of old Charles. God, he hated contemporary forensics, though he was sure he had studied enough manuals on the subject to make sure that he was doing it all the right way. After all, he had planned this for years.*

*Finally, he had Charles where he wanted him. And it was time; Charles was still heavily sedated. He'd never know exactly how he reached the pearly gates.*

*He loved his weapon of choice.*

*For a moment, he admired his handiwork. And then he struck.*

*His victim never uttered so much as a whimper.*

# 4

Ashley opened her eyes. Pale and surreal moonlight flowed through the gauze curtains and into her room, soft and evocative in the night. The white curtains shifted in the breeze. She had awakened in the middle of the night, not at all sure why. There should have been something, a loud noise, a gust of wind, a scream in the darkness, something.

She hadn't even been dreaming.

*Thank God!*

She was sure that there hadn't been any kind of commotion or noise. It was disturbing that she was so suddenly wide-awake, with no clue as to why.

She stood, curious, and walked to French doors that opened out to the wraparound porch, slipped by the hauntingly sheer curtains and out to the balcony, where she held the rail, as she had as a child, and looked over the beauty of the grounds. The moon was a crescent in the sky, and stars sparkled beautifully if opaquely. Rain might be coming, she thought. The ethereal light of the stars and moon—and the large lanterns at the front and rear doors of the grand old house—created a scene of misted and mysterious beauty.

So what had wakened her so swiftly and completely?

"Worry!" she whispered aloud. "'Hmm, Sherlock,' said Watson, 'there shouldn't be any werewolves out tonight. Werewolves need a full moon, so I believe!' Oh, God, I'm talking to myself again!" she moaned.

But—what?

Charles Osgood was still missing.

Jake was coming. That was certainly something that had to be haunting her mind—and maybe the mere thought of Jake, in the flesh, had never really allowed her sleep.

She began to wonder if Charles Osgood was really alive and well, and had returned tonight, wanting to play some kind of demented joke on everyone to prove that he really had been the right choice to play Marshall Donegal. The thought of Charles Osgood running around the property in the perpetuation of some kind of a hoax was irritating—but left her hopeful as well.

She found herself looking out to the graveyard.

She thought she saw a light flickering there.

"Damn it!" she whispered.

From her vantage point on the second-floor porch, she could see the ghostly white tombs and vaults, the weeping angels, mournful cherubs, praying saints and all the exquisite mortuary art to be found here.

She needed to put the nonsense regarding Charles out of her head and start remembering that she ran a business, a bed-and-breakfast and living museum. And, yes, Charles was on her mind, but there were still other problems that could arise.

Ah, yes, Jake always kept her grounded, and he always had that half smile on his face, the charming light in his eyes, and when he was there, she was whole.

Somehow, knowing that Jake was coming gave her that strength!

*Brilliant woman! So, push the man away!*

Still, just thinking about him…

Something was going on out there. It was her property, and it was going to stop. She was sick of wondering what had happened and what was going on. She was going out to discover just what the hell that flicker of light might be.

Indignant, she turned back and put on the pair of sandals by her bedside, found her white robe and hurried out of her room. She could hear the horses whinnying and neighing, as if something in the night had disturbed them as well. But she didn't head for the stables—they'd had problems before with local teens thinking it would be great to get high and play in the old Donegal graveyard. And although guests were always asked not to tramp around the grounds after eleven, every once in a while they had a ghost hunter who just had to be in the cemetery at midnight or beyond.

She crossed the stretch of lawn that led toward the old cast-iron graveyard gate. The gate, of course, meant nothing, since the stone wall surrounding the family "city of the dead" was only four feet tall.

The gate was open.

Kids would be kids. When she had been young, she had held some great slumber parties, and her guests had gone into the family cemetery at night, and they'd told ghost stories with flashlights aimed at their faces. But it was her home; her family graveyard. They had never been destructive.

Perhaps such an old, private cemetery on a property now run as an inn was just too big a temptation for people.

A few years ago, some young people from the local high school had broken one of the cherubs that had graced the walk near the gate. That might have been an accident; they'd caught the culprits, and the boys had said that they'd been terrified—chased by the ghost of a Confederate soldier. Their imaginations at work, Ashley was certain, and she hadn't particularly wanted that group severely punished—she was angrier with the teens who had left beer cans, cigarette butts, the tail ends of joints lying around…and had written a bunch of voodoo symbols on the tombs. Once caught, they, too, had claimed that ghosts had chased them out, but in that instance, Ashley was damned sure that the only ghosts had been the spirits they'd imbibed, and the weed.

She realized how ridiculous she must look, wandering toward a cemetery in a white nightgown and robe; if there were kids there, she'd probably scare them to death herself. The gate was open wide enough to let a body slip through. She did so, careful not to touch it as the old iron creaked.

Even she, who had lived here all her life, imagined that a cherub ever-so-slightly turned its head to watch her walk by.

She paused, listening, and realized that she heard only the rustling of the trees, the grand old oaks that stood sentinel along the walls, shrouded in moss. And yet, there seemed to be soft voices in the night. The sound possibly created by movement of the air, the natural settling of the earth and manmade structures as well. Still, it was almost as if she could hear her name spoken softly, urging her on, calling to her.

But then she heard something that wasn't the whisper of branches moving or the moan of the soft breeze. It was like a thump or a rhythmic tapping sound, and it was coming from just down the path and to the right, from the large and beautiful vault where her ancestors had been laid to rest. She hurried silently along, wanting to catch the prankster red-handed.

"Charles? Charles Osgood? Is that you? Show yourself. The reenactments are not a joke! Don't ruin it all by being a jerk!" Ashley called out.

She turned the corner and stopped dead, a scream rising in her throat. As if on cue, a drifting cloud un-curtained the moon, and the Donegal family vault glowed in opalescent majesty. Mist swirled at the base. An angel rose high atop the chapel-like roof, hands folded, eyes lifted to heaven.

The body of a man dangled from the base of the angel, the straps of his backpack caught upon the marble structure, his feet just brushing the ground. His cavalry hat covered his face, and blood, from a series of wounds to his abdomen and chest, streaked down his torso and limbs and pooled at his feet.

Terror filled her; she stared, blinking. Too afraid to run, too afraid to allow her trapped scream to escape, a confusion of thoughts tearing through her mind.

For a moment, it was as if her mind hit Pause on the horrible image before her.

Her home was haunted. This was the ghost of Marshall Donegal, the valiant man who had died there defending his property in 1861.

If she stepped forward, his head might rise with the hollow, skeletal grin of a man dead more than a century and a half….

She heard the rapping sound again. It was the dead man's sword, rapping, tapping, against the tomb.

And it snapped her out of her paralysis.

At last, she screamed.

This man wasn't a ghost.

He was never going to grin at her, or anyone else.

He was real, and he was certainly dead, murdered and in the cemetery, where she now stood alone with nothing at all to defend herself. She closed her mouth quickly, cutting off the sound of her scream.

She had been right to worry, and to search. She had felt even last night that they had to find Charles Osgood. And now, she had found him.

But the prank had been pulled not *by* him, but *on* him.

And it was fresh blood that dripped beneath his dangling feet.

A killer might still be here, watching from the shadows that melded with the mist in the darkness of the graveyard.

Donegal Plantation. Few plantations rivaled it. A haunting opaque white shimmer in the moonlight, the building rose up on the bank in all its majesty. It sat before Jake Mallory as it had all his life; a stunning representation of a bygone era.

Nowadays, the very circumstances that had defeated those who had lived here long ago were the ones that made the area a place of such amazing history and beauty. The war had scarcely begun when the Union might had throttled the city and parish of New Orleans, and, for miles around the city center, the surrender that had seemed like such a tragic disaster had kept enemy forces from laying waste to the magnificent houses that had been built when cotton had been king.

He remembered the first time he had come here; his parents were friends with Ashley's parents. He remembered the first time he saw her, hiding behind her mother's skirts. She had been five; he had been eight.

Compare that to the last time he had seen her. The way the light had gone out in her eyes. She had built a wall around her heart and soul that was as impregnable as brick.

He was still damaged goods himself. He had learned to cope with what he was because of Adam Harrison and the team he had put together in a way he had never managed on his own. Maybe because he had discovered that he wasn't so strange. Still, the images that lived in his mind would always create a divide with Ashley.

There had been good times, though. Their parents had played as a team in pool tournaments. Jake and Ashley had come along, played in the various game rooms offered by different venues, shared sodas and snacks. But more than pool had kept them together as friends when they'd been really young. Once, they'd been part of a garage band together; they'd been pretty good at that, too. And when the three years between them had seemed unbridgeable and they spent most of their time within a year of their own age group, Ashley had come to him upon occasion with her dating dilemmas, or to comment on his dating choices. He smiled as he thought about Ashley and remembered the way her lips would purse when she was trying to tell him something. Somehow, someway, Ashley had retained something of the Southern belle in her behavior; the word *bimbo* would not cross her lips, nor would she tell him that his latest crush was a slut, a tramp or trailer trash, nor would she use any other such derogatory term. The question was always, "Seriously, Jake, is she what you're really looking for? I'm not certain that her behavior is really...nice. But, hey, you want what you want, right?"

Nighttime here really seemed to be a time warp back to the past. Tonight, the house, seen through the veil of oaks that led to the sweeping entrance, seemed to stand guard upon a hill. A soft breeze caused the branches to sway in the ethereal light, and the path to the house might have led right into a different time and dimension. There was nothing to mar the perfection of the picture; whatever cars might have been there were hidden away in the car park, and the view he saw was one of sheer magnificence.

He drove up the vast and sweeping, oak-lined drive from the road. Once upon a time, the road had been a carriageway, and the rear entrance from the road had not been considered a grand entry at all. The grand entry had faced the river. Some things had changed. The mighty barges bringing cotton down-river were outdated. Still, with the working sugar mill and Beaumont plantations as the nearest neighbors to Donegal, and both a mile away, the view of Donegal, even by night, was spectacular.

It was quiet when he parked; yet just yesterday there had been hundreds—possibly thousands—of people crawling all over the place, from the reenactors to the visitors who flocked here on the day of the actual reenactment. That thought made him smile as well—in comparison to the real battles that had taken place during the war, the skirmish here had been nothing. But Donegal Plantation had always been home to those who knew how to survive. When Marshall Donegal had been killed, Emma Donegal had raised her son and daughters on her own, and she had kept the plantation thriving, even under Union rule. It was sad—and probably not at all fair—that legend had her as the one to slip out into the skirmish and kill her husband. Her motive was supposedly the fact that she didn't agree with his management of the plantation, or with the management of their slaves, several of whom he was supposed to have slept with, along with quadroons at the quadroon balls in New Orleans, and the wives of a few of his best friends. Their daughters, too. But those rumors weren't anything new. People loved to speculate. He knew that neither Ashley nor Frazier believed in the rumors regarding Emma, and he didn't take them very seriously, either.

He parked the car directly before the house and got out. He knew that he wouldn't be out here at all, and the team wouldn't be on call, if Adam Harrison hadn't been old friends with Frazier Donegal.

An inexplicable discomfort settled over him. It

was late, of course, and he was miles and miles away from Bourbon Street, where the parties were just hitting their stride. Out here, the world was sleeping.

Still, he hesitated.

Lights in the large old stable building showed him that tourists were still quartered there, and he even saw some light emitting from the smaller stables, still in use, behind the large barn structure.

The house looked ominously quiet.

He walked around the side of the house, not certain why he was experiencing such a distinct impression that something was wrong. And then he knew. As he stood there, he saw a figure in white come tearing out of the graveyard.

For a split second, he was paralyzed. She looked like a phantom, a stunning vision from the past, a gorgeous ghost in a long, flowing white gown, her golden hair caught in the wind.

It wasn't a ghost; it was Ashley.

She looked just as she had looked in his dream: a shimmering figure standing upon a roof with the floodwaters rising. She looked as she had looked, reaching out for him and yet trying to warn him of something horrible and dark that loomed behind him. Her fingers had slipped through his...

He couldn't let that happen now.

He raced across the grounds, hearing earth and gravel crunch beneath his feet. "Ashley!" he called her name.

She stopped; she stared at him with huge blue eyes

the size of saucers, like a doe caught in the headlights of a car.

She still saw him as a pariah.

"Ashley," he called again. She screamed and started to run away.

*They hadn't parted that badly.* She wasn't seeing him, she realized. She was still imagining whatever nightmare had caused her to run.

She turned just as he reached her, and they collided and fell to the ground. She struck out at him from below, and he caught her arms, perplexed and yet aware that she could deliver a solid blow if she chose. She seemed to be fighting for her life.

"Ashley! It's me. Jake. Jake Mallory!"

She went dead still. He realized that she was trembling violently.

"Ashley, it's Jake. Come on, Ashley, whatever else, you've known me all your life! It's Jake. What is it, what are you running from?"

Her trembling subsided.

"I found him," she said. "I found him."

"Found who, Ashley?"

"Charles. Charles Osgood."

Dead. She'd found him dead, of course. No one acted like this unless they had seen something really terrible. Certainly not Ashley Donegal.

"Where?" he asked, easing back.

He wanted to fix things for her. This was Ashley. Certainly, one of the most beautiful women he had ever known and once loved. He wanted to hold her and tell her everything would be all right….

But it wasn't, of course. She had found a dead man.

He rose quickly, taking her hand to bring her to her feet. "Where, Ashley?" he asked again, his tone quiet but authoritative.

She blinked and seemed to gain possession of herself again. "The graveyard. The family vault," she said.

"And he is dead? You're certain?"

"Oh, yes."

He pulled out his cell phone and dialed 911, and carefully gave the address and the situation. Ashley stared at him while he did so. If Jackson Crow was already on the case, then they had federal jurisdiction. But they needed a medical pathologist out here now, and, naturally, they'd have to work closely with the local police.

"Go on inside," he told her. "The police are coming."

She shook her head. "I'm with you. I'm not moving. I mean, I'm not moving if you're not moving."

"Someone needs to tell your grandfather."

"He's smart—he'll figure it out when he hears the sirens."

"When he hears the sirens, he'll be worried about you."

"I'm staying with you!"

He wondered if she was actually so shaken that

she was afraid to head for the house herself—afraid, perhaps, of everyone on her property now.

"All right, but we need to keep a distance from the actual...scene," he said.

"Corpse," she said dully.

He walked back to the cemetery. She hadn't released his hand. She wasn't going to.

They had to part momentarily to slip through the gate without opening it further, and Jake was loath to make any changes to the scene. A stone cherub seemed to follow their passage through the rows of vaults, shimmering beneath the moonlight.

He didn't have to ask her to lead him; he knew exactly where to find the Donegal vault.

It was the largest, the most ornate and the most beautiful in the graveyard. When they turned the corner in the center to reach it, he stopped, trying to take in everything that he saw before the local authorities came to assess the situation.

There was the vault. Cherubs and gargoyles guarded the iron-gate doors and the four corners of the tomb. High at the front was a life-size angel, and, caught upon its foundation by the heavy canvas straps of a period backpack, was the body of a man. He hadn't known Charles Osgood, and if he hadn't seen many a portrait of Marshall Donegal, he wouldn't have known that this wasn't a trick of time, that they hadn't gone back approximately one hundred and fifty years to discover a dead cavalry man in the cemetery.

*Convenient place to die. Or be murdered.*

But despite the blood that dripped from the body and pooled at the feet, he didn't believe that the man had been killed here. He had been brought here soon after death, but he hadn't died here. The body had been put on display. It was evident that whoever had killed the man had done so to be historically accurate—and to make sure that the world knew that a man had been killed just as Marshall Donegal had been killed long ago. Was it an assault on the Donegal family? Or had someone wanted this particular man dead and used the Donegal family history as a means of throwing off suspicion?

"He was so proud to be playing Marshall Donegal!" Ashley whispered.

"Stay here—exactly here," he told her.

He was afraid that she was going to cling to him, but she didn't. With him there, she seemed to be finding her own strength.

"I know. It's a crime scene," she said woodenly.

Jake, watching where he walked, searched the area surrounding the tomb. There was nothing there. The graveled paths around the tombs certainly didn't allow much room for footprints, and he didn't expect to find any. They would have to hope that the forensic team summoned could find fingerprints, hair, fibers, DNA—anything that might tell them who had brought the man to his death, and then here.

They could hear the sirens then, shrieking through

the night. And then voices as guests staying in the various rental rooms began to rouse.

"Get to the cemetery gates," Jake told her. "Make sure no one but the police comes through."

She nodded jerkily yet didn't move.

"Ashley!" he said, taking her shoulders. "You don't want guests wandering in here, and your grandfather will be coming out any minute, worried to death, and he is in his eighties!"

She snapped to finally and nodded, spinning about in a whirl of shimmering white. He watched her go, his insides twisting in a knot of pain. She didn't need this; she didn't deserve this. Of course, the dead man hadn't deserved it, either. As he heard the sirens come closer and closer, he pulled out his cell phone and dialed Jackson Crow. It hadn't been so important before that the team arrive quickly; now, it was.

He looked back at the corpse, and time melted away again.

Someone had reenacted murder.

# 5

---

Ashley stood shivering at the gates of the cemetery, trying to compose herself. She had certainly been in something like shock, but Jake was here, and now she was okay. It was bizarre that she was okay *because* Jake was here, but that was the way that it was; he was in control, and it brought her back to herself.

She had felt that she'd been losing her mind; the dreams had plagued her mercilessly, and Charles had been gone, and she had longed to see Jake.

And Charles was dead—and Jake was here. Really here.

And she had to quit behaving like a "dumb blonde" screamer out of an old movie. She started to move again, thinking that she had to get to her grandfather.

But she didn't get that far.

The first person to rise and rush out, hearing the wail of the sirens, was Cliff Boudreaux, and he didn't have far to come, racing out of his quarters in a flannel robe. His graying brown hair was mussed and he was barefoot, as if he had been sleeping. She saw that he first looked back to the house, but then saw her and ran to her instead, gripping her shoulders, his eyes filled with worry.

"Ashley? Ashley, why are you standing here like this? What the hell has happened?"

She stared back at him, suddenly more assured, and she was even angry again, furious. Someone had killed Charles Osgood. He could be petulant; he could be whiney; but he was a good man who, to the best of her knowledge, had never hurt anyone.

She felt all sense of trembling and shaking fade away completely. Yes, Jake had done that for her.

"Charles Osgood is dead. I just found him in the cemetery," Ashley said. "The police are on their way."

As she spoke, she saw that people were beginning to emerge from the far stables, where the rental rooms were.

"Cliff, I'm going to get my grandfather. Please make sure no one wanders into the cemetery," she said.

She turned toward the house, noticing Beth and her grandfather had come out to the riverside porch together and looked as confused as anyone else. She broke into a run, crossing the distance from the graveyard to the steps.

"Ashley!"

Frazier reached out, and she ran straight into his

arms. "I'm all right, Grampa, I'm all right. But I found Charles Osgood. He's...dead."

Frazier drew away from her, staring into her eyes. Beth let out a soft gasp but said nothing.

Ashley continued, "I thought I heard something in the cemetery."

"You heard something in a cemetery—and you hurried into it to find out what was going on? Lord, girl!" Beth said.

"I've lived my whole life with the family cemetery in full view from my window, Beth," Ashley reminded her. "And Jake's here," she added quickly.

"Jake's here?" Frazier said, and it seemed to make everything better.

"Yes, yes, Jake's here," she said, nodding. It might be best to let them think that Jake had been in the cemetery with her from the beginning.

Two police cars pulled into the front. The driver of the first seemed to hesitate a minute, but then he pulled straight on down by the side of the house, slowly passing the onlookers who had gathered outside. The second car came to a halt by the first. Ashley quickly ran down the steps from the porch to meet the officer who exited the first car. It was Drew Montague, who had been on call when she had reported Charles Osgood as missing.

"Well, Ashley, what's going on?" Drew Montague asked her. Behind him a uniformed man got out of the car.

"I found Charles Osgood. He's in the cemetery.

Someone bayoneted him and hung him on the family tomb," she said. She spoke to Drew but kept glancing at the other man who had approached them.

"I'm Detective Mack Colby, Miss Donegal, with the parish sheriff's office," he explained. He was so pleasantly nondescript, she wondered whether that was part of his act. "Can you take me to the body and explain, please, how you happened to discover it?"

"I woke up after I'd gone to bed. I thought I saw lights out there, and I went to investigate," she said.

"You ran into a cemetery in the middle of the night when you thought that someone might be out there?" Mack asked politely. He and Drew exchanged a glance. There was suspicion in his tone, despite the even level.

She let out an exasperated sigh. "I have lived here forever. My dead ancestors are in that cemetery. I'm not afraid of it!" she said. "The worst we've ever found before has been potheads and frat boys. I am not afraid of my own property," she said indignantly.

"Looks like you should be," Drew Montague murmured.

"Montague," Mack Colby said, "can you keep people away from the gates? The forensic crew will be here shortly. Miss Donegal, please take me to the body. Did you touch him? Are you quite certain he's dead?"

"He's dead. And, no, I didn't touch him," Ashley said. By then, her grandfather was by her side.

"Perhaps," he said icily, "it would be best if you investigated the dead man without giving my granddaughter difficulty?"

"If she's right, this is a murder investigation," Colby said, his eyes narrowing. "And you are—?"

"Frazier Donegal. We've not met, but you've surely known that this property was here and who owns it. My granddaughter insisted we call this man's disappearance in last night, afraid that something bad had happened. None of you seemed interested at the time."

More sirens blared in the night; a rescue vehicle came to a halt behind the police cars. Augie Merton, a medical pathologist from the coroner's office, emerged from the passenger's seat. He was a nice man; Ashley knew him. He sometimes came out to do lectures on Civil War medicine. Though the former New Yorker had lived in the parish for almost thirty years, he was still affectionately called the Yankee doc.

"Ashley, Frazier, sorry to see you here under unhappy circumstances," he said, coming forward with his black bag.

"Damn it, let's get to the corpse," Mack Colby said. "Lead the way. With any luck, no one has disturbed the crime scene."

"No one has. Jake Mallory is in the cemetery, watching over the scene," Ashley said.

Mack Colby stopped walking. "And who the hell is Jake Mallory?"

"An old friend," Ashley said.

"A good old boy. Great!" Mack Colby muttered.

"He's with the federal government," Frazier informed him.

"Feds have to be asked in. He'd best not be fiddling around in my jurisdiction!" Colby said.

"Frankly, I don't think he and his team *fiddle* with cases. I think they solve them," Ashley said, staring at him. Of course, she didn't really know much of anything about Jake's team, but this man was truly patronizing, and she was feeling just as indignant as Frazier.

Before he could respond, she said, "This way."

"Ashley, they can surely find the body on their own," Frazier said, worried about her and apparently not at all fond of Detective Mack Colby.

"I'm fine," she assured him. She mentally drew herself up, though it was difficult to do so with dignity when she was running around in a white nightgown.

She turned quickly, assuming that the men would follow. They did. It was surprising that Beth and Frazier chose to follow as well; she was certain that corpses did not fall into Beth's usual life. But she didn't protest; Frazier was proud and would insist on seeing what happened on his property. And there was no stopping Beth when she made up her mind.

When they reached the gate, Mack Colby said, "Stop! Who has touched this gate?" he asked.

Ashley turned to stare at him. "Possibly? Hundreds of people. Maybe thousands. There was a reenactment here yesterday. It was after the reenactment that Charles Osgood disappeared—something that we reported to the police."

"How long had he been missing when you called in the disappearance?" Colby asked.

"A few hours," Ashley said.

"You called in about a missing adult after just a few hours?" Colby asked, his voice level, and yet there was something suspicious in his tone.

"He had very badly wanted to play my ancestor, which he did," Ashley explained. "He should have been around to celebrate with the others afterwards."

Augie let out a sound of impatience. "Where is my body, please?"

Mack Colby lifted a hand, put on a latex glove with a snap, and pushed the gate open to a wider degree. Ashley slipped through, followed by her strange posse: Mack Colby and Augie, her grandfather and Beth.

Jake Mallory waited at the end of the path, before the turn to the Donegal family vault. Jake had always had a certain presence. His arms were crossed over his chest; he stood with his feet planted slightly apart and appeared formidable and authoritative as he stood there. Part of it was his height. He wasn't particularly heavily built, but his muscles were toned, his stance was straight, and, when he moved, it was with a swift agility one might not expect in a man so tall. He wasn't easily ruffled, and his temper seldom stood in the way of his intentions.

"So you're the fed, huh? Did you touch anything?" Mack Colby demanded. "And what the hell kind of federal officer are you?"

Jake remained calm as he reached into the pocket of his jeans for a slim leather wallet, which he opened and presented to Mack Colby. "Agent Jake Mallory," he said. Colby frowned, stepping forward to examine the credentials Jake had offered. His frown didn't disappear as he stepped back.

"How did you happen to be in the area?" he demanded. "And you do understand the concept of local jurisdiction? You have to be invited down if we have a problem, and I don't think that we'll have a problem here. We're capable."

"I'm sure you are capable. I'm a friend of the family. I happened to be on my way to the house. My boss is a friend of the Donegal family as well, and Frazier Donegal called him when Ashley was first worried about the disappearance of one of their re-enactors. If you'll check with your superiors, we have been asked to join in the investigation. Of course, we were looking for a missing man before. Now, we're looking for a killer," Jake said evenly.

Colby wasn't satisfied; his gaze remained fixed on Jake.

Augie cleared his throat. "May I get to the body, please?"

"A minute, Augie," Colby said. "They found a corpse—a man obviously not in need of an ambulance. I want the crime-scene people in here—I want pictures of the body *in situ*. I want every fiber, hair, fingerprint. And I want all the rest of you people out!"

"Detective, I'd like to stay," Jake said.

Mack Colby grunted. "Let me tell you—this parish has amazing forensic facilities. And we're not a bunch of local yokels just because we're in bayou country. You like to come down here from the big cities and—"

"I'm from Louisiana," Jake interrupted. "I was born and raised in Orleans Parish."

Mack Colby paused at that. He lifted his hands. "Fine. You stay." He turned around and looked at Ashley, Frazier and Beth. "All right. The rest of you—out!"

Ashley looked at Jake. He gave her a small, reassuring smile. Despite the fact that she was standing in her family graveyard with a dead man not far away in the middle of a bizarre night, she did feel reassured. In fact, she wanted to run to him. The breeze lifted her hair and touched her face, and she kept eye contact with him. Jake Mallory had always been steady and reassuring—when they were kids, when he teased her, when he taught her how to hold a cue stick, when he played his guitar and patiently went through a melody or a beat over and over again.

When he made love to her....

She had still thought that it would be awkward to see him again. They had been so close for so many years, friends and then lovers, and she had shut him out as cleanly as if she'd shut a door in his face.

Nothing like a dead man to ease the transition into seeing one another again, she thought dryly.

The thought brought a rumble of something that threatened to be hysterical laughter from her throat, and she swallowed it down quickly.

"Out," Colby repeated. "Good God, it's a crime scene!"

She nodded, turned and said to Beth and her grandfather, "Shall we?"

"This is my property," Frazier said to Mack Colby. "And I am a law-abiding citizen, a veteran of foreign wars, and, Detective Colby, I will be kept informed of what has happened and is happening on my property. I asked Agent Mallory and his team down—he is here on my request."

Frazier had said his piece. He turned to Ashley and nodded.

As they departed, a trio dressed in the parish's crime-unit jumpsuits paused for a moment to ask the way to the scene. Ashley indicated the path through the vaults with their decaying elegance and hurried on out.

More officers were on crowd control; two in uniform, flanked by Drew Montague.

"Someone want to talk to that group?" Drew asked them.

"I've got it, Grampa," Ashley said, hurrying forward.

One woman was weeping. Ashley quickly made her way through the officers and cars with their bright lights and reached the group of guests hovering by the old stables.

"As you know, we've just discovered a friend, dead, in the cemetery." She winced. Her words sounded like an oxymoron, though they were not. "We'll get you checked out quickly, and please, be assured, no one will be paying for the night."

She had to lift a hand against the bright car beams that were now on her. "Please come through the front door of the main house, and we'll be sure that you're completely cleared of all charges."

"I just want to go back to sleep!" one man called out.

She looked back at Drew Montague. He shrugged. "I guess it's all right. We had a body in a hotel parking lot once, and they didn't evacuate the hotel."

"All right. Anyone who wants to go back to sleep is welcome to do so," she said, hoping that was the right thing for an innkeeper to say under the circumstances. She didn't know anything more about crime and murderers than what she had learned on television and the news, but it seemed that someone had killed Charles Osgood and displayed his body in a certain way for a reason. The scenario didn't appear to offer danger to her guests for the rest of that night, especially since she was pretty sure the place would be crawling with police and crime-scene investigators until daylight and possibly beyond.

"Guess we'll be safe enough tonight, with the police prowling around everywhere," a woman said as if following Ashley's own train of thought.

"What the hell happened?" someone else demanded.

"We don't know anything right now," Ashley said. "The police are here. I'm sure one of the most important things is that no one goes near the cemetery until the scene is cleared by the police. And, please, of course, be very careful."

"Oh! He was murdered, he was murdered!" Another woman cried out. She was about fifty, in a house robe, and wearing curlers. "Oh, oh! We've got to get out of here, we've got to get out of here!" she cried, running forward and then running back.

"Calm down, Martha!" a man said firmly, stepping forward to grab her arm. "We have nothing to do with any of this. I'm going back to sleep. We'll check out in the morning."

"Please, all of you, I'll be at the desk in front. Stay the night, or pack up and leave. Whichever you prefer," Ashley said.

She noticed that Justin had appeared; he had come out of the stables alone, and she assumed that he had left Nancy with the children. He moved through the crowd and reached her side. "Charles?" he asked softly.

She nodded grimly.

"In the cemetery?"

"Yes."

"We searched there."

"I know. I was in there myself," she said dully. "I have to get in the house and start handling this situation. You have the children—I assume you want to get them out of here, and don't worry, we—"

"We're all right," he said quietly. "Don't worry about us. You've got enough on your hands right now."

She smiled and raised her voice. "Anyone who—"

"Not so fast!"

She turned around to see that Mack Colby was striding toward her. He gazed at her impatiently and addressed the crowd. "I'm sorry, folks. I'll need a few minutes with each of you before you pack up and leave. It can be tonight, or into the morning hours, but I'll need to question you all."

"About what?" Martha's husband demanded indignantly. "We had nothing to do with this!"

"You're here, and a man was murdered here. He took part in the reenactment, he disappeared and now he has reappeared—dead. You all were here. This is simple, people. Someone killed him, and you're all suspects until you're cleared. I'll need to question every single one of you!"

"Oh, my God!" Martha shouted. And then she dropped to the ground in a dead faint.

Jake called Jackson, sorry to wake him up, but knowing that Jackson needed to be advised immediately about the situation and the arrival of Mack Colby on the scene.

"All right. Tread carefully," Jackson said. "I'll call Adam right now and have him get hold of his congressional friends and make sure they speak with the local officials again. They weren't interested before—they'd already given us jurisdiction on the case. I doubt if there will be any trouble; Frazier Donegal is a force in this area, so it seems, and his contacts are endless. Do your best to get along with the local police. I'll pack up with Angela, and we'll be out right away. I'll have the others follow as soon as they've gotten their equipment together."

"Thanks," Jake said.

He hung up; the pathologist from the coroner's office had arrived. Jake continued to watch as the forensics team took pictures and combed the area. He remained a bit surprised that Mack Colby hadn't forced him out when he had finished listening to the pathologist regarding the corpse.

Of course, there wouldn't be a final determination until the body had been taken to the coroner's office for a full autopsy. But according to Augie in his preliminary findings, Charles Osgood had probably been rendered unconscious by a blow to the head—there was a pre-mortem bruise appearing on his forehead—sometime yesterday; death had not occurred until two or three hours ago, when he had, quite simply, bled to death. He had received five stab wounds to the abdomen area, apparently after his inert body had been hung from the angel, the wounds obviously caused by a sharp instrument. His blood had slowly oozed from his body, creating the puddle on the ground.

With any luck, the blow to his head had been severe enough to have kept him unconscious until death had come, though, since it had been more than twenty-four hours since he had gone missing, Augie suspected they would find drugs of some kind in his system. It seemed that the killer had been intent on keeping his victim quiet until the act of murder had been completed, but, at the least, he had saved Charles Osgood from the agony and fear that surely would have accompanied his death had he been conscious.

Jake waited while Augie's assistants brought the body down, carefully preserving the backpack and the straps that had kept him dangling from the tomb's majestic angel. Meanwhile the team searched the ground for possible footprints and used specialized lights to seek fingerprints on the tomb wall itself. There were hundreds of fingerprints, so it seemed, and the hundreds were atop more hundreds. In a small way, the Donegal cemetery was a tourist attraction in itself. The gates were usually locked, but the wall was really no obstacle, and someone might have forgotten to lock up again.

Jake wished them well. It was going to be a difficult and long haul, trying to sort evidence. Unless something could be found on the body or the backpack itself, any fingerprints or evidence could have belonged to any of the visitors or tenants who had traversed the cemetery.

He'd been to the reenactment at the plantation several times throughout the years. He closed his eyes for a moment, imagining it. The real battle had ended in the cemetery, oddly and sadly for Marshall Donegal, in front of his family crypt—he had bled out there, just like the murder victim, Charles Osgood. Jake found it curious that the body had been left so... displayed. And that the murderer had waited until now, more than twenty-four hours after the disappearance of the victim. If someone's intent had been just to ease Charles Osgood from his mortal life, that someone could have far more easily managed to stab him in the midst of the crowd that flocked around the reenactment. If the murderer had left him just lying there, the slim chance that it had been accidental—boys being boys and playing with real sharp weapons—would have existed. Someone, obviously, would have still been guilty of manslaughter, but the display meant murder for certain—and that the murderer wanted it known.

The body was wrapped, ready to be transported to the coroner's office.

"Dr. Merton," Jake said, addressing the pathologist. "Anything else you can tell me?"

"Augie, just Augie," the medical examiner replied. "Not yet—I have to cut him open. But I do believe that toxicology reports will prove that my assumptions are correct." He was quiet for a moment, shaking his head. "Seems like Miss Donegal was concerned from the start. If someone had paid more attention to her, he might have been found and saved."

"It's my understanding that they did search for the fellow. My bosses were called in because the Donegals were so concerned," Jake said.

"They didn't search hard enough, did they?" Augie asked. He looked around. "Must have been some feat—this man was no Tinkerbell. A hefty fellow. He was brought here before he was killed. That's evident by the blood patterns, I'd say, even though I'm not a blood-spatter specialist. Then again, I am an M.D., with a specialization in medical pathology, and I don't think anyone needed my expertise to see that the man was dead. Well, young man, if you need anything from me, you call me. Don't worry about blunderbuss Detective Colby. He's not a bad chap. We don't have this kind of thing happen often out here. Come to think of it, I've never seen anything like this—anywhere. But he's a decent fellow, just trying to play alpha dog right off."

"I'm sure we'll all be fine," Jake told him. He was done here himself; the crime-scene unit was still searching, dusting, taping and hoping for the smallest clue. There was nothing else he could do at the scene for the moment.

He followed Augie and the body out of the cemetery.

Returning to the lawn area between the house and the outbuilding, Jake saw that while the police were holding a line with their vehicles and a number of officers, the guests who had been staying at Donegal Plantation were now gathered up by the cottage, all speaking at once. Mack Colby was lifting his hands and trying to maintain some sense of order.

Ashley was still there, still the historical damsel in distress in her white gown. She knelt next to a woman who was sitting on the ground, head between her knees, and he could see the way that Ashley's jaw was hardening. Mack Colby was really beginning to anger her. It was a good thing the detective hadn't chosen to be a doctor, because his bedside manner would have killed many a patient before curing them.

Jake walked quickly through the crowd to reach her side, hunkering down by her.

"I need to get Martha into the house!" Ashley said irritably.

"That's fine," Colby said. "That's fine, but I repeat—no one, do you understand me? No one leaves. So settle in, folks, and if you're in a hurry to get out of here, try to be first in line for the questioning."

The elderly woman paled, and Jake stepped in hastily to curb what Ashley might say.

"May I pick you up?" Jake asked Martha. "With your permission, I can carry you in and set you on one of the sofas."

Ashley flashed him a glance of gratitude.

Martha placed a hand on his cheek. "Oh, yes, young man, please. My legs are feeling very wobbly."

"Thank you," said an older man next to them, obviously Martha's husband. "I don't think I'm quite up to lifting these days."

"Herbert, I am not that heavy!" Martha protested.

"It's not that you're heavy, my dear," Herbert said, "it's that I'm old."

Martha waved a hand in the air. Jake put his arms around her and lifted her, and Ashley led the way into the house.

"I'll need a room where I can be alone with each individual," Colby said, elbowing his way past everyone as he entered the parlor.

Tense and rigid, her lips pursed, Ashley directed him to a study on the bayou side of the house. Jake laid Martha down on the Duncan Phyfe sofa near the double stairway where her husband joined her, and followed Ashley and Colby.

The study was a pleasant room with a mahogany desk, computer, printer, and shelves lined with books and family pictures. It was a spacious room; two chairs sat in front of the desk, and a wingback chair faced the bayou-side windows. Mack Colby had sat himself behind the desk.

"I don't want to create any problems here," Jake said, his voice firm. "And if you question these people and have the courtesy to keep proper records, I believe everything will be in order. As I said before, the federal government was called in when this was a missing persons case. Since the victim was apparently kidnapped, the federal government has jurisdiction. But I suggest that we handle it as a joint investigation. It's a truly sad, horrible and bizarre situation, and I would think that all possible means of law enforcement would be indicated."

Colby stared at him as if he would implode. His face was mottled and almost as red as the pool of blood in the cemetery.

"Your behavior is outrageous!" Colby told him.

"No, sir. I suggest you call your superiors, at your leisure, of course. There's no reason that this can't be a combined effort, which is always best. There's nothing in the world like cooperation between law-enforcement agencies. You'll be so much more knowledgeable than we could possibly be on so many fronts."

Mack Colby kept looking at him as if he would finally pop, but he seemed to know that Jake was telling the truth. He leveled a finger at him.

"There's something fishy here. These folks called in the *feds* when a man had only been missing a few hours. A grown man. Someone knew something had happened to him, and if you're not going to get at the truth, I'll be making a stink they hear up in Washington and beyond!"

"Oh, good God!" Ashley, who had been standing quietly near Jake, exploded. "I'm the one who raised the alarm, and I raised it because *I know—knew—Charles Osgood!* He would have been here celebrating. He wasn't. I knew him, don't you understand?"

Jake set an arm on Ashley's shoulders. "Really, I think Detective Colby realizes that now—he is just doing his job. But we're all good now." He turned back to Colby. "Look, Detective, my team's expertise is in understanding why people behave the way that they do. And Ashley's intuitions assist us. Yes, we need to question everyone, but, because of the display of the body, it's evident that this wasn't simply an act of passion, a mistake or accident in the reenactment, or the casual act of a thief or drifter. This was personal, or, possibly, ritualistic. If you want to start with the guests who are down here for the first time, that's great. They can be cleared quickly, and we can begin to look at the people involved with Donegal, the reenactors and the locals."

Colby seemed somewhat mollified, but his facial muscles were still taut. He nodded jerkily to Jake. "Fine. You're sitting in? Or are you going to do the questioning?"

"I'll sit in and watch. Thanks. I think you'll ask

the right questions, and I can judge the responses. Ashley? Would you like to start bringing people in? First, guests—"

"Yes, guests who have never been here before. I've got it," she said.

He lowered his head, smiling. Ashley—tough Ashley—was back.

He settled into a chair. It was going to be a long night.

Martha could stand and walk and move, so it seemed most reasonable to let Martha, and then Herbert, go first. Ashley realized that she was trying to bring people in and out from a police questioning room as if she were still a hostess and it was a social situation, and she felt a little foolish at first but then decided it was the best way to keep everyone calm.

Beth pitched right in, brewing coffee and producing a nice array of finger foods.

Jake emerged from the room at one point, asking her to check her registration books and make sure that all guests still at the plantation were present, and also to give him a list of those who had left already.

She nodded, glad of anything to do that kept her moving and busy.

She realized that no one had really shed a tear yet for Charles Osgood. She felt like crying over his life then. He hadn't been handsome; he hadn't been popular. He had still been a decent fellow—always wanting to be handsome and popular. And now he was gone. And the question remained, of course: Had he been killed because he'd been Charles Osgood… or because he'd been playing the part of Marshall Donegal?

Finally, Colby had interviewed all of their casual guests, moved on to repeat guests and was ready to start on those who were close to the reenactment, the plantation or the family. Beth was surprised when she was called in, but she shrugged and went all the same. Justin followed next, and Ashley was close enough to the door to hear one of his answers to Colby.

"Oh, yeah. Of course, I brought my children along while I planned and plotted a bizarre murder. I've been hiding Charles under the kids' beds for the last night. Right, yes, of course, question away."

She grinned before moving on. She heard Jake patiently explain that they were hoping to find out if he'd seen anything, noticed anything or could give them any possible information.

Cliff went in after him, and while Cliff was being interviewed, she was startled to see that two new-comers—people she'd never seen before—were in the parlor, chatting with Frazier, who was still up, still making sure that he went the distance with his guests.

She hurried over to meet the couple. The man was tall, taller even, perhaps, than Jake. He obviously had Native American blood in his heritage somewhere. The woman was a pretty blonde, who almost appeared fragile.

"Ashley, Jackson Crow and Angela Hawkins," Frazier said.

She shook hands with both of them. "You're with Adam Harrison's team," she said. It wasn't a question.

"Yes, and we're so sorry that your missing person has been discovered dead," Angela told her.

Jackson nodded. "Will you bring me, please, to Jake and the local officer who is doing the questioning?"

"Absolutely."

"Beth will bring Angela up, assign them and Jake rooms," Frazier told her.

"This way." And she took him in.

Jackson Crow had a low, level voice, rich with authority. The door to the study had quickly shut behind him, but she had to smile, hearing the tone of his voice, through the wood paneling. He and Jake seemed to have the ability to be completely even-keeled—and yet say exactly what they meant in a way that brooked no interference.

She started to walk away, but the door opened and Jake came out.

"You and your household are to go to bed and get some sleep," he told her.

"Oh, I don't think—"

"We're almost done here for the night. Jackson is taking over," Jake told her. "I want to get some sleep.

You must need some, too. How about it? Where am I sleeping?"

She wanted to ask, *Could you sleep in the chair in my room?*

"I'm sure Grampa would have told Beth to put you in the Jeb Stuart room," she told him. "Do you want to get your things?"

He waved a hand in the air. "Right now, I want to crash. If I remember right, there's soap, shampoo, razors, toothpaste, you name it, in the rooms, right?"

She nodded.

"Then I'll run down in the morning. Come on, I'll walk you to your room."

Ah, yes, Jake could be the Southern gentleman. There was no "home" to walk her to now, so he'd walk her to her room.

"Hey, I live here," she reminded him.

"And I want to see you in. And lock your door."

"Oh, come on, Jake! I am not afraid of my grandfather or Beth—"

"Someone managed to get an unconscious, living man into the graveyard and to kill him there. Ashley, lock your door."

She nodded. They went through the living room, where Jake assured Beth and Frazier that they were free to get some rest; Jackson would deal with Mack Colby and arrangements for the continuing investigation. They'd see that Cliff got back to his place, that officers remained on the property until midmorning and that everything was locked up and safe.

Frazier kissed Ashley's forehead; Beth gave her a hug. She and Jake followed them up the stairs.

The Jeb Stuart room was next to Ashley's at the back of the house, so he didn't have to go far.

At her door, he said, "Good-night, and scream blue blazes if you need anything."

"Thanks, Jake."

He hesitated a minute. Jake had amazing sea-green eyes. They changed like the sea as well, but they were striking against his tanned face and auburn hair. She lowered her head suddenly, wondering why she had needed so desperately to step away from him.

Because her father had been dead. Dead. And Jake seemed to have spoken to him. Strange and scary— but, somehow believable. So her reaction had just been…fear.

Maybe even fear that her dreams should be believed as well.

"Hey, are you all right? Are you okay with me being here?" he asked her, lifting her chin and searching out her eyes. "The team is excellent. Angela and Jackson are amazing."

"I'm fine. I'm glad you're here. I mean, you know the plantation as no other investigator could possibly know it, and you know many of the people involved."

"That's true. I just want you to be all right…with me being here."

"I'm fine." She winced inwardly. "Jake, actually, I'm sorry. I know I overreacted, but…"

"Your father was dead," he said flatly. "That was the past. It's fine. I understand. Okay, as I said, I'm right next door. Just whistle—you know the old line!"

He waited for her to go into her room and lock the door; then she heard him enter his own room next door.

Ashley washed her face, brushed her teeth and realized she was still in her nightgown, but it was filthy, so she showered and changed. It was almost morning—no matter. She lay down and prayed for sleep.

It came.

The first pale rays of morning light seeping through the drapes woke her.

She frowned, still groggy. Was there someone at the foot of her bed?

*Jake?*

No, not Jake. It was a man in a Confederate uniform. He wore a sweeping, plumed hat. She knew who he was—her ancestor, Marshall Donegal.

She blinked; he would disappear, she knew.

He didn't.

She opened her mouth to scream, and he leapt to his feet.

"By sweet Jesus, did I breed a line of whimpering cowards? Ashley Donegal, pull yourself together! I'm here to help you."

# Interlude

The television stations had gotten hold of the information.

He was stunned; the body shouldn't have been found until morning. There should have been time for Charles to...ripen a bit.

But alone with his screen in front of him and dawn just breaking, he could see the reporter by the side of the road; a police car was blocking entry to the estate, but there was Donegal Plantation, as grand as ever, surviving time and death and change.

He didn't quite feel the satisfaction he should have from the kill.

Of course, it wasn't that he wanted to torture poor old Charles. He wanted the Donegal clan to suffer. It might have taken more than a hundred and fifty years for them to pay the piper, but they would be the ones to suffer. The sins of the fathers had to be paid.

The news crews couldn't get onto the property, so they were padding the broadcast with pictures. First, old Frazier. He could almost hear the old man's voice, rich but low, rippling along in that light accent like a roll of the Mississippi.

Then Ashley. The beautiful blonde, the belle, the last of the Donegal clan.

# 6

---

*Back at Donegal.* Jake couldn't settle in. He'd stripped down to his briefs but now lay staring at the double doors to the wraparound porch, the ceiling and around the room.

Back at Donegal.

Alone, he could remember why he and Ashley had parted. He would never forget the look in her eyes, the last time he had seen her. The look in her eyes... the way she had backed away from him.

They'd been friends forever. When they'd been young, the three-years difference in their ages had been gargantuan; as they had grown older, the annoying little girl had become inquisitive and fun. And he had loved to tease her. They'd argued incessantly; they'd done their best to beat each other at every game, to outrace each other on Donegal horses, and they'd laughed when they'd unseated one another.

Then they had grown older still.

And he had fallen in love. Maybe he'd been falling in love all his life, and he had just been waiting for her to catch up.

They'd flirted, they'd played, they'd kissed—and when he'd been twenty-two and she had been nineteen, the flirting and the stolen adolescent kisses had become much more. He'd never forget the night. He'd been due to leave for his last semester at Carnegie Mellon, and everyone had come in from the countryside to celebrate his last night home. They couldn't all crowd down to the bars on Bourbon or Frenchman streets, because several in the group were still underage, so they had rented out one of the old historic inns on St. Anne's. They had partied by the brick fire and then, sometime in the wee hours, he'd walked her to her room and gone to his…but seconds later, he'd heard a knock on his door, and Ashley had been there with this look in her eyes. She had asked, "Must you be *such* a gentleman? After all, you're heading back to college, and I'm off to school in Florida, and shouldn't we have a few memories?"

There had been nothing awkward about the night. Memory, of course, could alter and be selective, but he could still *see* the way she had looked that night, the brilliance in her eyes, the silky shimmer of her hair in the pale light and shadows. Clothing had melted away, and there had never been such a rush as just feeling her flesh against his. He hadn't wanted to leave after that night, but she had told him, "We've been best friends for years—you have always been a part of my life. You have a semester left, and I have faith and trust. A little thing like distance can't tear us apart."

Distance hadn't ripped them apart. Death had done so.

For him, it had been the odd beginning of another part of his life. For her, it had been the end. At a time when he should have been able to comfort her the most, he had become anathema.

But now, he was back at Donegal.

And a man had been murdered.

He stood up and got dressed again; he wasn't going to sleep.

Jake left his room, pausing to listen at Ashley's door, but all was silent. He flushed, glad that she didn't suddenly swing the door open and see him standing there.

Downstairs in the darkened dining room, he heard voices. Looking out, he saw that the police were still there—at least, the patrol cars.

A drone of voices from the study alerted him to the fact that Jackson was still in with Mack Colby, and maybe Cliff. He didn't know.

He frowned; the commotion from outside had grown louder. Curious, he walked out the roadside door and looked down the avenue of oaks.

The police were blocking the entrance to the plantation, but he could see that several news crews were out on the road. Crunching down the drive, he reached the officers. Drew Montague was standing in front of his police car, arms crossed over his chest, a look of pure annoyance on his face.

Montague saw him. "I don't know how the word got out so fast. They're like flies on a corpse. If you'll excuse the expression."

"Has anyone spoken to them?"

He shook his head. "I told them that it was a crime scene, and that they couldn't come on the property. That's all. Luckily, it is private property, so it makes it easier to keep them away."

Jake leaned on the police car next to Drew Montague, trying to listen. There were three reporters with their camera crews situated so as to pick up the plantation house in the background of their shots. He recognized the local network-affiliate anchorwoman, Marty Dean—he'd actually gone to high school with her—but the other two reporters were men he'd never noticed on the news before.

Perhaps they thought this story would be picked up by a national network. He was sure that the information that a man had been murdered on the property was out—they were living in the era of cell phones, texts and instant communication, and Donegal Plantation housed many guests.

He could hear Marty clearly.

"Donegal Plantation, historically a place of tragedy and loss, and filled with strange and eerie happenings throughout the years. Have the ghosts of Donegal arisen? Unconfirmed reports state that the body of a man in a Confederate uniform was found in the family cemetery on the estate. But other deaths have occurred at Donegal as well. Some are documented, and some are rumor, such as the hanging of a house slave after the murder of the master's wife during the first half of the 1800s. The Civil War–era master of the estate, Marshall Donegal, a brilliant tactician who might have served the Confederacy well, died within that cemetery. Perhaps he is still waging war against his enemies!"

That was too much.

Jake pushed away from the car and approached Marty. She saw him; her eyes widened, she smiled with pleasure.

"I see a Donegal guest now," she said into the microphone, nodding at her cameraman.

Jake felt the camera come his way. It didn't disturb him or stop him.

"Jake Mallory, one of our local heroes, seems to have been staying at Donegal Plantation. Mr. Mallory, can you tell us what has happened here? Some speculate that the ghosts are murdering people!"

"The police will give the media everything when they have something to say, Miss Dean. I'd just like to point out that Donegal Plantation is far more than a place of tragedy and loss. I think it's rather foolish for anyone to imply that ghosts might be running around murdering people. A man is dead, and first and foremost, his death is a sad occasion. I'm sure that everyone involved with *responsible* media will see to it that our sorrow over his death is respected and that an historic residence and business which has offered education and entertainment to visitors for decades should not be maligned in any way. Thank you, Miss Dean—I know that you will report responsibly."

He turned and walked away.

"Jake—wait!" Marty called after him.

He ignored her. The other two newsmen had seen him, and he walked quickly by Drew Montague. Montague grinned, liking what he had said. As Marty chased Jake, Montague stopped her.

"Crime scene, ma'am. I'm still not cleared to let you in."

"But you just—"

"Mr. Mallory is an invited guest at the plantation, ma'am."

With a smile, Jake kept walking. He didn't turn back.

There was just no way out of it.

Ashley felt the scream escaping through her lips, though it was more like a gasp or choke than a scream.

The ghost swore beneath his breath and faded into nothing, and she was left staring at an empty room, wondering if she could wake herself up. But she wasn't sleeping. She was wide-awake—and seeing things.

She leapt up and ran around, turning on every light in the room. It wasn't all that necessary—it was going to be light outside soon. But she didn't want the shadows that were created when the sun first began to rise; she wanted light, brilliant light, and a lot of it.

But she froze when she heard a light tap at her door and then a voice.

"Ashley?"

It was Jake. And she suddenly felt that dreaming about *him* had caused her to have dreams or nightmares about a body in the graveyard—*before* it had been there—and Confederate soldiers who somehow got into her room and faded away as swiftly as she could blink. She was overtired, she knew.

She was losing all grip on reality.

She walked to her door and threw it open, staring at him. "Yes?"

"I was just making sure you were all right," he said.

As at all times, he was so damned easy and confident. And he couldn't have heard her—the scream she emitted hadn't even been a squeak when finally uttered.

How the hell did he just know things?

"I'm fine, just fine." Was Jake's presence here making her *think* that she had seen a ghost?

He believed they existed, even if he hadn't said as much. And his special team seemed to have some kind of insight that others didn't have—surely that was why they were so *special*.

She was glad to have him here; she would have willed him here, if she could have done so.

But now she was frightened again.

"I know you think you...see things, know things, that others don't. But please don't suggest that the ghost of Charles Osgood is telling you things to tell me, all right? If you're an investigator, investigate. Real things. Blood. Fingerprints."

He stared back at her easily, with absolutely no show of emotion.

"I heard you walking around the room. I just wanted to make sure you were all right. I'm fairly new in my actual position, but Jackson has been with the federal government for years. He's excellent at following blood or DNA trails and fingerprints. Good night, again, Ashley. I'm sorry I disturbed you."

He headed down the hall. She watched him, her stomach knotting, her heart sinking. Well, she had to be looking like a schizophrenic now, welcoming one minute and greeting him like a shrew the next.

Because, once again, she was afraid. She was afraid that she could see things that others didn't sometimes, and that was truly terrifying.

This time, she couldn't shut herself away; she had to be reasonable, and she even had to learn to accept what Jake said. And what she saw.

A man had been murdered.

She needed sleep. Ashley decided to leave the lights on. It was nearly six now, she saw by the bed-side clock. Daylight would come quickly, but until then, she would be glad of the lights.

And the television! A television would distract

her. But when she turned on the television, she saw Jake. They were repeating a newscast.

She started to change the channel, but she paused, listening to him, his strong and authoritative manner—and the way he pegged the pretty anchorwoman. She had to smile.

She changed the channel. It seemed that half a dozen channels bought footage from Marty Dean's newscast. There was Jake, once again.

She hit the remote.

And again.

He couldn't possibly be on Nick at Nite! She hit the changer until she came across *Dora the Explorer,* and at last, satisfied, and hoping that maybe she'd even learn some Spanish through her subconscious mind, she eased her head down on her pillow.

And slept soundly and without dreams intervening.

Jake took time to speak with Jackson and Angela, choosing the study for the privacy it offered. He briefed them on the events that had occurred before their arrival, and Jackson told him about the last of the interviews.

"It's absolutely amazing that no one saw anything," Jackson said.

Jake shook his head. "No, not really. I mean, obviously, I wasn't here for this reenactment, but I've been here before when they've gone on. There's so much confusion. There's black powder in the air everywhere. When the fighting is over, everyone is paying attention to the riverside porch where Ashley and her grandfather are speaking, finishing up the event. It's a patriotic moment—everyone sings 'The Battle Hymn of the Republic.'"

"Did you know Charles Osgood?" Jackson asked him.

"I met him a few times years ago. He was part of the outfit, but his stepfather was alive back then, and so Charles wasn't asked to take part in the battle. There are only six Confederate roles to be played, and there is a strict pecking order to who gets to do what when."

"We need that pecking order written down," Jackson said.

"Here's the strange thing, from what I've understood so far. Charles shouldn't have been playing Marshall Donegal. The role should have gone to Ramsay Clayton, but Charles was apparently causing a stink about having to play a Yankee—they were short a Yankee—and Ramsay decided to let Charles have the honor and play a Yankee himself."

Jake realized that they were both staring at him. He sighed. "Slavery was obviously wrong, but for some reason, it's more romantic to be a rebel now. Especially if you are from the South. Don't look at me like that."

Angela chuckled. "Hey, I'm from Virginia. I've seen plenty a Civil War roundtable."

"Me, too," Jackson said.

"Then why are you staring at me like that?" Jake asked.

"I was staring at you because it seems that Ramsay Clayton is the first man we have to investigate," Jackson told him. He cleared his throat. "Get anything you can on the man off the computer. See if he made any waves anywhere—angered anyone."

Jake nodded.

"But first let's head down to the local police station. I want to see that our use of their forensics department is going to be respected."

Jake nodded again. He didn't really want to leave the house, but he usually accompanied Jackson on their police liaison.

"By the way, nice handling of the media," Jackson said.

"Oh? I thought I walked onto a live broadcast?" Jake said.

Jackson grinned. "Apparently, it was bought by several stations. Anyway, you handled the anchorwoman well."

"I knew her."

"Great. I'd bet big-time that she'll be traipsing around here a lot. You can take the press on this one, too."

"Sure. It's hardly my expertise—"

"No, you just didn't *know* it was your expertise," Jackson told him. "I'll meet you in front in five minutes," he added, rising to leave the room.

Angela was still there. She looked like an angelic

piece of fluff, but she could handle a Glock as if she'd been a shooting champ for a hundred years.

She set her hand on his. "I'll be here," she told him.

He grinned. "The place is riddled with ghosts, isn't it?"

"Probably," she said.

"Have you met any yet?"

"I haven't tried. But I promise I'll be getting right on that. And," she added, a curve to her lips and a light in her eyes, "you know me—I usually need a little time and quiet. God knows why—most ghosts are shy of disbelievers. You'd think it would be the other way around."

"You'd think Charles Osgood's spirit would be around here somewhere," he said.

"You never know who lingers and who moves right on," Angela said. "Remember, death doesn't make the soul all-seeing. Sometimes, ghosts don't know what's happened—we all know that."

"Great," Jake said. "Death is as confusing as life."

"Don't worry today," Angela said. "I'll keep my eye on your Miss Donegal—and her grandfather, of course."

"Thanks," Jake told her.

"Want to tell me about it?" Angela asked him.

He shrugged. "We were close, intimately close. Her father died, but I knew when he first went into emergency, and I shouldn't have. And I related a dream I'd just had about him, in which he said how much he loved her and that he was all right—and two seconds later the nurse walked in to say that he was dead. In that moment, I became a pariah."

Angela nodded sympathetically. "That's why we learn to keep our own council. But you're okay, right?"

"Yes, I swear it. Don't worry about me. I'm working, and my emotions won't sway me in any way," he assured her.

"Our emotions always sway us," Angela told him. "Just so long as they sway us in the right direction, we're fine."

He left her, ready to head to the front of the house. But he heard noise in the dining room and stepped in. Ashley was there, pouring herself coffee from the samovar on the buffet.

"Ashley, can you get me a list of the Yankees and the rebels who took part in the reenactment? I'm sure the police asked you for your rosters, but would you write up the names—and what they do and how long they've been involved with the plantation?"

She nodded. "Of course."

That morning she was in jeans and a T-shirt. She still appeared as gloriously beautiful as she had in flowing white. She had that same air of dignity that sat so well on Frazier.

And elegance. Even in jeans.

And she seemed to have forgotten her earlier tirade.

"Of course," she repeated. She looked away for a moment and then back to him. "Sorry about earlier. I was really tired."

"Don't worry. It meant nothing."

She looked down. "Of course not," she murmured. But she looked up again, frowning. "Are you leaving?"

"For a few hours—just down to the station. Angela will be here. And there are still two patrol officers getting your guests out and stopping others from coming in."

"Jake, I really can't believe that one of our reenactors could have done this. I've known most of these guys since I was a kid."

"Then you need to think hard about anyone who might have had a grudge against Charles—or Ramsay Clayton."

"No one had a grudge against Charles. They felt sorry for him all the time, if anything. And I really can't imagine anyone having a grudge against Ramsay. He's a pleasant person, not much of a temper—actually, a nice man. He had no problem with letting Charles take his place."

"He wouldn't—if he knew something was going to happen to the actor playing Marshall Donegal," Jake said.

She stiffened at that. "It was a last-minute change," she told him. "Why couldn't this have been a random killing?"

He paused, thinking that was obvious—except

that Ashley very stubbornly didn't want to believe that anyone with whom she'd been friends could possibly have plotted out the brutal killing.

"First, Ashley, simple logic," he said. "You have to know this area to have kidnapped a man and kept him hostage—even drugged—for that long a time. You'd have to know Donegal Plantation well to know the cemetery, how to reach the Donegal vault easily and to escape unseen."

"We're open to the public—we're a bed-and-breakfast. And the history of the place is written up in a number of books."

"Ashley," he said seriously, "a murder like that isn't a sudden act. It was preplanned, and preplanned carefully. Is it *possible* that a stranger came on a tour and devised a way to find notoriety? Yes. But it's most likely, considering human nature and behavior, that someone close to Donegal Plantation committed this crime. I'm sure that law enforcement will look at all angles, but we—the team—specialize in behavior—" he broke off; he didn't want to tell Ashley bluntly that they would also be seeking those *who weren't still living* for help "—and even the events that occurred in the past that cause someone to act a particular way in the present, and so, we'll put our focus on those who are close to the family and Donegal Plantation. I'm sorry, but I honestly believe you're going to have to accept the fact that someone you know is a murderer."

"You could be wrong," she said.

He had to grin ruefully at that. "Damn, you're still stubborn as hell. Think about it again, about everything I said. A random act of violence wouldn't explain someone holding a man drugged and hostage and then killing him with a bayonet—*as your ancestor was killed.*"

"But you could be wrong," she insisted.

He didn't answer. "I'll be back soon," he told her.

Jackson was waiting for him in the hall. He drove, and as he headed out, he looked back in the rearview mirror as Donegal Plantation became smaller and smaller, and disappeared in the trees.

He didn't want to leave. Not while someone was still out there.

"This," Beth commented, "is sad!"

She and Ashley were at the dining-room table. All of the guests were now gone, including Justin, who had taken his family into New Orleans. At this point, it was definitely going to be better to think about his children enjoying the zoo and the aquarium than hanging around Donegal Plantation.

Ashley looked at Beth, frowning, "Well, of course, it's sad. A man is dead."

Beth shook her head. "No, this—the two of us sitting here, drooping on our elbows, getting nothing done. That's sad!"

Ashley sat back. "They asked me for a list—I've done the list. I've checked on my grandfather—he's actually sleeping. There are two guys in uniform hanging around outside, and I'm not sure what else to do."

"Well, I'm going to cook." Beth stood up. "And I suggest that you go befriend the blonde cop who is wandering all over the house."

"Angela. Angela Hawkins?" Ashley murmured.

"That would be the name of the blonde cop or fed or whatever we have walking around," Beth told her. "Go on. I'm going to occupy myself. Alone. Go find the investigator. Maybe you can help her."

Ashley rose. "All right," she said.

She left Beth and looked through the rooms on the ground floor. Upstairs, she saw the door to Angela and Jackson's room was open; Angela was inside, sitting on the bed and staring into space.

Ashley approached the door. "Hello?" she said.

The woman started and looked at her, and then smiled. "Hello. This is a beautiful place. Absolutely beautiful."

"Thank you."

"I'm sure it's full of legends," Angela said.

"You bet."

"Want to share a few?"

"Oh, Lord, well…there are supposedly several soldiers wandering around. We had an actor die of a heart attack, in the 1940s, I believe, in the barn. Members of the Donegal family have died of old age. So, let's see, we're supposedly haunted by Unionists, rebels, actors—oh, a World War I cavalryman who died in France but made his way back here. The house was built in the early eighteen hundreds, so we've decades of ghosts running around," Ashley said lightly. "Then, of course, we have the rumored ghosts who really can't possibly exist—not here. Every plantation is supposed to have the beautiful slave girl who poisoned the mistress and was then hanged from one of the oaks. But it didn't happen here. Not that way, anyway. I've had guests, however, who swear they've seen her."

"Well, sometimes people see what they want to see, don't they?" Angela asked her.

"And sometimes, what they don't want to," Ashley replied.

"Really?"

"Finding Charles," Ashley said, looking away. It wasn't what she had meant at all. She had just met this woman.

And maybe it wasn't such a good idea to remain with her.

"Well," she said awkwardly, "thank you for being here."

"It's what we do," Angela said.

Ashley inclined her head. "Thank you anyway. I'll let you get back to—to whatever you're doing. Excuse me."

"Ashley!" Angela called when she would have walked away.

Ashley paused.

"I'm not sure what Jake told you, but we were

banded together because we learned how to blend our intuitions with logic, and even to analyze our dreams. Don't let any of that scare you. If you let yourself turn fear into careful thought, you'll discover just how much you may know yourself."

"I don't know who killed Charles, and I don't have a logical—or even illogical—thought on what might have happened. I wish I did," Ashley said. She gave Angela a forced smile.

"I'm here if you need me," Angela said.

"Thanks," Ashley told her and waved, walking away. She wasn't sure where to go, and she found herself returning to her own room. She lay down on the bed, remembering that she'd slept no more than two or three hours. If she tried closing her eyes, maybe she would sleep.

What now?

The world was strange; they were waiting. Waiting for what, she wasn't certain. The police seldom captured a murderer immediately, and they were in a very bad position here, since they depended on tourism and their guests to keep the place afloat.

"Ashley."

The whisper of her name brushed her ears, and she didn't trust the sound was real, or if it was all in her mind.

She kept her eyes closed.

"What?" she demanded crossly.

"You hear me. I know you hear me. It's so difficult to find someone who actually does."

"You're the illusion of a tormented mind," Ashley said.

She swallowed hard as something settled at the foot of her bed.

*Don't do it, don't do it—don't open your eyes!* she commanded herself.

"Look, I'm trying to help you. I swear. You're my great-great-great—I don't know how many greats— granddaughter, and I'd never hurt you, not for the world, but I'm afraid for you."

"If you're afraid for me, go away. You'll give me a heart attack. Or the police will have to collect me and put me in a straitjacket if you don't," Ashley said, still keeping her eyes tightly closed.

"Donegal women are not cowards!" he said.

"I'm not a coward. I'm trying to stay sane!"

"Open your eyes, young woman!"

She did so. She blinked. She wanted to scream, but, of course, she couldn't. Her throat was locked.

And he looked so damned comfortable. He sat on the edge of the bed, a handsome man. His hair was a darker blond than hers, long and actually curling around his neck. A large-brimmed, plumed hat sat atop his head, and he had brilliant blue Donegal eyes. His uniform appeared to be new, and in pristine shape, and bore Louisiana militia insignia. A scabbard held his sword in place around his hip, even as he sat, the sheathed sword at an angle.

He stared at her.

She stared at him.

Eventually, the lump went down in her throat. She wondered if she was dreaming again. She didn't think that she was. She could feel the pillows beneath her head, and the fabric of the sheets she lay upon. Daylight was streaming through from the balcony. She could see the sky beyond. She was awake, and she pinched herself to prove it, feeling a bit ridiculous as she did so.

"You really see me!" he whispered with pleasure.

"You're in my mind," she told him.

"Maybe, but you see me." She hated to deny a man such evident pleasure at so simple a thing.

"You're a ghost, haunting Donegal Plantation," she said flatly. She groaned. "No, haunting *me.* Why me?"

"Because it's in you—it's always been in you to reach me. And I've tried to reach you forever."

She didn't know that you could startle a ghost, but apparently you could, because he jumped when she suddenly sat up. She stood then and walked around, turning away and turning back.

He didn't disappear.

"You've been in my dreams," she whispered.

"Easiest contact," he told her.

She shook her head and then approached him, angry. "Then—you knew. You knew someone was going to kill Charles. Who is it? Damn it, tell me, tell me what's going on, and we can solve this. What did you see? What do you know?"

He rose to meet her. He was really quite the swash-buckling figure, and she could see where he had been an impressive man—until he'd gotten himself killed.

"Nothing," he said.

"What?"

"Nothing. I know nothing. Look, a ghost can't be everywhere at the same time. I've had this odd feeling for a long time that something was going to happen. Something bad. I've tried to reach you, to make your see me and be careful."

"You had a *feeling?*" she demanded incredulously. "You're a ghost!"

"I'm the ghost of the man I was, and the essence of what I was is still what I am," he said flatly.

She blinked, trying to make sense of what he was saying. "Explain that!"

"What remains is the soul," he said. "And the essence of our being. The body is fragile—it ages and it dies. But the soul, the energy of what we are, is what we always were." He searched out her eyes and tried again. "We learn through the ages, through everyone we watch. I've seen generations come and go, and I've shed tears that no one sees through many a tragedy. I touched your father once, but he does not remain—he went with your mother when the call came."

Her parents had gone on. She missed them, so much, still. The beginnings of tears tightened her throat.

She steeled herself, wondering if she could possibly be speaking to the ghost of a long-dead ancestor, or if the events had just become too much for her.

"You watched all that—but you didn't see who killed Charles?" she asked.

"No! I was with you and Frazier on the porch. I love the reenactments. Now, that is. But the first few years of my—*ghosthood?*—I was a bitter fool. I really was. I owned slaves, yes—it was a way of life, and we didn't really know any better. Really. I was bitter when we lost the war. I was bitter when the carpetbaggers came down. Then I began to learn. I began to watch the world as the years went by. I could see that I'd been—not a fool—but utterly ignorant to many truths in life. Now I've watched many young people go off to war, and I've seen the fallacy of our ways, and I'm glad we lost the war—we never should have fought it."

He was really there. Or, in her mind, he was real, and he was just like a reasoning, functioning human being.

Except that he was dead.

She shook her head again and realized she was doing so enough to give herself brain damage. She forced herself to stop.

"This is great," she whispered. "I'm seeing a ghost—and you can't even help me."

"I *can* help you," Marshall Donegal said.

"How?"

"I can do my best to watch the behavior of those

around us now even more closely, and I can do my best to stay near you and look after you. If you know I'm here and accept that I *can* be here, and you'll let me in, you'll hear me now when I know that there is danger."

"How did you know there was danger?"

"I could *feel* it," he said again, exasperated. "I tried to warn your great-grandfather when the old fellow was about to keel over in the barn. No one saw me—no one came to help when I screamed. Now that poor old bastard is spending his afterlife pacing out there in the stables, and he won't move on. I talk to him, and he doesn't hear me. He just waits for his opportunity to act out a long-gone and lamented war, and there's nothing I can do."

"You can't speak to other ghosts?" she asked him.

"Sometimes. Sometimes it's as if we never quite touch," he said sadly.

"It's not just one big old ghostly community out there?" she demanded.

"Some don't accept that they're dead," he told her.

"And others?"

"Others know, and they're not sure why they linger. Some just can't go on. And sometimes we can reach one another."

"What about Emma?" she asked him.

He turned away from her. "No," he said, his back to

her. "Perhaps she has gone on. Perhaps we are being punished. But, no, I can't see or reach Emma."

"Punished for what?"

He turned back to her, waving a hand in the air. "That's not important. What's important is that you have a killer on your hands. A cruel killer, one who mocked the way I died. I died for a cause that might have had serious flaws, but I believed that I was fighting for my family and my state. Why should we be mocked so?"

"We?"

"The Donegal clan."

"You think someone killed Charles—to hurt the family?"

"The days of cotton and sugar being a means to all ends has long passed—the plantation survives on the guests who come. Donegal does well because there are always visitors. If the place becomes known as the site of a heinous recent murder, the people will not come."

"Oh, well, that may not be true," Ashley said dryly. "It may attract more."

"It will hurt, I believe."

She pointed at him. "You're not really a ghost, and I'm not really seeing you. You are a creation of my subconscious, and you're logic—telling me that I can figure this out if I think hard enough."

"I'm afraid I'm not going away."

"I'll just ignore you."

"Then you'll be behaving in a most foolish manner.

Think about the day, about the event. Think about the men involved, Ashley. Your friend is right, and you know it. Someone close to Donegal Plantation committed that murder."

# 7

"No hairs, no fibers, nothing on the bastard but the wool of his uniform and fluff from a pair of cavalry gloves," Colby said, disgusted. "And, of course, there are so many fingerprints on the tomb, we can't begin to sort them. Same thing with tire tracks— there are none close to the cemetery wall, and there are thousands in the gravel and the road out front. We have begun to sort them out, but it will take a great deal of time, and when we have them, what will we have?" The man was clearly frustrated. "There was absolutely no sign of a struggle. There's no sign that Charles Osgood was dragged to the tomb. Science isn't going to point us straight to the murderer on this one, and we need warrants to just go digging into the personal effects of the hundreds of people who might have been around. He was killed with a bayonet, so getting a judge to move on collecting the weaponry used at the reenactment has been a piece of cake, but once we go beyond that…well, it will be hard to pinpoint the fellow—not unless he strikes again, or gets careless."

"Let's hope he doesn't strike again," Jake said.

"Well, of course. It doesn't look like a serial killing, does it? The way I see it, someone had a grudge on Charles Osgood and found a way to really drag out his death."

"We're grateful, Detective Mack, that your officers began collecting all of the rifles and bayonets used by the men in the reenactment, and that you've been so gracious to share information" Jackson said. "Profiling isn't an exact science. We all know that. And we don't believe we're dealing with a serial killer, either, but still, finding someone who holds a grudge—even finding out if there was a perceived slight to someone—can often help point law enforcement in the right direction."

Detective Colby nodded. "Fine. We'll track down people. We can narrow the field, but it will still be a big field." He was quiet a minute. "I heard you all did a damned good job in New Orleans. Some of the information seems to be a bit vague. Do you people mind-read, or something like that?"

"We explore history—history in time, and history as it pertains to individuals," Jake said smoothly. He had a feeling that with Colby, they'd be thrown out if they were to mention the fact that they sought out ghosts.

"Detective," Jackson said, "we're truly grateful that you're allowing us to work with you. I believe that the cemetery was thoroughly searched when Charles first went missing. When his body was discovered, he was still wearing his uniform, so he was held from the time he disappeared until he was found. He was apparently held in a drugged condition, and perhaps the murderer was able to go about his customary life while stashing his victim somewhere. But if we have alibis for the time before the body was found—we know he had only been dead for a few hours, tops—then we can eliminate those people and concentrate on the lies someone might be telling, or on alibis that might have a few holes in them."

"You know there were hundreds of people on that plantation for the reenactment," Colby said wearily. "We're on it, but the manpower needed for that kind of investigation is great." He was quiet for a minute and said grudgingly, "This is a sensational case. We're, uh, grateful that you're here, too."

"Thank you," Jackson said.

"It's a needle in a haystack," Colby said.

"What about the bayonets of the men who were already gone that day?" Jake asked.

"If the men were gone with those bayonets, they couldn't have killed him with them," Mack Colby said.

"*If* they were really gone, which, of course, your men will find out," Jake said. "I don't think that any of the men who were playing Yankees—who had left the property already—are guilty, but I believe that two of them are local, Southerners who had ancestors who did choose the Northern side. Once we eliminate—" Jake began.

"We'll get every weapon. Every blade," Colby said grimly. "They'll be wiped clean, of course. But sometimes, no matter how you wipe down a blade, the forensics folks can still find a miniscule dot of blood. I'm doubting it with this guy, though. This damned thing was planned out."

"Yes, it was," Jackson said.

Mack Colby seemed pleased Jackson agreed with him.

"How much of the property was searched by your men?" Jake asked.

"We had an entire team in the cemetery," the detective said. "And, of course, I had officers comb the area around the cemetery as well."

"I think we need to extend that search—take it to a daylight level," Jake said. "If I had committed such a murder, I wouldn't have kept the murder weapon on my person anywhere. If you're found with the murder weapon, it's most likely you're the killer. He's gotten rid of that bayonet—and I believe it might well still be on or near the property. He might have been on the property *after* the murder, or nearby, and I just don't think he'd risk being found with the weapon."

"Hell, we don't even know how the bastard got his victim there, with no one at all seeing him. The plantation was still crowded—lots of folks staying over," Mack said.

"The river," Jake said, imagining the scene in his

mind's eye. "He might have come by the river. The cemetery abuts it. Easy enough to take a rowboat, tie her up, drag your victim in and disappear the same way—you'd never have to go by the house or the out-buildings," Jake said.

"I'll have a team back out there by this afternoon," the detective assured them. "I'll muster up our best techs to go over the property again, and call in some divers. It will take me a few hours, of course."

"I'll do the dive myself," Jake told Jackson.

"Surfer boy, that's a hard current—you'd better be a damned good diver," Colby told him.

Jake held his temper and smiled. He didn't look like a "surfer boy." He had just stepped on Mack Colby's toes the first night of the crime by being there when the body was found. Colby had accepted them; he even seemed to like Jackson. But Jake had been there when the body had first been discovered, and Colby seemed to have a bit of grudge because of it.

"I used to scrape barnacles off shrimp boats, and I've fixed a few motors in the Gulf and the Missis-sippi. I'll be careful," he said pleasantly.

He thought that Colby would sniff out his disdain, but he didn't.

Adam Harrison's reach was long. The investigation was theirs, not that they had any problem working closely with the local police. Mack Colby just had a chip on his shoulder, even though he was trying to pretend it wasn't there.

"And, of course, we are talking muddy water and hard currents. I'll sure be grateful for the help of your police divers," Jake said.

At his side, Jackson grinned and lowered his head to hide it.

Colby was mollified.

Jackson and Jake left the police station. "You really know that muddy water so well?"

Jake laughed. "Yeah, I actually do. But I have to admit, I'd be in the damned muck anyway even if I didn't. There's just something about that damned detective. And I won't go alone. I know that Cliff Boudreaux is a diver. Cliff has been on the plantation forever. His dad was a manager and tour director here, too."

"Cliff Boudreaux took part in the reenactment and has lived at the plantation forever," Jackson said, looking over at him.

"Right—that's what I said."

"And that makes him a suspect," Jackson reminded him.

"An unlikely suspect," Jake argued. "Cliff has been an open book. Two of his ancestors were Donegals."

"That could make him a prime suspect," Jackson said.

"I knew him when I was a kid," Jake told Jackson.

"He's still a suspect. I want to believe we can communicate with the dead at times," Jackson said gruffly. "I don't want any of us joining them. I won't let you go alone."

Jake didn't argue.

When they reached the house, Jackson motioned for Jake to follow him. They went up to the bedroom Jackson and Angela were sharing to find her at the desk lost in thought.

"Everything is all right here, right?" Jackson asked.

Angela looked up in surprise at his entry.

"Any sense of…anyone who might be able to help us?" Jackson asked.

She quirked a brow. Jackson knew that the world wasn't always what it seemed, but he still had trouble just asking her if she might have met a ghost who could flat out tell them the truth about the situation.

"Don't you dare laugh at me—I'm letting the house get to know me. And, Jackson Crow, you know as well as I do that we're unlikely to come across an entity who just happened to see the whole thing. If the ghosts haunting the cemetery are active, they probably get the hell away when a reenactment takes place because people are everywhere, and if they're just reliving the fight—well, then they don't see anything but what was. Some of those entities have been around forever, but still can't quite reach out and touch anyone, much less a newcomer to the property. Give me time." She looked at Jake. "And give Jake time. He knows the place. And those who might still haunt this house and these grounds know that Jake is familiar here. And Ashley."

"Ashley?" Jake said, frowning.

Angela nodded, looking at him. "I think that Ashley has a sense that there is more—and I think it terrifies her. Maybe she'll come around. You can't force ghosts—and you can't force anyone to admit that they might see ghosts."

"The murderer was alive," Jackson said. "So let's concentrate on behavioral analysis of the living for the moment."

"It's possible that someone wanted Charles dead— and killed him here," Angela said.

"Too pat, too hard and too complicated. If someone just wanted Charles dead, there were easier ways to kill him."

"A narcissist," Jackson said. "He's sure of himself. He believes in his intelligence and his ability to carry out the plot."

"So we're looking for someone who isn't stupid," Ashley said.

"The police will be working hard on the masses and their alibis. I think we have to look at the probable first. So we'll go with the fact that we believe that it's someone close to the family. We all thought that from the beginning. Initial instinct is a good place to start. This is someone who, I believe, is a functioning psychopath. He's living with the belief that he's been harmed in some way by the people here, or even by the plantation itself."

"I agree," Jake said.

"Even then, we have to start narrowing down the suspect pool," Angela reminded them.

"I'd say we can get it down to a handful soon enough. Prove where people were physically, and we'll find out answers. Or, at least, get the number down to where we can apply some pressure and perhaps cause this particular person to break. I don't think that he's well. This is the kind of murder perpetrated by a person with some kind of mistaken belief in the righteousness of what he's doing. We just have to figure out who is really a concerned friend—and who is wearing a mask of friendship. I believe that he'll eventually break."

"I'm just afraid of what might happen if we don't find him quickly. He may start to spin out of control before he breaks, and that could be really dangerous," Angela said.

"That could be fatal," Jake said. "We need to take care—great care."

Jackson nodded. "Go work with Ashley now," he said.

Jake went back downstairs and found Ashley in the study. He sat down in a chair across the desk from her and surveyed her. She handed him a sheet of paper. It was filled with the names of those who had played rebels and those who had played Yankees. There was a little paragraph about each man's family, employment and character that followed. He smiled, looking down at the sheet.

The first name on it was Cliff Boudreaux. And Ashley had typed, *You've known him almost as long as I have. Cliff, competent, good-looking, strong, self-assured. Tour guide, jack-of-all-trades. We all know he has family blood and that he loves the family.*

Mentally, he added Jackson's note: because of that very family association, he may have underlying feelings of resentment, as in, he has as much right to the property as Frazier and Ashley.

Following Cliff's name was Charles Osgood. *Not* a suicide. Underlined three times. *An accountant, always an in-between man, not bad-looking, not a charmer. Thrilled to play Marshall Donegal; change happened at the last minute.*

Charles was followed by Ramsay Clayton and then by Hank Trebly, which made sense. Hank was involved with the sugar mill on the cemetery side of the property.

*Hank Trebly,* Ashley wrote, *reminds me just a bit of a hobbit. A little short, a little squat—I know you know Hank. Fortysomething, balding a bit, always chewing his lower lip, concerned with politics, and the environmentalists coming after the sugar mills. I hear he's a good guy, though, insisting that corners never be cut, and that they follow regulations to a T.*

Jake looked up again, smiling as he caught Ashley studying him with serious eyes.

"What?" she asked.

"Nothing. This is perfect, actually."

"You sure?"

"Jackson's specialty is behavioral science. This is exactly what he'll need. He hasn't met these people, and your information is the kind of thing that a behavioral scientist works with. Perfect," he told her.

She nodded, but her gaze shifted toward the door. He looked around. There was no one there. Was she praying someone would come get them both out of here?

"You okay?" he asked her.

"Fine," she said, not taking her eyes from his again.

He turned again, feeling as if someone were behind him; no matter where she was looking, it was as if she had seen something.

But there was no one there.

He looked into her eyes questioningly, but she had her hands folded on the desk, and she maintained eye contact. He looked back to the list.

*Griffin Grant, affable fellow, think you've met him, though his uncle used to do the reenactments. Adores the place and the playing—he's a CEO, VP (?) at a cable company out of New Orleans. Early thirties, good-looking, sharp and well-dressed, nice sense of humor, especially considering the fact that he's a total business geek.*

*Toby Keaton, owns Beaumont, but you know that. Medium height, medium weight, early forties, thinning hair. Our families have always gotten along well—starting from the beginning of the "survival by tourism" days. We do Civil War and reenactments; he works on Creole history, the real day-to-day work involved in such a plantation. He's always been part of the reenactment.*

*John Ashton, nice guy, his father did the reenacting in the old days. He's in his late twenties, bookish, glasses, even has special wire frames just so that they work for the reenactments. He runs a tour company in New Orleans, and has long been a good friend of the plantation.*

Jake looked up at Ashley again, seeing her and imagining the reenactments as he had seen them so many times before. He knew the positions the men would take—he could run it in his own mind easily. "So, Charles winds up playing Marshall Donegal. The rebel troops are complete with Cliff, Griffin, Hank, John and Toby. Ramsay goes off to be a Yankee."

"Yes, Ramsay went off to join the Yankees, and that group included two locals, men you know as well—" Ashley reached over to tap the paper "—Michael Bonaventure, from New Orleans, bar owner, has a place off Royal Street, and Hadley Mason, an engineer from Lafayette. Justin Binder is from Philadelphia, and he was here with his mother-in-law and two children. He's a widower. The other two Yankees were Tom Dixon, from New York City, and Victor Quibbly, from Chicago, and they both left the morning after the reenactment."

"They flew out from New Orleans?" Jake asked.

Ashley swung around in the chair, hitting the on button on the computer that sat on a stand next to the desk. She nodded. "We know when everyone is coming in and out from different cities, because we try to arrange rides. Yes, Tom left on American Airlines at noon the following day, and Victor was on Continental fifteen minutes later. Cliff drove them to the airport, I believe."

"Can you think of anyone else who is closely involved with this property or with the reenactment?" he asked her.

"Dr. Ben Austin—he's a practicing M.D.—and John Martin, our biggest sutler, or vendor. He was here with his wife, and they were at the party—you know, the wind-down in the house. Every one of those folks was there—except for Charles, of course," she said.

He nodded. "Change places?" he asked her.

"What?"

"May I get on the computer for a minute?"

She stood up, walking around the desk. As she did so, she looked at the door again, frowning. He followed her line of vision but saw nothing.

Jake sat at the computer and started punching in keys. He could access sites that the average person couldn't because he had the proper codes.

"What are you doing?" Ashley asked him. She hadn't taken his chair; she stood at the edge of the desk.

"Simple elimination," he said. "Two Yankees in

the clear—they indeed flew away. Their names are on the manifests for the flights."

"Wouldn't the police be checking on that kind of thing, too?" she asked.

He nodded. "Yes, but in my mind, the more people I know to be eliminated entirely on my own, the easier it will be to home in on what really happened. And Jackson is a stickler. He's a team man—it's the way he's always worked. People make mistakes. *We* can make mistakes. Anyway, I know we're down to a few-score people."

"A few score," she repeated, wincing.

"Don't worry. That number will go down quickly," he assured her.

Once again, she wasn't looking at him. She was looking behind him. He turned quickly, wondering if he didn't glimpse a shadow…something. Ashley was definitely acting strangely.

Donegal was known for being haunted. Maybe that was why she had fought all her life against the possibility that ghosts could be real.

And maybe, she was just beginning to feel or see something….

There was a tap at the door. Jake was surprised by the way Ashley seemed to all but jump out of her skin.

Frazier poked his head in. "Lunch is served. An excellent meal, it appears."

Beth had cooked—and cooked, and cooked. She had gone for just about every staple known to

Southern Louisiana—corn bread, jambalaya, craw-fish étouffée, gumbo, turnip greens, pecan pie, bread pudding, shrimp salad and more.

It astounded even Ashley that she could have prepared such a feast so quickly, but then, when the reenactment wasn't taking place and they weren't investigating a murder, Beth did run one of the finest restaurants in the area. There was still a crowd for lunch; Jackson, Ashley, Jake, Frazier, Cliff, Beth and herself.

She noted—as she was sure Cliff did—that their guest investigators did not treat him as a suspect; they treated him as one of the family, which, of course, he had always been. Growing up, he'd been the big brother Ashley had never had, even though he was about thirteen years older than her and had been actually managing much of the plantation while she'd still been playing with her dolls and video games.

At the luncheon table, she wasn't being haunted by an annoying Confederate in full dress uniform. He wasn't in the dining room. Not at the moment, and Ashley was grateful for that fact. He'd been in the office with her when she'd been giving Jake the list, and he'd been terribly annoying, wanting her to punctuate every detail regarding every man. She kept thinking that Jake would turn around and see him standing there, laugh and tell her that the fellow was an actor hired to torment her.

But Jake didn't see the man—so she was the scary one after all, suffering from strange delusions about the dead. They were all probably brought on by the murder.

During the massive meal, they all spoke as casually as possible in the aftermath of a brutal, senseless killing. Jackson and Jake relayed the conversation they'd had down at the police station until Cliff had left them, saying that he had work at the stables.

Ashley pretended to listen attentively while wondering again if she had imagined that a ghost— looking as real as flesh and blood—had carried on a meeting with her. She looked here and there around the room, wondering if Marshall Donegal would appear in the flesh—or the appearance of flesh!—sweeping off his great plumed hat and setting a booted foot upon a chair, perhaps.

But though he had been a pest in the office, he didn't show. She was so busy worrying that he would, however, that she barely heard what was being said. She wondered if Frazier had ever seen the man—or even Cliff. After all, one way or another, they were all related.

Then one word that Jake uttered brought her to.

*…diving…*

"Diving?" she asked.

"I believe that the murderer might have thrown his weapon into the Mississippi," Jake explained. "He's organized, and intelligent. Such a killer would know that the murder weapon would be searched for immediately, and that he couldn't be found with it on his person or his property. So if it were me, I'd throw it in the river as quickly as possible. Actually, I think the killer had Charles with him, maybe drove him away after the reenactment and then brought him back here in some kind of a boat. That being the case, he'd have thrown the weapon into the river while he returned to wherever he had come from by boat."

"Unless, of course," Ashley said, staring back at Jake as if she dared him to agree, "the murderer held Charles drugged on the property. If that was the case, the killer could have taken him into the cemetery, where he bayoneted him to death, and went on to return to his room. The river has a terrific current, too."

"That's possible, too," Jake said evenly. "But I think he threw it in the river—the weight of a weapon could have easily caused it to sink."

"I'm not a suspect, am I?" Beth asked.

Ashley straightened, looking around the table at the three investigators.

Jake smiled and answered. "No. It's highly unlikely that you have the strength needed to carry out what was done."

"Thank the Lord!" Beth said.

"But *Cliff* could be guilty," Frazier said.

"We certainly hope not," Jackson said.

"Wait!" Ashley protested. She didn't believe that Cliff could be guilty, but she didn't believe that any of the men who had acted like children on the day of the reenactment could possibly be guilty of such a heinous crime. "Who's going diving? Aren't they sending out police divers?"

"Yes," Jake said, frowning slightly. "I'm assuming that at this point they'll be along really soon. But I want first crack, before the water is churned by a team of four or five."

"But—are you authorized?"

"We are working co-jurisdiction," Jackson said, glancing at Frazier. "Adam's your grandfather's friend, and Adam has the influence to make a great deal happen."

"Ashley, you know that I know what I'm doing," Jake told her. "I'm going to get started now."

"I'll work with you," she said.

"Ashley—" Jake began.

"No one should dive alone," she reminded him primly. "The water is brown—even with lights, vision is limited," she said. "You need a dive buddy. And it's my property."

"Ashley," Frazier said, "my dearest grandchild, my old heart is still ticking. It's still my property. You two children can fish through the regulators, tanks and masks we keep because of work that has to sometimes be done down by the bayou."

Frazier had spoken lightly, wanting to ease the tension with smiles. He managed the feat.

"Grampa!" Ashley protested.

"Well, don't look at me!" Beth said. "Dive in that nasty old muddy water? No, no, dishes look much, much better than diving in the Mississippi!"

"I was planning on working with Jake, too," Jackson said.

"That's fine. But I'm going," Ashley said firmly.

"All right. Let's get on it," Jake said.

Half an hour later, the divers were nearly ready. Ashley had opted for a dive suit—she didn't like everything in the Mississippi touching her bare skin. Jake and Jackson had eschewed the idea of suits and were just in swim trunks, booties, gloves and their masks and regulators.

Angela, Beth and Frazier had come down to the embankment near the cemetery while they checked and rechecked their equipment and the flashlights they'd be working with.

Angela had watched Jake walk over and over the embankment near the cemetery wall. He found a spot that seemed to satisfy him.

"Here," he said, looking at them all.

Jackson, apparently, knew what he was talking about. He came over and hunkered down next to Jake, inspecting the ground. He stood after a moment. "Hard to tell, but possible. We'll go in here. Time for tanks, children," he said.

The three assisted each other, buckling into the heavy dive tanks. "You're just walking in, right?" Angela asked. "Seriously, shouldn't we be waiting for the police? They'll have metal detectors—"

Jake lifted a rod he had on a cord at his wrist. "Jackson has one, too," he told her.

"It is one big damned river," Frazier said. "And then there's the bayou—"

"I don't think so, sir," Jake said. "This is how he managed the movement of the body. This is where he'll have ditched the weapon."

Frazier nodded. He gazed at Ashley, and she knew that he was worried about her. It was only fair; she was worried about him. She blew him a kiss.

"I'll follow the current and watch for you down by the public ramp," Angela reminded them. "Don't try to get back—I'll be there."

"Keep up with us," Jake warned, catching Ashley's hand.

Pride dictated that she draw away, pride and maybe fear that it was too easy to depend on him so swiftly. But she didn't draw away; they were diving together, and she wasn't going to be uncooperative.

They eased into the water over the embankment, a difficult task as it was shallow next to the levee and they sank into the mud. She immediately felt the strength of the current, and she knew what Jake was thinking: if the killer had indeed followed this route, he had gone with the current in whatever little boat he had been maneuvering. He wouldn't have used a motor; a motor might have been heard.

The brown, muddy waters of the Mississippi covered their heads, and they went with the current themselves, using their flippers to thrust them downward. Ten feet, twenty feet, thirty feet…forty feet. She'd been in the water here before, but only ever to clear growth from the seawall or work with their little strip of dock. The water was filled with silt, and everything before her eyes was curtained behind a brown haze. The sun didn't penetrate deeply.

A massive catfish glided by them, taking a look, moving off quickly. They passed over the ruins of a broken-up tugboat. Gar drifted by, and in the few feet she could see ahead, even with her diving light, Ashley saw that a blue suckerfish was watching them avidly. There seemed to be little else of interest. Diving in clear waters was beautiful, but the Mississippi wasn't clear. It seemed as if the light dimmed quickly, as if the riverbed sucked it up into the mottled brown darkness.

She heard the rhythmic sound of her regulator, air moving in and out of her own lungs. She usually loved that sound. She glanced over to see that Jake was still moving fluidly at her side, inspecting the river bottom as they drifted along, barely using their fins, the current was so strong.

She tried to give her concentration over to the task at hand.

She felt a jerk on her hand; she turned and saw Jake's blue-green eyes through his mask. He motioned that they needed to go down. His metal detector had come upon something.

Fighting the current, they shot downward, only to discover car parts that had been in the river long enough to acquire massive growth. She and Jake, with Jackson close behind, started to move onward again.

She wasn't at all sure how she saw it, but suddenly it seemed that something bright flickered in the glow of her beam.

She started toward it.

A jerk on her ankle made her panic for a moment; alligators didn't usually travel out into the depths of the river—they preferred the bayou and the shallows. But it would be quite ridiculous if she were to be consumed by a natural predator she knew and respected in the hunt for a human monster.

It wasn't an alligator; it was Jake. He frowned at her, indicating that she wasn't to take off without him.

She nodded and pointed. Then, of course, her beam picked up nothing, but he nodded and followed her downward.

They were in an area of soft packed mud and underwater growth. At first Ashley thought she had imagined the glitter in the water. It was dark, and with the current, once the muck was disturbed, it spread out, creating an even darker brown haze.

Then she felt Jake squeeze her hand, and he indicated the metal detector.

There was definitely something there.

They had to move quickly, because the water around them was becoming browner by the second. There was nothing easy about maintaining their position in the water; they fought the current hard. But Jake was digging in the mud, and she did the same.

There, beneath one of the plumes Jake had just started.

She saw it.

It was still in excellent shape; it looked as if it had just been set down on the river bottom. The 1853 Enfield rifle that shot a Burton-Minie ball still had its bayonet, which had surely glittered in the glow of her flashlight, soundly attached.

It was the weapon that had been carried not just by the defenders, but by all of the federals on the day of the skirmish that had taken place in 1861. It would have a thirty-nine-inch barrel with three grooves, and the stock had three metal bands, so that it was sometimes called the popular "three-banded" rifle. Reproductions of the rifle were carried by all the reenactors. At the beginning of the war, it had been quite typical, appreciated on both sides of the great conflict.

She pointed; Jake reached down a hand and collected the weapon by the stock. He nodded to Ashley and indicated that they head toward the riverbank.

They emerged about a hundred feet shy of the boat ramp. Sludging up the muddy bank, Ashley saw that Angela had been true to her word and was there leaning against Jake's car down by the public ramp.

She saw them right away and came hurrying toward them, heedless of the marshy terrain. She had something in her hand, which turned out to be a large plastic bag of some kind—an evidence bag for the weapon retrieved. Angela, apparently, had had faith in their findings, while Ashley had to admit she hadn't expected that the four of them would find anything in the Mississippi. Of course, this team had probably been trained, but then again...

She had been the one to spot the weapon.

"You found it!" Angela cried, wrinkling her nose as she stepped into a deep pit and struggled to free her foot.

"Ashley actually made the discovery—without a metal detector," Jake said. He held the weapon out while Angela opened the bag.

"Wait!" Ashley said.

They both paused, staring at her.

She studied the weapon.

The manufacturers of historical weaponry were good—really good. They could replicate weapons to a T.

But there was something about this one.

She didn't touch it, but she moved closer. Mud encrusted the weapon, and there was no choice. She delicately took a finger protected by her diver glove and dusted aside a speck of the mud.

And it was there. Deeply, roughly gouged into the stock near the barrel, there were initials.

She looked up at Jake and Angela, chilled to the bone.

"This weapon is real. I mean, authentic to the period—and our house. It belonged to Marshall

Donegal. You can see his initials right there, MPD. He carved them by hand himself with his knife. Marshall Patrick Donegal."

# Interlude

*He watched it again. There she was, that blasted reporter, talking to Jake Mallory.*

*Mallory, so cool and solemn and yet easy with the reporter, revealing nothing at all.*

*They didn't have good new footage to show; so far, none of the reporters or their crews had been allowed on the property, and thus they had nothing new to say. Of course, the world now knew that Charles Osgood was dead, and everyone everywhere was deliberating. It was absolutely amusing to discover just how many people were certain that a bitter Confederate ghost had committed the crime.*

*Or even a Yankee. Hell, four Yankees had "died" on the property that day.*

*Ridiculous. No one was putting blame where it belonged. Or maybe they were.*

*The canned video was replaced by the reporter again, the pretty woman who seemed to have a hard edge. It was the hardness of a woman who wanted to rise in her field and was willing to do just about anything to do so. She'd sleep with the boss while making her cameraman traipse through dangerous territory before setting her pretty face in front of the camera. She'd sleep with the producer. He knew that look. He'd seen it often enough in the business world. With men, it just meant that they'd stab you in the back; with a woman, it meant that she'd do just about anything.*

*The reporter's face was replaced again by the image of a sea of pictures; they were artistically angled in the shot, from, clockwise, left to right, Frazier Donegal, Emma Donegal, Marshall Donegal and Ashley Donegal.*

*Ah, and it seemed that the generations had taken DNA from all—Ashley looked like her great-great-however-many-grandfather, and like Emma Donegal. All these decades later.*

*The newscast ended.*

*He should have felt satisfied. He'd caused the havoc he wanted. They were never going to catch him; there was just no way to prove that he had done any of this.*

*But then the newscast changed; there was a "this just in!" alert.*

*The reporter came back on. Anchorwoman Marty Dean identified herself again and announced that police believed that they had the murder weapon, an historic Enfield rifle once owned by the Civil War master of Donegal Plantation, Marshall Donegal. Tests were being done by forensic experts, seeking proof that the weapon, pulled from the Mississippi, had indeed been used in the murder.*

*Naturally, Marty's station would be right on the investigation, bringing news about the heinous events at the plantation the second they became available.*

*He clicked off the television, startled.*

*The weapon shouldn't have been found so*

*quickly. He had left no traces; he had ditched the damn thing in the Mississippi River, and he had been careful in every possible forensic way.*

*He paced, trying to calm down, and he did.*

*They had the weapon. Even if they found old Charles's blood, they could never trace it to him. Even if they knew how he had gotten there and killed the man, they couldn't trace it to him.*

*Pity, though. The image must have been so brilliant, the dead man—dead. Blood dripping. He'd been in Marshall Donegal's uniform. The possibilities for amazing ghost stories were endless....*

*He sat down again. It wasn't enough. It wasn't going to really choke the life out of the place.*

*So...*

*They'd be watching the cemetery. And they'd be watching the river.*

*There was always the bayou, and before you reached the bayou from the house, there were endless trails with pines, giving way to marshland....*

*"'It is well that war is so terrible—lest we should grow too fond of it,'" he whispered aloud, quoting Robert E. Lee, the South's— no, the country's—greatest general.*

*He smiled, his faith in himself restored.*

*"It is well that bloodletting is so complicated—because it is so actually sweet and entertaining!" he said.*

*The killing was the best.*

# 8

The Enfield and bayonet had been turned over to the forensics lab, and there was nothing to do on that angle but wait—and, determine, of course, how the priceless family heirloom had gone from its glass-encased place of honor in a small attic museum that guarded such precious pieces into the hands of a murderer, and then into the river.

Frazier was horrified. Of course, it had never been locked up. They didn't lock up their artifacts at Donegal Plantation. Marshall Donegal had been buried with his dress sword, but not the Enfield rifle he would have carried into the war. At his death, Emma had kept the weapon above the fireplace in the rear parlor, should they come under attack again at any time. It was most likely that she kept it there until her death in 1890. One of her children had probably moved the rifle and other artifacts from the mid-1860s to the attic. Frazier knew that his father had been the one to purchase the box it had been displayed in now. No one had even known it was missing; when they all returned to the house, he asked Ashley a dozen times at least if she was sure that the weapon they had found had been Marshall Donegal's, and he had gone upstairs himself to assure himself that the box was empty.

It was.

The reality of the Mississippi River was that it was not the nicest place in the world to dive; returning to the house—once the initial questions were asked and answered—Jake hurried up to his room and straight into the shower. He was sure the others were doing the same. But he had barely stripped out of his swim trunks when there was a knock at the door. He frowned, wrapped a towel around his waist and went to it. He opened it a crack.

Ashley was out there. She had stripped off her dive suit and wore a terry robe over her bathing suit. Her hair was still damp and tangled from the water, but she looked restless and uneasy.

He opened the door fully without moving aside.

"What? Is anything wrong?" he asked.

She looked at him with her huge sapphire eyes. It was suddenly impossible—despite the five years that had passed since they'd been together—not to feel an uncomfortable rise of his libido.

God, he'd loved her, always. *Not true,* he tried to correct himself. Once, she had been a bright, entertaining, but annoying little precocious kid. But not long; she'd caught up so quickly. And when he had realized that he'd teased her the same way boys had teased girls they had secretly coveted since the beginning of time, he had just fallen head over heels. It was the sapphire of her eyes, maybe. The perfection of her skin, the softness and the glitter in the color of her hair. Ah, but that was just lust. He'd loved her tomboy antics, the way she could ride, race, challenge, laugh, and argue her side of any matter. It was the sound of her voice....

"Well, a man is dead," she said flatly. "Killed—with a family heirloom!"

He started, his reverie fading. "Yes, we all know that. Is something wrong? I need to take a shower."

He was a fool, of course. She was standing there; he was standing there. He was naked beneath the towel; she wore flimsy pieces of a bikini beneath a terry robe. He had never really fallen out of love, and he'd have to be a hell of a lot older or infirm to fall out of lust.

But that wasn't the point here.

What was the point?

He didn't know why she was here. He didn't want to be used because he was convenient and her world was going to hell.

*Yes, I do want to be used!* his mind raged.

No.

"Ashley, let me jump in the shower, and I'll be right with you," he said. "I suggest you do the same. You wear even river mud well, but I think you'll be more comfortable without it."

He stepped back and forced himself to close the door.

His shower was pure torment.

Marty Dean sat at her office desk, studying her phone, and wondering what she could say once she'd reached Jake Mallory. She'd had such a crush on him in high school. His guitar had gained him quite a reputation, and he'd played with some pretty extraordinary bands. Everybody had a crush on Jake! And he'd just gotten better, really. Some of those boys—the big football-hero types—were just downright pudgy now. And Jake? He still had those probing eyes, that sculpted face, those shoulders.... It had been something to see him again. And he had looked right at her—and not given her a thing.

Well, she thought, pouting, he'd come around. He was a man, and she knew how to make a man come around.

Her pout became a frown. But, of course, he was at Donegal Plantation, and he and Ashley Donegal had been quite a *thing*. If he was sleeping with her again…

Hmm. The promise of an affair might not do it.

Maybe she had to promise that she would promote Donegal Plantation, though she would love it if there were a mystical ghost story involved.

She was still pondering the mode by which she would get him to agree to an interview when the switchboard signaled a call for her.

"Line four," the operator told her.

"Who is it?"

"Some man who insists you're going to want what he has to give you," the operator told her, bored. "Look, I'm not the FBI. I don't know who he is. You said to send through anything promising—"

"Yeah, yeah, I got it, thanks."

She picked up the phone.

"Marty?"

The voice was deep, quiet and husky.

"Yes?" she said. "Who is—"

"You want an interview. You want to know what's really going on. You want to break it free. Well, I'll do it for you."

Jake! It had to be Jake. Oh, and he was FBI now, or something governmental, and he was one of the big shots on the case. But he did remember high school, did remember that they'd flirted and teased and that she'd been the hottest thing in his class.

"Oh, you sweetie!" she said. "Thank you, thank you! Can you come in—"

"No, but you can come out," he said. "I'll tell you where to leave your car so that it's not seen. And I'll tell you the easiest way to get to me. No cameras. This is between you and me. But it will help you get to the truth. I can't say more—you have to really solve this on your own after what I tell you. But I won't speak if there's anyone else there, so come alone. I mean it. Don't tell anyone where you're going. I can't be involved in this when the news gets out."

"All right, all right. Where should I be? When?"

She listened. She hung up, delighted.

Her secretary stopped her as she headed out for her car. "You have the newscast at eleven, remember?"

"I'll be back. I've got a lead. I've got plenty of time. I just need to meet with an informant—a local informant. It pays to be me!"

Marty tore out of her office, mentally planning her speed. How fast could she go without being in danger of the cops stopping her?

*Pretty damned fast,* she told herself.

Oh, this was it! This was it! The case of a life-time.

By the time Jake came downstairs, he found that he was the last to do so. The others were arrayed in the roadside parlor, seated in the big wingback chairs by the fire and the massive Duncan Phyfe sofa. Jackson's hair was still wet, so he had obviously just arrived. Ashley had showered and changed into jeans and a tailored blouse; her damp hair was tied in a queue at her nape.

"The house itself is seldom locked," Frazier said as Jake entered the room. "We're a bed-and-breakfast. We have a restaurant, and we're open to the public. God knows when the rifle was taken. I haven't been up to that little attic museum space in years." Frazier glanced over at Ashley. "Have you been up there?"

She shook her head. "Sally Mayfield, one of our housekeepers, last did a dusting up there three or four weeks ago, I think. Sally would have noticed if something had been gone, and she would have told me. So I'd say that it had to have been taken within the last three weeks."

"When were most of the reenactors here last? They still meet ahead of time, right? And what about Civil War roundtables? Frazier, you used to have them here now and then," Jake said. He heard the front door open as he was speaking; Cliff had arrived to join them. He glanced over at Jackson for a silent communication.

Cliff remained a prime suspect. They needed to keep a close eye on him.

Ashley didn't want to believe it. He didn't, either. Cliff had always been around when he'd been younger; he'd always been strong and steady and decent, and he loved Donegal Plantation, just as he'd always loved the family.

Frazier was thoughtful. "Yes, of course. I'm not sure of the date of the most recent."

"We had a meeting out in the barn about two and half weeks ago. The out-of-towners weren't here, but the rest of us were," Cliff volunteered.

"Everyone?" Jackson asked.

"Every one of the locals except for John Ashton," Cliff said. "He had a tour group in the city that he had to take out himself. Some bigwigs from the tourist board. And obviously, out of our group, I have continual access to the house. And I suppose I have the physical ability to have done all of it, while, no offense, Frazier, I don't see you committing this crime at your age, and I sure as hell don't begin to see Ashley or Beth committing it. I wish I knew how to clear myself, because no matter what you all say or how you act, I know damned well I have to remain a prime suspect."

"You even have motive," Jackson said pleasantly.

"Yes, I should own the house. But..."

"But?" Angela asked gently.

"Whoever did this might want the whole place to fall apart. Let's face it, if the place is tainted by a recent murder and a killer who isn't caught, people could be afraid to come. I'd never want to do that," Cliff said.

"We all survive because of Donegal Plantation—well, except for Beth, who could get a great job anywhere," Ashley said. "But Cliff is right. There's no reason for him to want to lower the value on this place. Besides, Cliff doesn't even have to wait for Frazier and me to die—he owns a piece of the land, and he has a lifetime lease on his apartment in the stables."

"Bitterness," Jake said. "I mean, if we're looking for motive. Let's face it, this whole thing is sick. Cliff, you're the outsider. You were the product of an illicit affair, historically speaking."

"Two illicit affairs, really," Cliff said. He never took a seat; he stood there and shrugged sheepishly. "I can't prove anything, but I'll answer any question you may have. Obviously, I didn't stash a body in the stables—they were searched. Of course, I could have stashed the drugged body of our friend in my apartment and joined the group. I would have had to have been terribly crafty, though, since the place was teeming with people, and the entrance to my apartment is easily visible from the grounds."

"And how did you return the body, then—by the river?" Jake asked him.

"You might have done that to throw off suspicion," Angela told him.

"I might have," Cliff agreed. "Except that I didn't. I'm going to feed the horses," he said, then, "But I'm available to you anytime—I won't be leaving the property." He smiled. "See you all at dinner?"

"We're having crab cakes. My best!" Beth assured him.

When Cliff left, there was an uncomfortable moment of silence in the room.

"I don't think—" Ashley began.

"None of us wants to think, but we have to weigh all the factors, eliminate the impossible and start looking at the possible," Jackson said to her gently. "Sometimes a killer wants to inject himself into the investigation."

"Cliff isn't—"

"It's not impossible, Ashley," Jackson said.

"It is impossible," she said stubbornly. "Cliff is part of the family."

"In the old days, brothers would kill brothers to be king," Jackson said.

"Look, Ashley," Jake said, leaning toward her. "Hopefully we'll be able to clear Cliff soon."

"So, we're all careful. We all stick together, and we keep doors locked. Agreed?" Jackson asked. "I've got Will and Whitney on their way out here now with some new equipment, and Jenna is interviewing Justin Binder and his family in the city. I'm going to pay a call on Ramsay Clayton—I believe he's still in residence at his old family home down the road—and have a talk with him. There are still a couple of uniformed officers outside, but I think part of the team should always be at the house. Jake and Angela?"

"I'm here," Jake assured him. "I'll get on the computer."

Jackson nodded. He looked down at Angela and squeezed her hand, and Jake knew that her assignment was to discover what she *felt* about the house.

Frazier walked over to Ashley. She stood quickly, hugging him. He hugged her silently in return. "I'm for a nap," he said. "At my age…" He apologized to the others.

"I'll be in my room, too," Ashley told him.

"A nap sounds good to me," Beth said, yawning. "And then dinner."

Angela laughed. "Oh, my God, after that delicious lunch you prepared! I'm not sure I'll be able to eat dinner. I'm going to…search the house. Combine a little work with exercise."

"Search for what?" Ashley asked her.

"Evidence," she said softly.

Ashley shook her head. "But that won't help us. Every man had access to the house at some point. What evidence could we possibly find that would be evidence? And the cops have been here, too."

"I never really know what I'm looking for," Angela said. She glanced at Jake. "But it's good to walk around and think and look, and then you sometimes find what you didn't know you were looking for. If that makes sense."

"I'll be in the study," he assured her. "If you need me."

Beth and Frazier headed for the stairway, arm in arm as they walked up the stairs.

Ashley lingered until she was alone with Jake. "Cliff didn't do this," she said with finality.

He walked over to her, placing his hands on her shoulders. "Ashley, honestly? I don't think that Cliff did it, either. But it's not going to hurt to be careful, to be with someone, to keep the doors locked, right?"

"I can be careful," she murmured, bowing her head.

He lifted her chin gently so that she met his eyes again. "Hey," he told her huskily. "Remember when we first decided we wanted a rock band and we set up out in the stables? The poor horses! Cliff never said anything. He just moved the drum set into the front yard and told us that birds liked music more than horses—especially heavy metal."

She smiled. "My father let us move the drum set into the old smokehouse." Her smile faltered. "Jake, my father has never come back from the dead," she said.

He was puzzled. She wasn't angry with him, and she wasn't even turning away from him or trying to escape him.

"I never meant to hurt you," he said.

"Well, I probably managed to hurt myself," she murmured. "You…scared me. You really, really scared me," she told him. She was silent a moment, looking at him. "But you should know. My father isn't here."

She flushed as if she had said more than she had meant to. She backed away from him. "I'm—uh—I'm going to go to my room," she said.

"Into the land of digital reality for me," he told her and headed off into the study while she walked toward the stairs.

The subtle, almost elusive scent of her perfume lingered, and he had to force himself not call out her name, not to draw her back to him and demand that she understand. Time had done nothing to lessen his feelings for her.

He wanted to hold her; he wanted the truth. He wanted to make the losses and traumas of her life go away. And, that, of course, was impossible.

They could do their best to find the killer. That was what he could do for her, he thought.

But when he sat behind the desk in the study,

he didn't turn to the computer. He sat in the chair, scanning the space around him. "Where are you, damn you?" he whispered aloud. "Emma Donegal, I saw you. You knew something was wrong. You wanted me here. Please, won't you come and help me now?"

Ashley headed for her room, still feeling a flush on her cheeks. Well, she was a fool. She'd turned away from Jake Mallory, cutting him from her life as if she had done so with a sharpened blade. What was she expecting now, and what the hell had she been doing, throwing herself at him just because she was scared?

"Well, I am scared," she said and then winced, wanting to nip in the bud the fact that she was talking out loud to herself far too frequently now.

She threw herself down on her bed and closed her eyes. She didn't see him; she didn't feel anything at all, but she knew that Marshall Donegal was there.

"You have to go away," she said. "You were trying to make me look like an idiot in the study, and I was a nervous wreck all through lunch, thinking you'd make me do something stupid. If you're my ancestor, and you love me so much, will you quit tormenting me?"

She felt a shift of weight. He had taken a seat at the foot of the bed. She opened her eyes at last.

"If someone comes at me with a weapon, can you protect me?" she demanded, sitting up to stare at him.

"Will that ghostly blade save my life? If not— Where is this going?"

"Can I protect you? That depends. I am fairly powerful. Being as I am requires concentration and practice, and I was always a disciplined man."

"Right. So you got into a barroom brawl and died before the war really began," she said dryly.

He seemed to stiffen. "You're wrong. I didn't get into the brawl. Peter O'Reilly got into the brawl. I dragged him out of the place before it turned into something right there, though that might have been a mistake. God knows, if we'd brought troops in, the Yankees would have been killed on the spot or hanged for being spies. But I didn't want murder committed. Hell, I lost my own life because of it."

"O'Reilly?" Ashley asked. "That would have been Charles Osgood's great-great-great-great-stepgrandfather, right?"

Marshall Donegal nodded, rising and walking to look out on the river. He lifted his hands. "I lose track of the generations…but, yes. He wasn't a bad fellow, just the kind who was quick to anger and to feel an affront. He was eager to 'whomp those Yanks!' He survived the war. I saw him here once, when he came to pay his respects to Emma. He was minus his left leg. It made him a different man. Emma was sorry for him, of course. She offered him work. But he went into New Orleans and became a printer."

"Even so, do you think that someone's ancestor knew this and thought it was a justice that Charles should die since his ancestor brought about the whole thing? Maybe one of the Yankees!" Ashley suggested.

"One who perished?" Marshall asked her.

"Possibly. I mean, if the rebels more or less caused it all because of Peter O'Reilly, and four of the Yankees died, maybe it was a sick kind of late-blooming vengeance."

"Even I'm aware—perhaps more so than anyone— that the war is long, long over," Marshall said. "Other wars have raged since, and will rage in the future," he added sadly.

"Yes, but whoever did this has to be sick. You don't drug a man, hide him for a day and half and then take him and bayonet him to death and hang his body off a tomb's angel if there isn't something really wrong in your psychological makeup," Ashley said flatly.

"Why would someone avenge someone after a hundred and fifty years?" Marshall demanded.

"I don't know, but Cliff is a prime suspect because of his family relation," Ashley said. She frowned and then gasped. "I can't believe I forgot. We do have that old plantation story about the master who supposedly slept with a slave. Were you involved?"

He was quiet, and he gave her a curious, sad smile. "Not me, and not any plantation master," he said quietly.

"But you know who?"

"Haven't you ever studied the records?" he asked her.

"Of course, but the baby who was Cliff's great-great-whatever just seemed to appear, and he was raised by Harold Boudreaux and grew up after the war on the property."

"After the war. I was dead, remember?"

"Yes, but there's no exact age on what records we do have," she reminded him. "The records for the slaves on the property were kept at the chapel, and the bible recording all the births disappeared sometime during the war, so the lists we still have don't have birth dates on them."

"Cliff's great-great-great-great—I believe—grandparent wasn't a Donegal man."

"Then—who?" she asked.

"It was Emma," he told her quietly.

Words and numbers seemed to blur Jake's vision, but he did feel that he was gaining ground.

Cliff Boudreaux could not be eliminated. Nor could Ramsay Clayton. John Ashton was easy to eliminate. There were pictures of him in New Orleans on the web the day following, and he had gotten an interview on one of the local channels to talk about the history surrounding the city—and to plug his own business. He had been on an evening show that broadcast at seven, and he had been going to give a tour that night that included the broadcaster. It didn't take long to verify the fact that he had led the tour, as he had said on air. He hadn't been at the meeting that had taken place approximately when the Enfield rifle and bayonet had most probably disappeared.

In like fashion, verifying their location at the time the drugged-but-still-living form of Charles Osgood had been taken into the cemetery and murdered, he managed to clear the field of all the Yankees except for Justin Binder. Tom Dixon had attended a party with his wife and children in New York that had gone on 'til midnight, and Victor Quibbly had already been in Austin, Texas, on a business matter.

He looked at his remaining list and his notes. Cliff—no one wanted it to be him. Ramsay—had he set up Charles Osgood? Hank Trebly—why? Sugar interests. Toby Keaton—okay, so he owned Beaumont, the Creole plantation next door, but he was never in competition with the Donegal family…or it didn't appear that it could be so. Griffin Grant—no amount of searching showed exactly where he had been, other than that he had shown up at his office for the usual workaday world on Monday. He hadn't even taken the day off, as so many had. Three others to look at would be the sutler, John Martin, Justin Binder, who had stayed in New Orleans at a chain hotel, and Dr. Benjamin Austin, who lived in Francisville and had not had office hours after five on the day that Charles had actually been murdered.

He sat back for a minute, closing his eyes. They could be way off. Anything *could* have happened. But he was pretty sure he was on the money, and he knew that Jackson would agree with him. Eliminating the household—Beth, Ashley and Frazier—left those who were closest to the household. He knew Ashley, and if he hadn't known her, he'd still know that no one could have acted the terror she had shown when he had come upon her. Frazier couldn't have pulled if off physically. Beth had no interest in the family; she hadn't even really understood the history behind what was going on, and she didn't have the strength to manage the feat, either. He'd pulled up everything he could find on her on the computer anyway; she couldn't have any determination to avenge a long-ago ancestor. Her family hadn't been anywhere near the United States during the war. So, using logic, it seemed to be down to Griffin Grant, Cliff Boudreaux, Ramsay Clayton, Hank Trebly, Toby Keaton or, less likely but still possible, Dr. Benjamin Austin or the sutler, John Martin. He put the last two at the end of the list. Concentration first—Ramsay Clayton and Cliff Boudreaux.

How in hell to prove that it wasn't Cliff?

He looked at the phone on the desk and noted that there was a button to call directly to the stables.

Cliff answered quickly. "Yes?"

"Cliff, I'm going to be honest. I want to eliminate you as a suspect. Would you be willing to let a forensics team go over your apartment and car?"

There was silence, dead silence, on the other end.

Then Cliff answered him, his voice tight and hard.

"Whatever it takes, whatever it takes. Bring it on, my friend."

As he hung up, his eyes on the desk phone, Jake felt that someone was watching him.

He looked up, and his breath caught in his throat.

It might have been Ashley—Ashley in her attire for the drama they played out at Donegal Plantation.

But it wasn't.

It was the woman he had seen in Jackson Square in New Orleans before he had even known that he was going to be coming out to Donegal Plantation.

Emma. Emma Donegal. He could see the door through her misty form, but he could also see her face clearly. It wasn't as if he could really hear her voice, and yet he could; it was inside his head.

"Come!" she said urgently. "Please, come."

He forgot about Detective Mack Colby and the call he had intended to make to get Cliff's apartment searched. He followed the ghost out of the office and through the house.

And on out to the stables.

Cliff was there, sweeping hay from the slab of concrete in front of his door. He looked up at Jake with guarded eyes.

"Are *you* doing the search?" Cliff asked him.

Jake felt about two feet tall. He had known Cliff for years; he could remember many more occasions with the man than what he had mentioned to Ashley. Cliff had patiently corrected him and taught him about riding, horses, shooting and the plantation itself dozens of times throughout the years. They'd gone out in alligator season together, and Cliff had taught him that even if the creatures were predators, they had their place in life. They had to be hunted to control the population, but they didn't deserve to be tortured because man had unbalanced nature. A clean kill: a good shot between the eyes. That was the way to kill a gator.

He had taught him other things. Things like balancing his weight with that of the horse he was riding, how to sit a jumper and how to calm a horse when they ran into a bear in the woods. He'd taught him how to hunt fowl, and, in return, Jake had taught Cliff how to hold a cue and shoot a break that could nearly clear the table.

"No, Cliff, honestly, it's because I want you cleared. I don't want anyone who doesn't know you the way I do not knowing that they can trust you," Jake said.

Cliff studied him and then nodded. He leaned on the broom. "You come out to go after Ashley?" he asked. "You ask me, she shouldn't be out alone right now."

The ghost of Emma Donegal had disappeared when he'd reached the stables.

But now he knew why he was here.

"Where is Ashley?" he asked.

"Just ten minutes ago, she came running down and asking me if there was any problem with taking her mare out for a ride. Said she needed to clear her head, and a ride around the property always did that for her. I was going to let her have a few minutes and then take a ride myself. I just don't feel right about her being alone."

"Hell, no!" Jake said. "What horse can I take?"

"If you head to the bayou, you'll find a concrete marker. That's where Emma had Harold Boudreaux buried," Marshall had told Ashley. "But don't go now, young woman. Show some sense of self-preservation. There's someone out there bent on hurting Donegal Plantation, and you are the last of the Donegal family."

"Cliff is a Donegal!" she told him.

"No, my dear, not really. Emma wasn't born a Donegal."

"Yes, and I'm not sure exactly what the relationship is, but Cliff's great-grandfather and a young woman born a Donegal got together in the 1920s, so, yes, he is a Donegal!" she said.

"Well, yes, I suppose you're right on that."

Marshall Donegal had followed her when she went out to the stables, determined on riding. He kept trying to dissuade her while Cliff kept trying to dissuade her.

Before she'd mounted up on Varina, she'd given Cliff a huge hug. "I love you, cousin!" she told him.

Cliff had looked at her strangely and then shook

his head. "Look, Ashley, you don't have to defend me. I didn't murder anyone."

She'd grinned at him. "I never thought you did. I just wanted to say that I love you!"

She hadn't bothered with a saddle; she had to find out if there was really a stone near the bayou. If so, she wasn't imagining the ghost. He was really there, telling her things.

Or she was imagining the ghost, and he was really suppressed memories in the back of her mind. Whichever. She wasn't doing well fighting the concept of imagining Marshall Donegal, so she might as well try to use what was happening. And it didn't look as if she'd be running to Jake for comfort. She'd be business, strictly business, from now on out.

She thought that she had ridden out alone; she should have known better. Marshall Donegal was riding behind her—on a ghost horse, of course. His mount was a beautiful roan, complete with all his Confederate trappings.

"Dammit, woman! Let me lead!" he called to her.

She felt something as he and the roan seemed to pass through her. Then she took off through the woods, following him.

They rode for twenty minutes. Then the ghost horse let out a whinny and stopped, and her haunting ancestor slipped from his mount and walked down the trail to a large pine. He tried to rip away the vines and grass and weeds that grew around the base; Ashley saw that the grass moved, but little else happened.

She began the task herself.

She gasped out loud. It was there, a large, flat, stone marker. One word had been crudely etched into it.

FRIEND.

Ashley sat back on her haunches and looked up. Marshall Donegal leaned against the tree, watching her.

"Why? Why did Emma bury him out here? There's a tomb for the slaves—and then the servants—who stayed on to work the plantation," Ashley said.

"Emma was truly a wonder," he said sadly. "Any rumors you heard about fights between us—or my indiscretions—were stories created because people need stories. We fell in love, and when that first blush of love was gone, we still loved one another deeply. She was a strong woman. She held the place together after I died—with the help of Harold Boudreaux. In 1864, they became lovers. The world would never have accepted it. Even after the war ended, they would have been in grave danger. There was a pecking order for those of mixed blood in New Orleans, you know that. Quadroons were all the rage to become a man's mistress, and the Quadroon balls were infamous. But after the war, the KKK was started up, and if they had been discovered, Harold most probably would have been burned on a cross, and Emma would have been subject to rape and ridicule. They had to keep their affair entirely secret. So he raised their child as one of his own. Another of the former slaves—a young woman of mixed blood herself—was accepted as the child's mother."

"Did you mind? Did you hate what happened?" Ashley asked him. "I mean, as a ghost, were you bitter or…can you still hurt?"

"My soul can know agony," he said quietly. "But did I mind this? No. I loved Emma with my whole heart. And a dead man knows that the color of his skin doesn't mean a damned thing. I admired Harold. I loved what he did for my family, and how he taught and defended my children. No, I didn't mind. Not this. I just thought you should know. Maybe it can help you in some way."

They both started at a sound that seemed to come from the woods that led straight to the bayou. Ashley quickly stood up. "Probably a raccoon or even a squirrel," she said and grimaced. "Maybe even a gator." She walked toward her mare.

It wasn't a raccoon, squirrel or gator. As she mounted, she heard the noise from the woods by the bayou again.

"Quickly," Marshall said. "I'll hold the path!"

"But it may be nothing."

"You're alone out here. Get back to the house! Please!"

She almost laughed and reminded her ghost protector that he was dead.

But she didn't. She turned to ride, finding the

quickest path back to the house and kneeing her mare to a gait that would lead it at all speed through the trails without killing them both.

But as she made her way homeward, something darted into the path in front of her.

Varina reared, and she wasn't as prepared as she should have been. She cursed herself for her carelessness as she felt herself fly into the air.

And land hard on her rump in the middle of the dirt path.

As she quickly stood, rubbing her injured section, she realized that it had grown late.

Darkness was falling, and she was alone in the woods.

Even her ghost was far behind her now.

# Interlude

*People were easy.*

*Pathetically easy.*

*Once you knew what they wanted and you dangled it before them as you might dangle a carrot before a horse, they came. They came— just as the stupid animals they were in truth.*

*She barely saw him coming.*

*She got just a glimpse of him.*

*During the phone call he'd made to her, she'd guessed that he was Jake. She'd giggled.*

*He'd almost giggled, too, it was so damned perfect.*

*And what an idiot woman. You'd think they'd have to get through some kind of school to broadcast the news. But a pretty blonde was all you had to be, it seemed. Maybe not. Maybe others were smarter.*

*He watched her when she came staggering along the overgrown and marshy trail near the bayou, swearing as she did so. Actually, he watched her for a while. He didn't know what it was about her that had made him want to do this. He'd plotted and planned his first kill forever; he'd thought that it would be his only kill. But he started hearing the voice again. She was nosy. She was going to start dredging things up and just might have some journalistic abilities. The voice said that she needed to go. And looking at her, he had begun to anticipate the kill.*

He glanced toward Beaumont; he could see the plantation through the trees. But there was nothing going on there—the plantation offered its last tour at four, and people were usually off the property by five. Even the actors and historians would all be by the road now, ready to head out.

She stumbled her way to the small clearing. Her little red spiked heels were completely ruined, and her jacket was torn. But though she was irritated, she wanted the story more. In fact, when he came upon her, she was looking down at her shoes and cursing about how much they had cost her.

"Damn it, what the hell are you doing here?" she demanded, tossing back her head of bleached blond curls. "I was expecting—"

She never voiced what she was expecting. He was quick. The needle got her with such speed that she barely gasped, much less managed to get out a scream.

As she fell, he heard the horses. He heard the rummaging over on the next trail.

He had to move with speed.

He rolled her down to the true swampy area just before the bayou.

He held her head under in just a half foot of water.

She didn't struggle. She was out, and she was easy to kill.

When she was dead, he couldn't help but roll her over. He smiled, looking at her face.

*That pretty, bitchy face, all clotted with mud now. Her lashes were slipping. False lashes; she'd been all makeup and hype and selfishness. Actually, he'd done the damned world a favor.*

*She wouldn't look so good on the eleven o'clock news now. Of course, they wouldn't find her right away, and they wouldn't expect to find her out here.*

*But somebody was out here now. He had to move.*

*And move quickly.*

# 9

She stood in gathering twilight, cursing her mare for throwing her.

Poor mare; it wasn't her fault—she had been startled. *Scared.*

"Damn you, foul rodent!" she cried into the bushes. She swore softly; it was time to walk, and walk quickly. "Last time I follow a ghost into the woods!" she muttered.

Was it a ghost? Was there really a ghost? Or did she have deep-seated memories that she needed to address, and seeing the ghost of Marshall Donegal was a way of doing it? Hmm. That would be a good one for a shrink.

Maybe, just maybe, people did see ghosts. And maybe it was some kind of a gift, and she'd been far too terrified to ever recognize the possibility before.

Jake had that gift—that sixth sense or intuition. And when he'd come to her with it, she had simply panicked.

Well, too late on that one!

She paused; she heard something coming from the pines and brush closer to the bayou. Gator? It was unlikely that one of the giant crocodilians she'd known all her life was going to come this far in off the bayou and stalk her.

She quickened her pace.

Of course, she knew that even on land an alligator could move damned fast as well.

But, no. The woods here were filled with birds, the bayou was brimming with fish and there were plenty of small mammals. A gator had not had a whiff of her and decided that it was time for his evening meal.

She heard it again. Definitely not a gator, because she kept hearing the rustling, would stop—and then the rustling would stop as well. A beast of prey would come straight for her.

She started to run. As she did so, she heard a thrashing in the woods ahead of her and then from one of the other trails.

She swore and looked around her. There was a fallen slender pine near her, leaning against an oak. She tested the trunk carefully, found that it would bear her weight and crawled up to the branches of the hardier oak. She kept crawling, hoping that whatever was out there didn't climb trees.

The thrashing around her grew louder, as if amplified in the thickening darkness of the night. She finally realized that she could hear hoofbeats, and a rider was coming for her. She waited, barely daring to breathe.

Of course, Cliff knew that she was out here. When her mare came back without her, he'd be on the trail, coming to find her.

But even as she heard the sound of a horse, she saw something dark below her. Not a creature—a man. A man who looked like a shadow because he was dressed in black: black boots, jeans, sweatshirt and hoodie. He moved with his face lowered, and in the darkness he might have *been* a black shadow.

Was she seeing shadows now instead of ghosts?

No, he was real.

He was approaching the tree; he paused as if listening.

She heard her name called through the trees. And she no longer heard the sound of hoofbeats.

For a moment, the entire world seemed silent. She waited, not daring to breathe.

Darkness fell in earnest, but the moon prevailed.

And then, naturally, the moon was covered by clouds.

Ashley cursed herself for starting out alone tonight. She had to breathe; she tried to do it silently.

And then, though she couldn't see him, she was certain that the man below her in the dark hoodie was looking up.

Did he see her frozen there?

She held her position. She couldn't tell if he was there or not anymore; his form seemed to have been swallowed up by the blackness of the ground below.

There was rustling.

There *was* someone below her, someone who seemed to be stalking the area.

Something banged against the tree. A man's hand?

She started to slip; she felt a splinter of bark shoot into her hand and barely kept from crying out. She tried to shift her position and fell, a scream escaping her lips at last.

She landed hard on human flesh, toppling the standing man to the ground. Panic seized her and she shot out a fist, striking anywhere she could as she tried to rise. She made it halfway to her feet when she heard him shout out.

"Bloody hell, Ashley! Why are you hitting me, damn it?"

Jake.

She went still and started trembling. For a minute, she still had to wonder if he'd been in the pines before the bayou, stalking her.

But then both heard it; more noise coming from the trail.

"Ashley! Jake! Where the hell are you two?"

That was Cliff's voice.

And from the bayou, another voice.

"Hey! What's going on in there? I have a gun, and I know how to use it!"

Jake scrambled up, half knocking Ashley over but then drawing her to her feet.

A light suddenly glared into the darkness, and they both raised their hands to protect their eyes. Cliff came trotting up on his favorite mount, Jeff. He dismounted in the little clearing where he found them.

"Cliff!" Jake said.

"Where's your horse?" Cliff asked.

"Where is your horse?" Ashley asked Jake.

"Mine is tethered down the road—he meant you!" Jake told her, irritated. "What the hell are you doing, skulking around in the woods by yourself? Jesus, Ashley, how much of an idiot are you?"

He was clearly upset, but he took a step back. "Damn it, I would have thought that you had some sense."

She heard the safety slide on Cliff's shotgun, and she felt a millisecond of fear again.

She was wrong; Cliff was bitter, and he was going to shoot her in the woods.

"Someone is coming," he said.

A minute later, his shotgun aimed at the clearing, Toby Keaton came into view. Seeing them, he lowered his weapon.

"What is this? A family meeting? You guys scared the hell out of me! What's going on over here?" he demanded.

"I was out riding. Some fairly big mammal scared

Varina, my mare," said Ashley. Ruefully, she added, "She threw me."

Toby looked at Jake, standing beside her, and Cliff, seated again up on Jeff.

"With what went on—you all damn near scared the death out of me. I mean, this side is your property, but I'm just a spit across that bayou. You've got to warn me when you're going to be rustling around by the water at night. I can tell the difference between the sound of a gator and the sound of folks stomping around in the woods, you know!" Toby said.

He was clearly shaken.

"Toby, I'm so sorry," Ashley said. She looked at him. His black jacket didn't have a hood.

But he might have a hoodie stuck down beneath his coat; his shirt was black as well.

"How did you get over here, Toby?" Jake asked him, as if reading Ashley's mind.

"I live next door, remember?" Toby said, exasperated. "One of my hounds was going crazy, but he lost the scent at the water. I don't come out at night without a shotgun. God knows when you're going to come upon a doped-up schoolkid, a gator or, hell, a damned poacher! Or just a nutcase now, like whoever did in old Charles."

"I'm sorry. Toby, how did you get here?" Ashley repeated. "Have you been over in the woods right by the bayou?"

"I came over in my little aluminum canoe," Toby

said. "I heard all manner of rustling—and it's turned out to be you!"

He shook his head. "Look, Ashley, I know we're all kind of scared right now, so maybe you could quit with the trail riding in the middle of night until they find whoever killed Charles!"

"She won't be out alone again," Jake said firmly, in a voice that seemed to scrape all the way down her spine. "It's pitch-dark and chilly out here, and the mosquitoes are big enough to rustle the woods themselves. We're going to get on back now."

Toby clicked on his own high-beam flashlight. Once again, they protected their eyes.

"Toby!" Ashley said quickly.

"Yes?"

"Were you under this tree a few minutes ago?" she asked.

He looked at her and squinted. "No. Well, hell, I don't think so. I didn't know what the hell was out here—I was moving around quiet as I could, trying to listen. Why?"

"I—I thought I might have seen you," she said.

"Well, if you'd seen me, it would have been nice if you'd said something," he told her indignantly. "I'm getting back."

Toby turned and started tramping down the trail. They could follow the glow of his flashlight as he headed for the bayou.

"What was that all about?" Jake asked Ashley.

"I climbed the tree because…because I was afraid.

I thought something was stalking me. I saw someone beneath me, and it scared the hell out of me," Ashley said.

"What were you doing out here?" Jake demanded, perplexed.

"Riding!" she snapped.

"Well, he's right. You shouldn't have been, and you damned well better not do so again until the killer is found."

"And what if you brilliant people with your brilliant team never find the killer?" Ashley demanded.

Jake didn't answer. Cliff did.

"Then we won't be out here, period. The plantation will go down, and the Donegal family won't own it anymore. You'll see sugarcane here, just like you see it beyond the cemetery side."

Jake was staring at her; she could see that in the glow of the flashlight Cliff still held on the little copse where they stood.

"We'll find him. We'll find the killer," Jake said, and he turned away. "Come on, you can ride with me."

She was angry...and worse, she realized. She was still feeling rejected, no matter how stupid any of it might have been—even if she *had* been the one to put a block on him years before.

"I'll ride with Cliff," she said.

Cliff was startled, but he looked down at her with a shrug, sheathed his shotgun in his saddle and shifted the light in his hands to reach down for her.

"Let's hope Varina made her way home—and that your grandfather hasn't gone out and had a heart attack!"

With Cliff's strong grasp, she leapt up behind him on Jeff. Ahead on the trail, finding his way through the dark, Jake mounted up on his horse.

They made a silent trek back through the woods to the house.

Approaching the stables, they saw that Varina had indeed made her way home. She was walking around in the center of the stables as if she were teasing the horses who were still in their stalls.

"I've got the horses," Cliff said gruffly. "You get in the house, Ashley, before Frazier realizes that you're not around anywhere."

She started toward the house. Jake was right behind her. She felt him come closer and closer, but she didn't realize he was going to stop her until she felt his hands on her shoulders.

"What the hell were you really doing?" he demanded.

"Riding. I do it all the time."

"Right—after a corpse is found in the cemetery."

She turned around and stared at him.

"A murdered man!" he said with some force.

"Look, this is my house. I live here, and I don't think I'm under suspicion—by anyone's standards. I'll ride when I feel like riding!" she told him.

She was startled when she suddenly saw him take a breath and smile.

"What?" she demanded.

"I'll just talk to Frazier," he said and walked past her.

"Damn it, Jake, stop!"

He did so, turning back to her.

"I—I heard a rumor after the reenactment," she said. "I heard that Emma Donegal was actually Cliff's ancestor and not one of the men in the family. She could never admit—not at that time—that she had an ex-slave, Harold Boudreaux, for a lover, or that she'd given birth to a child of mixed blood. But she loved him, and I heard that there was a gravestone out there. She had him buried out by the bayou. I thought if I found the stone, it might all be real. I went to find it."

He paused, watching her for a moment. "And did you find it?"

"Yes, it's there."

"It has his name on it?"

"The word *Friend* was carved into it."

He was quiet, and his silence seemed to scream that a stone that said *Friend* didn't really mean a thing, and that it was incredibly stupid at this time to be wandering around in the woods looking for the headstone of a man who might or might not have been an ancestor's lover.

Before they could argue further, the riverside door opened and Beth stepped out. "There you are! Goodness, I was starting to get worried. Jake, Jackson got back, and he's looking for you. Crab cakes are on, and it's time for dinner!"

Ashley turned from Jake and looked at Beth, forcing a cheerful smile.

"Crab cakes! Better yet, *your* crab cakes. Do we have a minute to wash up? Should I call Cliff?"

"I'll get him on the house phone, honey. You run on up. Angela has given me a hand in the kitchen, and it will all be on the table in ten minutes, so hurry it up, girlfriend! And, we've got more company!"

Ashley looked at her, puzzled.

"Will and Whitney?" Jake asked.

"Yep. They're as nice as they can be!" Beth told Ashley.

Ashley didn't doubt that the pair was exactly that. She was surprised to feel a little tug at her heart, created by the sound of pleasure in Jake's voice.

His friends were there. Maybe Whitney was more than a friend.

She suddenly felt out of step with his life and ashamed of herself. Jake had been the best friend in the world; she had loved him. She had turned from him. He deserved a little happiness.

"It will be great to meet them," she said.

She flashed Jake a quick smile, and hurried on into the house.

It was odd, but somehow the arrival of Will and Whitney—with all their paraphernalia—was like a breath of fresh air.

A horrible murder had taken place, and they were in the midst of a rough investigation. But Whitney's vibrant personality made its mark on the solemn household. As they sat down to dinner, she explained the setup that she and Will had carried out.

"Don't worry—we haven't put cameras in anybody's bedroom," she said, "but we do have the house nicely wired for sight and sound. Ashley, you haven't seen it yet, but there's a bank of screens in the living room. We have cameras aimed in both of the parlors, out to the front, out to the back and over the cemetery. Tomorrow we'll set up over the stables. That way, we'll be apprised of any unwanted visitors on the property. And—" she hesitated, casting Jake a questioning look "—and we'll be aware of anything that might happen inside the house as well."

She looked at Jake again.

Do they know that we investigate for paranormal occurrences or help? she seemed to be asking.

"I think what you've managed in a few short hours is amazing," Jake told her. "A camera setup like this will definitely catch anyone trying to play games in the cemetery again. But we have to rig by the river as well."

"They've done that," Jackson told him. "We got here at about the same time, and I asked them to make sure the back wall of the cemetery and the river were both in view on our screens."

"Did you have an interesting interview with Ramsay Clayton?" Jake asked him.

"Ramsay swears that he gave Charles the role out of the goodness of his heart. He also said that he'll be back in New Orleans by tomorrow or the next day. He's buying a guard dog and a pistol and getting a permit—he's afraid that whoever killed Charles might have really been targeting him," Jackson told them.

"That is a possibility," Jake agreed.

"Yes," Jackson said simply. "He asked the police for protection. They couldn't give him anything full-time, but they have patrol cars watching his residence while he's here. He said that when he goes back into the city, he's going to stay at a hotel for a week." Jackson smiled. "The casino hotel—there's lots of security around it. Unseen, half the time, maybe, but it is there."

Cliff let out a dry laugh. "Ramsay is a crack shot. But a dog is a good thing to have. Dogs really have a sixth sense. We used to have a dog."

Ashley smiled. "Brutus," she explained. "He was a Rottweiler, and I loved him to death."

"What happened?" Jake asked. He'd never met Brutus.

"He loved me in return—but he hated the horses and tried to bite them all the time, and they tried to kick him. He went to live with my mom's cousin in Gainesville. They're still happy as clams, I believe," Ashley said. She looked at her grandfather. "I should call Gina. She's probably heard all this on the news, and she'll be worried."

"Already called her and assured her we were fine," Frazier said. "She wants you to come stay with her and Brutus. I said it wasn't a bad idea."

"Oh, no. I'm not leaving," Ashley told him. She stood and walked over, slipping her arms around him. "We didn't do this, and Donegal Plantation itself is being victimized." She stared across the table at Jake. "This team will find the killer."

No one said anything for a minute. Frazier patted Ashley's hands where they lay against his chest.

"Well, a hotel at a casino might not be a bad idea," Beth murmured. "Ramsay might have it right."

"I personally couldn't afford a casino for more than a night!" Whitney said.

Ashley walked back to take her seat again. "Sounds like Ramsay's really scared. Doesn't sound like he could be the killer," she said.

"Lots of killers are good actors," Jake said.

"Crab cakes, children, crab cakes!" Beth said. They all looked at her. She smiled. "Hey, we can't live and breathe this every second. We'll lose our minds."

"Beth is right," Frazier said. "Whitney, why haven't I ever met you? Have you ever been out here?"

"Oh, yes! On a school bus with a swarm of children, I'm afraid, but I've been here before. It's a beautiful place, Mr. Donegal."

"Frazier, please," Frazier told her, smiling. "It's great that you're so kind as to respect your elders, but I am just Frazier."

Frazier was a grandmaster at heading his household; Ashley seemed quiet during the meal, but Frazier and Beth drew out the newcomers. They learned, of course, that Will was originally from Trinidad, that he had been a musician and an entertainer, specializing in illusion, before he had gotten into law enforcement. Whitney had been a filmmaker, and she loved film—and the world.

When the meal had ended, Jackson nodded to Jake, and they went to the study together. Jake brought up the lists he had made during the day, along with what he had discovered or not about his defined list of suspects. Then he told Jackson about the events in the woods.

"So, Toby Keaton appeared right in the middle of the chaos in the woods?" Jackson asked.

Jake nodded. "He'll bear further investigation. Basically, he and Hank Trebly are the only neighbors. Well, it's a sugar plantation-slash-mill on the other side, but the two of them are definitely close enough."

"What about the 'Yankees'?" Jackson asked.

"Justin Binder is the only man still without a reliable alibi. He was here the night that the body was found. He didn't leave until the police cleared him."

"Tomorrow we'll pay a visit to the sugar mill. And we'll drop in on Toby Keaton, too."

Jackson stood, ready to leave the room first. Jake

hesitated a minute, and then rose to follow him. "By the way," Jackson told him, pausing at the door.

"Yes?"

"Angela says that the house is riddled with ghosts, and half of them don't know that the other half are around. And none of them is talkative."

"Well, it is a plantation," Jake said, not yet wanting to talk about Emma Donegal. "What self-respecting plantation comes without its share of ghost stories?"

Jackson studied him and nodded. "Right. Naturally. Maybe we should let the owners tell us about a few. Let's hear what they have to say."

They went out to the front parlor where the bank of screens was set up. Whitney and Will had created their own little viewing station, pulling a few of the big wingback chairs in front of the screens. Whitney turned, seeing him.

"Hey! I brought something of yours from the hotel that you forgot, and I can't believe that you forgot it," she said.

"What?" he asked, puzzled.

"Your guitar," she said.

He raised his brows, opened his mouth and said nothing.

His guitar.

He'd never left his guitar anywhere; it was a beloved Fender.

Ashley and Donegal Plantation. They could make him forget anything.

He was surprised to see Ashley walk over to the guitar; Whitney had set it against the wall by the fireplace. She gingerly touched the case and looked at him, a nostalgic smile on her lips.

"You still have the old Fender," she said.

He shrugged.

"Play something," Frazier told him. "Looks like we're all in for the night."

"And the nights aren't easy to get through," Beth said.

Jake looked at Jackson, who nodded. *This is just what we need.*

Jake took out the guitar, sat and tuned it. He looked at Ashley. "Still play the banjo?" he asked her.

"Yes, badly," she told him.

He laughed. "Go for it!"

She hesitated, but Frazier said, "Come on, Ashley. For the love of God, let's have some music. We need something."

She hurried up the stairs and returned. Jake looked at her and smiled. "'Never Marry an Ugly Girl?'"

She nodded. They both played and he sang, and they encouraged everyone to join in on the chorus. Once they had started, they fell in together.

As if five years had never gone by.

They played Arlo Guthrie, and Cliff sang, and even Frazier did a rendition of a Frank Sinatra tune.

It went on for about forty-five minutes, and then Jake drew off his strap and set the Fender down. "Hey, let someone else do the entertaining now.

Ashley, tell them some of the ghost stories about the place that have some merit."

"Oh, well," she murmured.

"There's Marshall Donegal, of course," Frazier said. "The poor fellow must be turning in his grave at all this."

"What about Emma Donegal?" Whitney asked. "Wasn't she accused of having killed her husband and somehow covering it all up with—'the Yankee did it!'"

Ashley spoke up indignantly. "That's not true at all, and I don't know where that story got started. There were several diaries kept by the men who survived, and the surviving enemy even told the story the same way. Emma was innocent."

"Ah, well, I thought she was supposed to haunt these halls."

"Maybe. She died here," Frazier said. "By then, of course, her daughters were married and her son had children."

"Where did she die?" Whitney asked.

"She was in the Jeb Stuart room," Ashley said.

Jake started; that was something he hadn't known. And it was strange, of course, because he'd always stayed in that room when he had been a guest at the plantation. He lowered his head quickly. Did Emma appear to him because she felt she knew him?

"There was a fellow who had a heart attack before a reenactment and died in the stables," Cliff offered.

"I swear, now and then I think I see a shadow out there."

"Marshall Donegal supposedly guards the plantation in death, just as in life," Frazier told them. "I'm sad to say, in all my days, I've never seen a ghost."

"Have you ever *felt* one?" Ashley asked him.

He grinned. "Lots of times. I believe that there are spirits here, spirits of the past, of happiness and of trauma. But if we have ghosts, they're here to guard us, to watch over us. There's nothing evil at this plantation," he said firmly.

Ashley spoke slowly. "There's nothing evil at the plantation," she repeated and looked around. "But the living can certainly be evil. Do you think that… sometimes people create evil where there was none, because they believe that it existed in the past, and they encourage it in the present?"

"There's a lot of that going around," Jake said. "Take prejudice, for example, and the old hatreds people never let die. But, yes, Ashley, people can certainly perceive a wrong and turn it into a personal vindication. And it's possible that's what happened here—either that or someone's personal agenda. Who would benefit if this plantation went down? If we can't find discover why anyone would have hated Charles—or gone after Ramsay Clayton—we have to find out who wants to see you go down like a sinking ship."

"No one," Ashley said.

"No one that you realize," Jackson told her.

Beth ended the evening by rising. "I'm going to bed. And, may I say, I'm delighted to have you all in the house!"

Night again, darkness, and the hour growing later.

Jake stared at the ceiling.

He remained disturbed at finding Ashley in the woods, though he wasn't sure why. It seemed apparent that they had all frightened each other.

Was that all that it had been?

Ashley had been up a tree. Well, she had heard Toby Keaton. Toby had said that he'd heard commotion—Ashley. And then him—and then Cliff riding behind him.

Screw it.

He couldn't sleep. He rose and walked to the double doors that led to the wraparound porch. It occurred to him that a gymnast could easily figure out a way to enter the house by means of the porch. The house did have an alarm system, but, as Frazier had said, it was a bed-and-breakfast. They catered to the public. The doors were seldom locked, so it was doubtful that the alarm was often activated.

Out on the balcony, he stared at the night. The moon was now up, its light was shining down with a benign glow. He looked to the cemetery, at the ghostly and beautiful tombs.

And he looked toward Ashley's room, and then started, because, as if he had willed her there, she appeared on the balcony, encased in her gossamer white robe.

She looked his way.

He smiled.

"Couldn't sleep," she said.

"Neither could I."

They stared at each other as heartbeats went by. She kept her distance.

"Your friends are very nice."

"We're a good team."

"Whitney is a doll."

"She's like a little sister."

"Ah."

He laughed. "Really."

She walked to the railing, looking out as he had done.

"The river looks so peaceful tonight—and beautiful in the moonlight."

"Not so great when you're in it," he said.

"True. The police have the rifle and the bayonet at their forensics lab?"

He nodded. "They crawled all over the property today, too. I didn't think that they'd find anything, once we—you—had already found the weapon."

"Will you really solve this?" she asked.

"Yes."

"You're so certain."

"We have to be."

She pushed away from the balcony and looked at him. "Oh, come on, Jake! I'm not walking to you again. I already made the play, and I fumbled badly."

For half a heartbeat, he was still. Then he moved. He covered the distance between them and pulled her to him. He didn't believe he was being used; he wasn't sure he cared. Something, whatever lay between them, surfaced with the music, in the woods, even as they argued. He'd been looking for it without even being aware ever since he had lost her.

Feeling her in his arms, he found it.

He lifted her chin and touched her lips with his, and when he kissed her, she returned it with a passion and hunger that made his knees weak. He had to pick her up and sweep her off her feet quickly—while he still could.

He did so.

"Your room or mine?" he whispered against her lips.

"Either!"

He chose his own. He was certain that Emma Donegal knew all about this desperate kind of love and would leave them in peace.

He lay down with her on the bed, falling into the cool, clean touch of the sheets and the gossamer mist that surrounded her. He smoothed down the white flurry of the gown and met the crystal beauty of her eyes. She stared up at him with complete openness and trust, and he longed to ask her why she had turned from him so completely, but he didn't dare take a chance with the moment, because it was fragile. He found her mouth again, rubbing his thumb gently over the dampness of her lower lip, cherishing the contours of her face. Then his mouth found hers, and again their kiss was instantly hot and wet and filled with passion and hunger. As they kissed, they fumbled with one another's clothing, his easy since he was wearing nothing but briefs, hers a bit more complicated since she wore the light robe and a sheath of silk beneath. But making love had always been easy and natural for them, and in seconds he was feeling hunger and awe that he should be lying here with her once again. She was as smooth to his touch as the silk of her gown, and he swept his hands over her shoulders, cradled her breasts, pressed his lips to her collarbone and shuddered with the pleasure of simply touching her, feeling the pressure of her body, the tug of her fingers in his hair.

"Jake," she whispered.

It was as if there should have been more, but it didn't need to be said.

"Ashley." He murmured her name in return, his lips against the taut sleekness of her abdomen.

Her fingertips played over his shoulders and teased down his spine. He tried to hold on tightly to every moment, knowing moments could become nothing more painful or sweet than memories.

His thought eclipsed to the back of his mind as he rose against her again, found her lips and felt her tear away then to press her mouth against his chest, to press more fully against him. She was a naturally exotic lover, sensually seductive, writhing or undulating just to cast the ultimate moment of arousal in any given place upon his body. He made love to her torso, breathing in the scent of her, tasting the erotic aroma of her soap and essence with his kiss. Her breasts were beautiful and perfectly formed, her waist winnowed away to nothing and her hips were pure fascination. He couldn't touch them enough with his caress, with his lips, with his hungry kiss. As he moved against her body, he felt her breath, felt her body giving, yearning. He moved lower against her form, kissed her thighs, caressed her sexuality and grew ever more urgently in need as he felt her response to his touch. At last he rose above her, hungrily capturing her mouth once again. So entwined, he sank between her thighs and entered her. Sinking slowly into a state that was sure heaven, only to be followed by the blinding light of movement, urgent and passionate, and the explosive feel of her beneath him, undulating, tightening, wrapping around him and giving to him.

Her fingers gripped his shoulder, his back, his buttocks. She wound her thighs around him, and they seemed to rocket with the need and energy of lightning. Thunder tore into his heart, and storm winds created by their mingled breath. The world was still, nonexistent, and everything. And then he felt her gasp, felt the give of her body against his, and he allowed himself to climax, feeling as if he had emptied his body and soul. Giant shudders ripped through him in aftermath; he held her closely against him, and they eased back into the night, back into the bed, back into each other.

*I think that I have loved you all my life.*

The words didn't escape him; he somehow held on to that modicum of control. Instead, he just held her. Yes, he had loved her. Yes, she had turned away from him. And no, he had never really understood. Maybe she hadn't herself.

He hadn't allowed himself to become a pitiable hermit; he had lived life, and he had enjoyed it. He had even had other lovers.

Never like this.

And it was frightening to be with her again. He'd gotten his soul back once. He didn't know if he'd ever be so lucky again.

So he didn't speak. He just felt their breathing subside together. He listened to her heartbeat, and to his own, and it almost seemed that they there were in a harmony of motion.

"Jake," she said softly.

"Ashley," he murmured.

She was silent for a minute, and he wondered what she had really wanted to say. Was it possible that it would have resembled his own thoughts?

"I'm—I'm so glad that you're here," she said.

"So am I," he told her. "So am I."

He didn't ask her questions; she didn't try to explain. They lay together and drifted, and awoke, and made love again.

And in the end, he slept with her in his arms.

Slept deeply, plagued by no nightmares.

He had been adrift in a boat, knowing that there were those who had to be found. He had seen Ashley, and he had reached for her, and her fingers had slipped through his again and again.

But now he had caught her.

And he could dare pray that the nightmares had really ended.

# _Interlude_

_Tonight…_

_Tonight had been exhilarating!_

_There had been those moments of stark fear; fear that he would be discovered and caught in the act, that he would be captured._

_There had been those terrible moments of indecision._

_And yet there had been Ashley._

_Ah, Ashley! If she'd been alone, and come upon him, he could have handled her, of course. Not that she was easy—no, not Ashley. She always had been a fighter._

_Difficult to think of her in a coffin, set in a vault and left to disintegrate into dust and bone fragments._

_He didn't like to think about Ashley dead, not really._

_But the aspect of killing her was suddenly… so seductive._

_Charles was a big old ugly lug; he hadn't felt much of anything. Marty Dean was a bitch, pure and simple, fake breasts, fake hair, fake smile. He'd felt a pleasure in killing her that he hadn't felt with old Charles._

_If he had to kill Ashley…_

_He would definitely want her drugged. He would want to see her die without a crease in her beautiful face, without a cry of pain. She would be his then, if just briefly._

_Ashley was special. She would fit the bill_

*as no other could, and she would also fulfill something in him, some need he hadn't known he had....*

*Well, not really.*

*He broke out suddenly in a cold sweat.*

*Tonight...*

*Tonight he had almost been caught.*

*No.*

*He was getting better and better at what he did.*

*And they never would catch him.*

# 10

Ashley awoke alone.

She was in the Jeb Stuart room, so she hadn't imagined a wild and passionate sexual experience.

In her mind, she had to admit, the fear had existed that she had dreamed the whole thing.

But, no, she had been with Jake through the night, and that made her wake with a smile. She rose, found her clothing, slipped into it and nearly opened the door to the hall. Remembering that her house was now riddled with cameras, she decided to reach her own room through the wraparound porch.

She showered quickly and headed downstairs. It was late; it seemed that breakfast was long over; there was no one in the kitchen or dining room, but Beth always had coffee on, so she quickly poured herself a cup and decided to start looking for the others.

Walking into the roadside parlor, she discovered that Whitney was in front of the bank of screens, comfortably curled into one of the wingback chairs.

The coffee cup nearly fell from her hands as she

realized that one of the screens showed the back of the house—and the wraparound porch.

Whitney heard her there and turned around. Ashley's horror must have been clear on her face, because Whitney smiled. "Hey, don't worry! I'm the only one on now. And if there's anyone in this world who can't look at the two of you and know that something is going on, that person is certainly blind."

"I—I—I just—"

"Quit stuttering!" Whitney said, laughing. "Sit—join me."

Ashley sat in the chair next to her. It was amazing—the young woman, and Will, she presumed, had managed to place the cameras so strategically that the whole of the house was covered.

The outside and the public rooms.

There were no screens that covered the bedrooms, just as Whitney had said.

"So…"

"Jackson and Jake have gone to the sugar mill, and then they're going to stop in on Hank Trebly," Whitney said. "Angela is upstairs with a few folks from the police forensics team—they're trying to discover anything they can about who might have stolen the Enfield. Will has gone to get Jenna. You haven't met her yet, but you'll love her!"

"Beth? My grandfather?" Ashley asked.

"Jackson and Jake are dropping them off at a diner down the street—they needed to get out for a bit," Whitney explained. "Don't worry—they'll get them on the way back. Beth suggested that they wait for you, but your grandfather was insistent that you get some sleep."

"It was good to sleep," Ashley admitted. "So, what have you seen on the screens? Anything—besides me sneaking back into my own bedroom by way of the balcony?"

Whitney smiled at that. It was an honest smile. Ashley thought that she and Jake really were just friends. Caring friends, but no more. And it was easy to understand. Whitney was impossible not to like.

"I'll roll some tape. It's interesting," Whitney said.

She hit a button on her remote and directed Ashley to watch the top screen. She did so. The screen captured the area between the stables and the cemetery.

Shadows seemed to undulate on the screen.

"What is it?" Ashley asked her.

"The past?" Whitney queried in return. "It's hard to say. Skeptics would swear that you're seeing movement because of clouds and the moon. I think it may well be the movement of ghosts." Whitney looked at her; she wasn't joking. "It seems that sometimes energy remains—energy from a particularly traumatic event, such as men dying in battle. Some people believe that such hauntings are repetitious—it's just the energy, running in the same pattern over and over again. Then, of course, there's what they call an intelligent, or active, haunting. That refers to a ghost or ghosts who still have their wits about them. And they don't repeat an action over and over. They move about and watch the world."

"Oh," Ashley said simply.

Whitney smiled again. "So, what kind of haunting do you know best? I have a feeling about you. You're like Angela—you just don't know it yet."

"Pardon?"

"Everyone is afraid at first," Whitney told her.

"Afraid?"

"Of ghosts, of course," Whitney said.

Ashley just stared at her.

Whitney continued. "The thing is, most of the time, they just want to help. They've made their mistakes. They want to keep others—especially their descendants—from making the same mistakes. I know that this house is haunted, but ghosts, in my experience, don't want to meet everyone. I believe, though, that the ghosts very much want to meet you. They love you. They want to shield you from all danger, and they want to preserve Donegal Plantation, too, because it carries an important lesson. The place is all about the path that we've taken as Americans, the good things and the bad. The sane among us don't want to repeat mistakes of misunderstanding, cruelty to our fellows or war."

"I believe we do a good job with education here," Ashley said. She realized that her voice sounded raspy. She took a long swallow of her coffee, afraid to say anything else.

Whitney smiled and shrugged. "Anyway, that's what I believe," she said softly. Then she added, "Hey, that was great last night—the music, I mean."

"Jake and I played together...before," Ashley said.

"That was obvious. You're really good together," Whitney said. "In many ways." She set the remote down, stood and stretched. "Hey, want to introduce me to the horses? I love horses, and I never get to ride. I'd love to meet them. We're certainly safe enough—the place is surrounded by cops at this moment, and besides, Angela is here. She made some of the best scores ever at the target range back when she was a cop."

"It's hard to believe Angela was a cop," Ashley said.

"That's like a fairy-tale princess in a patrol car, huh? But, hey, even Disney princesses are toughening up these days. We're all capable of many things, right?"

"So I like to believe," Ashley said. "Is it all right to leave the screens unattended?"

Whitney nodded. "Everything is taping." She hesitated. "Okay, so half my job today is to make sure you're safe. We might as well enjoy it, right?"

Ashley smiled. "Yes, and I love our horses, too. Come on out and meet them."

It was obvious Hank Trebly wasn't pleased to see Jake and Jackson—he left them sitting patiently in his waiting room for an hour.

He nodded curtly to them after emerging from his office and motioned to them to follow. He didn't shake their hands, even though he'd known Jake before, just as Toby Keaton had known him, from the days when he had been at Donegal Plantation constantly.

"I don't know what you think I can tell you," Hank said, pulling out the chair behind his desk in his office and taking a seat. "I was there, yes, of course. But I didn't see anything. And I told that to the police. They sent a man around right after, you know—right after they found the poor bugger's body."

"You weren't particularly fond of him, were you?" Jackson asked.

Trebly immediately took a defensive tone. "What was to like or dislike? He was O'Reilly's stepson, and he didn't really belong. I mean, he never even took his stepfather's name. He was…just this big nothing, always there, always wanting to be a part of it all. He didn't have anything to add to any of our conversations in a roundtable. It was his place to play a Yankee, but he whined so much Ramsay gave him the role of Marshall Donegal. But I didn't hate him. And, sweet Jesus, I could never do that to another human being! I mean, why in hell would I?"

"Well," Jake said, "there's that bid you made to take over the Donegal property."

"What?" Trebly said, sitting up straight. His eyes narrowed. "Frazier Donegal told you that?"

"No, actually, Frazier didn't tell me," Jake said.

"It's public record. Right after Frazier's son, Patrick, died, the property fell into bankruptcy. You went to the bank, trying to coerce a sale."

"I—well, that's just pure bull!" Trebly said, but his face had gone pale. "Look, I was willing to help Frazier out."

"I don't think so," Jake said. "There were also plans on file to expand the sugar mill and the sugar fields."

Trebly sat back and stared at them hard. Then he dug around in his desk for a business card and tossed it over to Jackson. "I'm done speaking with you. If you need anything else from me, you can call my attorney."

"Thank you," Jackson said, rising. "We'll do so."

Jake stood behind him. Trebly didn't rise; he looked like he was going to explode.

"You shouldn't have come back here, Jake Mallory." His voice broke. "You're not wanted in the area. That was obvious after Patrick died."

"This is what I do," Jake said.

"You shouldn't have come back," Trebly repeated.

Jake shrugged and started out. He was surprised when Jackson lingered. "Is that a threat, Mr. Trebly? Because if so, you just threatened a government agent. I could actually have you brought in for that."

Trebly rose at last. "I didn't do it, damn you, and I don't know anything about who did. I didn't like Charles Osgood, but Ashley was probably the only person who felt sorry for him—or even felt genuinely bad that he was dead. Hell, yes, we could have used that land, but I didn't force the issue. Old Frazier pulled it together. We aren't expanding, and I didn't kill Charles Osgood!"

"Thanks for your time, Mr. Trebly," Jake said. "Jackson?"

Jackson turned around at last and they left the offices and the mill building.

"The man is an ass!" Jackson said.

"Maybe. But I believe him. I don't think that he did it."

Jackson shrugged. "Right now, I can't really tell. He was shaking, and he looks as if he might have really high blood pressure. He's not in the best physical shape, and we are looking for someone with strength and dexterity."

"Let's move on to Beaumont," Jake said.

Jackson nodded. "We'll pick up Frazier and Beth, drop them back at the plantation. I don't want them deciding to get back some other way."

Jake didn't reply. Jackson was worried about the plantation household.

So was Jake.

As long as the cops were still on duty, treating the entire plantation as a crime scene, the plantation itself seemed safe.

But that's where Charles Osgood had been found. *Safe* was the last word he'd use.

\* \* \*

"This is my favorite, my mare—even though she gave me a toss last night!" Ashley said, stroking Varina's soft nuzzle. "On this side, next to Varina, you have Jeff—after Jeff Davis, of course—and at the end, down there, Bobby—for Robert E. Lee."

"A true Southern stable!" Whitney said.

"Not really. Across there you have Abe—for Abraham Lincoln—and then Nellie and Tigger. Go figure. We just weren't consistent, I'm afraid. Actually, Jeff is Nellie's offspring, so we did name him, but we named him Jeff because we already had a Varina!"

"They're beautiful," Whitney said. "I wish we could go riding."

"We can go riding," Ashley said. She saw Whitney's face. "Oh, that's right. I'm not allowed to go riding. It's light out, though. So can I go with you?"

Whitney was thoughtful for a minute. "I'll give Jake a call."

"I thought Jackson was the head of the unit."

"Jake gave me the order." Whitney grimaced.

"Look, I went out late yesterday afternoon, and I shouldn't have, but honestly, I didn't think Varina would throw me. And nothing happened, really. We just all scared each other."

"And Toby Keaton showed up, and no one trusts the man at the moment," Whitney said.

"And Cliff," Ashley added.

Whitney watched her, nodded, and slowly smiled.

"You think we're full of it for suspecting Cliff, don't you?"

"Yes."

"I'm sorry. He is a suspect."

"Right, so I've been told—because he has access, he has motive," Ashley finished.

Whitney drew out her cell phone. She turned away from Ashley, putting through her call. Ashley could hear Jake's voice on the other end of the line, but she couldn't make out his words.

But Whitney was smiling when she hung up.

"We have permission? I'm shocked," Ashley said.

"He's just trying to protect you, you know," Whitney said.

Ashley smiled. "Yeah," she said quietly. He was trying to protect her. "But you know what? I may not have been a cop like Angela, and I may not be a crack shot—but I did grow up here, and I do know how to use a shotgun. Guess I'll go drag mine out."

"I'll get Angela. Jackson and Jake are almost back with your grandfather and Beth. If you get the horses saddled—and I'm a decent rider, not great— we can head out as soon as they drop off Frazier and Beth."

"Are they staying?"

"No—they have another stop to make. They're going to have a talk with Toby Keaton," Whitney explained.

Whitney headed back to the house, her dark curls

bouncing as she walked. Ashley was about to knock on Cliff's door and find out if he'd mind helping her saddle up the horses, when he walked out.

"We're expecting a load of hay," he told her. "I imagine the cops will let that through. Seems like they've been doing a good job, though. I haven't seen any reporters around for a while."

"Maybe they've decided that peering in from the road just isn't that exciting," Ashley said. "Apparently, they've got something going with the police. I think that a police spokesperson has been handling news on the investigation. Well, actually, what do I know? We're all at the house having the same experience."

"Cops are supposed to come out—or forensic people, whatever they are—and go over my apartment," Cliff said.

"And you don't mind?" Ashley asked him.

"I want to be cleared," he said.

She smiled. "You're clear in my book."

"Well, and that's what counts to me. But I don't want to spend the rest of my life with people glaring at me if they don't catch the bastard."

"They'll catch him," Ashley said.

"How do you know that?"

"Jake said so," Ashley told him.

Cliff nodded. "Well, God knows—I hope so. I pray so, Ashley, I really do."

They looked at one another as they heard tires on the gravel near the front. Walking around, they saw that a white minivan had just pulled into the front.

Will Chan emerged, followed by a tall, slim, red-haired woman.

"Hello!" she called out, seeing them watching her from a distance.

She said something to Will, who nodded and grinned. He went for the bags at the back of the car while she walked over to them.

Her brilliant green eyes shone out over her easy smile. "Hello, I'm Jenna," she said, offering her hand.

"Jenna, lovely to meet you. We've been expecting you, of course," Ashley said. "Welcome to Donegal Plantation."

"It's brilliant," she said. There was a lilt to her voice, very soft, and yet it spoke of an Irish background.

Jenna looked at Cliff and seemed to assess him quickly. "You're—"

"Cliff. Cliff Boudreaux. Suspect," he said dryly.

"Ah, well, we're all suspect at one time or another, aren't we, then?" she asked.

"If you say so, Jenna," Cliff said. He was grinning; the two were looking at one another with amusement and something like an instant rapport. Ashley found herself amused.

"I'll bring you into the house, Jenna, and show you to a room. There are a few left to choose from—" Ashley began.

"I can—and have—slept on many a floor. Put me

wherever you would like, and I'll be just fine," Jenna assured her.

"Oh, Cliff, would you saddle Varina, Nellie and Tigger for me? Whitney wants to go riding, and Angela is going to come, too."

"Riding?" Jenna's eyes lit up.

"Cliff, add Jeff to the horse list, will you?"

"Oh, I think she'd do well on Bobby. You're a rider, aren't you, Jenna?" Cliff asked.

"I like to think so," Jenna said.

"Bobby, then. Bobby it is!" Cliff said.

"Are you joining us?"

"Can't," Cliff said. "We're expecting a delivery. But hopefully we'll get a chance somewhere along the line to head out together."

"It's a date," Jenna said.

Bemused, Ashley led their new guest to the house.


Frazier and Beth were still sipping coffee when Jake and Jackson went in to pick them up for the ride back to the house.

They both looked a little brighter for having escaped the house for a while, but Beth was grave.

"We have another missing person," Beth said.

"What?" Jake asked her.

She lifted her coffee cup and indicated the television above the diner's counter.

"The news just had a thing about it. That reporter—I think you knew her?—Marty. Marty Dean. She didn't show up for work today, and her station has plastered her picture on the news a dozen times. See—it's who you know," Beth commented to Frazier. "This woman was a newscaster—people saw her every day. So they ignored us when Charles disappeared, but they're all over it now because she's missing."

"It's true," Frazier said. "Her coworkers believe she wouldn't miss work. Ashley was upset about Charles. She knew him. She knew something bad was going on when he turned up missing. But Charles didn't work for a news program, and neither did Ashley. If I hadn't known Adam—"

"Think about the people who don't know Adam, either," Beth pointed out.

"They might have found Charles alive if anybody had really been looking," Frazier said.

Jake stared at the television. An old Western rerun was playing.

"What did they say about Marty Dean?" he asked.

"She rushed out on a tip yesterday afternoon, said she'd be back for the eleven-o'clock news, but she didn't make it," Beth said. "She still hasn't shown up."

"But she was in New Orleans, right?" Jackson asked.

Beth nodded. "Yes, she disappeared from New Orleans."

Jake looked at Jackson. He had a bad feeling—a really bad feeling.

But the police in New Orleans would certainly be on the disappearance. Forty-eight hours or not, the media would be forcing them into action.

"Let's get them back and look in on Toby Keaton," Jackson said.

It was nice, riding with the other women, even if their previous acquaintance made her the odd man out.

Jenna was a welcome addition. She was sweet and energetic, but it was really the accent, Ashley decided. Americans loved accents from the British Isles, English or any variety, whether Irish, Scottish or Welsh.

And Jenna oohed and aahed over the river, over the cemetery, over the horses, over everything. She seemed to love Donegal Plantation, and as they rode, she told Ashley that her expertise was in nursing.

"A federal agent—in nursing?" Ashley asked.

Jenna waved a hand in the air. "I have other talents," she said.

"Oh?"

"I'm not as good as Angela," she said flatly. "But I speak with the dead."

"A little subtlety might be in order!" Whitney called out.

Ashley twisted around in the saddle to see Angela, who was also rolling her eyes.

"The cameras, the shadows, Jake…is this a *paranormal* unit?" Ashley asked.

"No—we're a regular unit," Angela said.

"We're a special one," Whitney told her.

"We look for what's real," Jenna said. "But we may be able to find what everyone can see by seeing what everyone can't. There, does that clear it all up?"

"Just like Mississippi mud," Ashley said.

"Jackson came from a regular behavioral-sciences unit," Angela said. "Then Adam Harrison formed a team when Senator Holloway's wife, Regina, died. Jackson knew all about forming a team and learning each member's specialty, but Adam had done the legwork already, finding those he wanted."

Ashley studied them all. "I know the case, of course. But people were saying that ghosts had killed Regina Holloway. I suppose we're in much the same position here."

"Exactly. Here's the thing. Jackson knows that things happen out of the norm, but he's also aware that living people usually prove to be behind it," Angela explained. "He's a true skeptic—a prove-it-to-me man. The thing is…"

"The thing is what?"

"Ghosts do exist," Whitney said. "And no one sees them more clearly than Angela."

Ashley looked ahead as they rode on.

Had Angela seen Marshall Donegal yet? She hadn't seen him herself today. Maybe he had decided he might find a more intelligent *life* force in someone else?

Angela smiled. "Well, I also believe there has to be

human evil involved. But...Whitney is telling you the truth. We investigate for ghosts. Not because they're evil, though, honestly, evil men make evil ghosts. They'll encroach on someone's mind, but they can't carry out evil deeds. It's like hypnotism. If it's something you won't do, you still won't do it, no matter how a ghost tries to play with your imagination."

"Wait a minute. It sounds like you're saying 'The ghost made me do it!'" Ashley said.

"Not at all," Angela said gravely. "What we're saying is that...well, if the evil in a man's soul or spirit remains behind, it can act as fuel to someone who is already a madman. But most of the time, those souls that linger are yearning only to bring something to right, to protect those they might have loved. To bring about some kind of resolution or conclusion."

"Interesting. What about a ghost who lingers over a hundred and fifty years?" Ashley asked.

"I'm sure that ghosts have lingered much longer," Angela said. "Sometimes they're just waiting to be freed. And, I imagine, sometimes they like being ghosts and doing what they can for the living. God knows, I don't have all the answers."

"But—you talk to ghosts!" Ashley said.

Angela smiled. "Yes, but you see—they don't have all the answers, either. This direction we're riding in—it's toward the bayou and the plantation next door?"

"Yes, our best trails are out this way toward the

bayou. Just past the outbuildings on the other side, it all turns into barbed wire for the sugar fields."

"There have to be gators out here," Whitney commented.

"There are. We leave them alone, they leave us alone," Ashley told her. "And you'll only see them when we're right on the bayou. They seldom venture as far as the riding trails. They like their watery habitat."

"Alligators. Ugh," Jenna said, shuddering.

"To tell you the truth, we worry more about the snakes," Ashley told her.

"Oh, great! It might be about time to head back, eh, friends?" Jenna said.

"Just a bit farther, please," Angela said. "I want to see the Creole plantation."

"The bayou is between our property and Beaumont," Ashley told her.

"That's all right. I just want to see it from here," Angela said.

"It's just up ahead. There's a twist in the trail that goes right down by the bayou," Ashley said.

"You'll be able to see it from across the water there."


Jake parked in front of Beaumont.

It was an entirely different place from Donegal Plantation, not as grand, and there was no canopy of oaks along a sweeping front drive. By car, the house was reached by a massive gravel parking lot in front. Wooden fencing surrounded the residence itself, which was only two stories. Jake had been in Beaumont himself, and he found it as fascinating as Donegal, just different. Here workrooms and space for the animals had once taken up the first floor, or raised basement, while the household had always lived in the second floor. Like many of the other plantations, Beaumont had been a working sugarcane farm, and the outbuildings remained as they had been, important parts of the tours that were given here. The Creole way of life, rather than that of the English planter, held sway here.

Toby Keaton had inherited the house through his mother's side of the family. She had been a Thibadeux, from an old French family. His father, whose family line also went back for generations, had hailed from the English who had settled in the Garden District of New Orleans. Toby had been divorced for years; his one son, now in college, was being groomed to take over the family business when Toby grew weary of it...or willing to give up being the one in charge. Jake could remember meeting Josiah Keaton; he had been a handsome yet solemn young teen when he had last seen him, aware of the responsibility that would one day be his.

"Intriguing place," Jackson said, sliding his sunglasses down on his nose as they emerged from the car.

"Toby runs a good business," Jake said. "He and Frazier have always supported one another."

Jackson looked at him. "But Donegal Plantation has become a bed-and-breakfast. Beaumont has to be doing better."

Jake shrugged. "It pulls in a higher gross, yes. But the expenses are higher, too."

"Still, Toby Keaton could want Donegal to go down. And last night, when you went after Ashley, the man made an appearance in the dark—on the other side of the bayou."

"True," Jake said.

Before the path that led to the house there was a little kiosk where tickets could be bought. A woman wearing French Creole Empire–style clothing, circa 1820, was behind the counter.

"Hello," Jake said. He flashed his badge; he didn't know her. She was young and had probably taken work here to get through school herself. "We're looking for Mr. Keaton. Can you tell me where to find him?"

"I wish!" she said irritably. "He hasn't been around this morning—and he's supposed to be handing out paychecks. His car is here, but he is not."

"He lives here," Jake said politely. "He has to be somewhere." He pointed to an overhang in the parking area; there was a shiny new Honda parked there. "Is that his car?" he asked.

"Yes." She flushed, looking at Jake. "I'm sorry, Officer. I just don't know where he is. I've tried his cell phone, but he wasn't answering. I opened the sales window at ten, just as I'm supposed to do. Everyone who is supposed to be here working is—you can ask Dan out by the field, or Martha, who gives the tours up at the house. Maybe one of them has seen him."

Jake glanced at Jackson and thanked the girl. They walked up to the house, where a costumed interpreter—Martha, he assumed—met them at the door. "The next tour starts in thirty minutes," she said cheerfully. "You're welcome to explore the grounds while you wait."

Once again, they produced their badges.

"Oh, dear!" Martha said. "What's wrong? Oh, is this about poor Mr. Osgood?"

"We need to speak with Mr. Keaton," Jake said.

"I wish I could help you, sir. Mr. Keaton hasn't checked in with any of us this morning."

"Is that unusual?" Jackson asked.

"Well, yes, of course. He is a hands-on man where business is concerned," she said. She was thoughtful. "Well, of course, there was the morning after he'd met with a few of his cronies, and we found him passed out in one of the rooms we show. It was rather frightening. We have mannequins in that room to add to the historical setting, and there was the monsieur, the madame, the *jeune fille*—and Mr. Keaton, all messed up and on the bed between them all! My poor guests—"

"He's not there now, you're certain, is he?" Jake interrupted.

"Oh, no! I've had several tours through the house already today!" she said. "But I don't suppose that anyone has searched all the outbuildings. There isn't a guide stationed in every one. We have a girl who comes in at ten—"

"Excuse me. I understand there's someone in the field we might talk to?" Jake interrupted again.

"Oh, yes, silly me, I do go on. I can see Dan now—he's in the straw hat, over down by that wheelbarrow."

"Thank you," Jake told her.

He felt a growing concern as he and Jake walked down the expanse of sloping lawn to find Dan, a tall, muscular, African-American man sorting through an enormous pile of produce.

Jake remembered Dan, though he doubted that Dan would recognize him.

But Dan did.

"Is that you, Jake Mallory? Sad things going on, sad things! Why, I remember you riding like wildfire all over that big plantation next door," the man said to him, giving Jake a brief hug.

"Good to see you again," Jake said. "We're here looking for Mr. Keaton."

"So am I," Dan said. "Paychecks are due today, and if you don't remind that man, he doesn't remember to pay us."

"Do you mind if we start searching for him? Have you been in all the outbuildings today?"

"I gave tours in the old kitchen and the smokehouse. I have been in all the slave quarters. They should be open, though. Martha walked around and unlocked them as soon as we came in and saw that Toby wasn't around."

"Thanks, Dan."

"I'll give you a hand, if you need," Dan offered.

"That's fine, Dan. It won't take us long," Jake assured him. "You seem busy."

"I'd like to get these to the kitchen, but if you need me, just holler."

They started for the row of old wooden slave quarters. But before they reached the first, a bloodcurdling scream stopped them in their tracks. It came from the other side of the bayou.

The scream was followed by a volley of gunshots.

# 11

Ashley had heard the grunting long before they'd reached the bayou.

"What in the Lord's name is that?" Angela demanded.

"Gator," Ashley told her. "Sometimes it sounds like you stumbled upon an entire pig farm. That's the noise alligators make."

"Should we come any closer?" Whitney asked.

"We're fine. We just stay on the road and make sure that we don't bother them. Remember, we don't bother them, and they don't bother us. They're really not insane predators chasing everything that moves," Ashley said. "They can move on land, and move fast, but, usually, they hunt in the water. They wait for their opportunity, and they snap, and then twist and turn in the water, drowning their prey. They're as instinctive as other predators—they don't want an eye gouged out by a flailing claw or the like. If you go to any of the gator parks, you'll hear them sound like that when it's mating season, or when an employee is about to hand out the chickens—dead, of course."

She was in the lead, but Whitney was right behind her. Ashley had twisted in her saddle to speak, and so she didn't know what Whitney saw when her eyes suddenly went wide and a scream escaped her lips.

Ashley turned back; she didn't scream. She let out a gasp of horror and pulled out the shotgun she had opted to bring along on the trail.

She could see why the gators were going crazy.

They had been fed.

Some were on the embankment; some thrashed in the water, adolescents and adults, maybe eight to ten in total. It was difficult to tell, because they were snapping at one another, the large ones going after the smaller ones. But they were all hungry for human flesh.

A number of the beasts had already started in on the bodies; it almost appeared that they had been playing with mannequins. The two bodies in the water were muddied and mangled beyond description, certainly, at this point, past any sense of pain or horror. It was impossible to tell if they'd been dead when they'd been discovered by the alligators, or if the gators had gone entirely mad and attacked two human beings.

Usually, upon discovering large dead prey, an alligator would drag it around until decomposition and the water softened down the bones, but when they started fighting over prey, it was like a scene out of a horror movie. The bodies might have been toys being ripped apart by children; the snapping jaws landed on limbs, and they were ripped cleanly away.

Ashley took aim at the head of a large adult, aiming right between the eyes. Her shot was true; the jaws clamped shut, but then the gator began to sink. Behind her, Angela was taking aim with her pistol. Ashley shouted, "The eyes! Strike between the eyes!" Luckily, the horses had grown up around hunters, and though Varina had thrown her before, the sound of the gun didn't bother any of the horses.

Ashley emptied the second barrel of her shotgun, horrified at what she was seeing and equally horrified that she was killing so many of the beasts who were only acting as nature intended; she felt a sinking certainty that the alligators hadn't attacked standing adults. They wouldn't have needed to, and they wouldn't have attacked unless an idiot had gone with food and become part of it. They would, as they were doing, go for a tasty morsel of meat that was dead and decomposing.

Angela was shooting with a pistol, and her shots riddled the air as Ashley reloaded.

The scent of dead alligators mingled with that of ripped flesh—and more fights erupted, but the sound of the shots was finally entering into their lima-bean-sized brains, and they began to move off at last. Ashley and Angela stopped shooting.

Whitney, as stunned and shaken as the rest of them by the bizarre and horrible spectacle, fumbled for her cell phone. But before she could dial with her trembling fingers, they heard shouts.

Across the bayou, men burst through the trees. Jake and Jackson were followed by Dan, Toby Keaton's manager. He was armed with a shotgun, while Jake and Jackson had drawn pistols.

They didn't need to fire; they clearly saw the carnage, and it was evident that they were equally stunned and appalled by the sight.

"Ashley! I'm getting the bodies out. Cover me," Jake shouted, his voice stretching across the thirty feet of muck and water. He stared at the women on the horses, and back to the water, at the gators now whipping their tails to escape, and back to the dead creatures, floating absurdly between what remained of the human corpses.

He started into the water.

"Jake!" Jackson roared.

Jake looked up. "I know what I'm doing, Jackson. Aim for the head, the eyes if you can, if anything starts to come near me."

"Jake, don't!" Ashley screamed.

But even Jackson seemed to know that Jake was right and motioned him forward. To discover anything—*who* the mangled bodies had been—they had to get them out of the bayou. Now.

Jake, maintaining a grasp on his pistol, walked carefully into the slick muddy water of the bayou, and seemed to sink into it slowly. The deepest water here was about five feet; his head was still above water when he pushed his way past a dead alligator and reached the first body. Grasping it around the shoulder with his one hand, still watchful of any movement near him, he eased back to the bank with it. Watching, Ashley still couldn't tell if the mud-encrusted pile of death was male or female. She could see that it was missing limbs.

She wiped sweat from her brow, barely blinking, watching the water for any sign of movement. An alligator could have been lurking below and heading out to strike beneath the surface, but there was no way for the great jaws to snap shut on a standing man unless the beast twisted and turned, and she would see that motion.

She heard Whitney chanting behind her.

"Jake, come on, Jake, Jake, Jake...."

He went back for the second body while Jackson and Dan pulled the first up the bank. Dan was already on the phone, Ashley saw out of the corner of her eye. Help would be coming soon.

Not soon enough for those being dragged from the bayou....

She saw a ripple in the water twenty feet from Jake. There was no way to take aim between the eyes, so she calculated a few feet before the ripple and shot, and then shot again. Willing herself not to fumble, she tore at the packaging of a cartridge and loaded again.

But the ripple bobbed to the surface; she'd made a clean kill, and Jake grasped the remains of the second body and dragged it to the embankment. As he crawled out, Jackson reached down to drag him from the water and up the slick, muddy embankment.

He stood up; his eyes met hers across the water, but he wasn't smiling. He was grim.

"We found Toby Keaton," he said dully, his voice barely carrying across the water.

"God in Heaven! God in his Heaven!" Augie breathed, looking at the corpses. Jake knew, of course, that finding a corpse in situ was the best possible place for a medical pathologist to first encounter a murder victim, but if they hadn't intervened, there might not have been actual body parts to be discovered. Toby Keaton was already missing a lower leg and his left arm, and the woman—*Marty Dean,* of all people—had lost her right arm to the shoulder and was missing a calf and foot on the opposite leg. Lain out, high on the grassy embankment of Beaumont, they formed pieces of a grisly human puzzle. Ashley, Angela, Jenna and Whitney had described their discovery of the bodies—and the gators—once the authorities had arrived and ridden back to Donegal Plantation.

"Can you tell me how they died?" Jackson asked Augie.

Augie, down on his knees near the heads, looked up at Jackson. "Are you kidding me?" he asked.

"I don't think they were killed by the gators," Jake said.

"I agree, but I'm going to have to get them back to the office to determine an exact cause." He indicated the places where flesh had been torn away. "These pieces have most probably been consumed, but I'm not seeing a blood flow on the bodies or in the water that would indicate that their hearts were still pumping when the alligators attacked, and liver temperature suggests that they've been dead for hours—twelve to twenty-four—but they've been in the bayou, so that can mess with temperature. I'm not seeing any gunshot wounds or slashes that look as if they were made by anything but giant snapping jaws. Frankly, I wouldn't trust any of my own findings in these circumstances until I've had time at autopsy. Jesus! Jesus, Mary and Joseph!" Augie finished, crossing himself.

"Might be the same, though," Augie added after a moment.

"Same as what?" Jackson asked sharply.

"I found massive doses of benzodiazepine—a sedative—along with chlorzoxazone—a muscle relaxant—in Charles Osgood's body. I believe that Charles was held unconscious and controlled by the two drugs until he was taken, still unconscious, to be killed at the site in the cemetery."

Jake looked at Jackson; they both held silent. Drugs were involved. Either they might start looking at M.D.s or pharmacists—or at robberies of pharmacies and doctor's offices.

*Such as the offices of Dr. Ben Austin?*

Jake decided to see what else Augie could tell them before assuming that these two had been killed the same way.

Mack Colby arrived. Both Jackson and Jake stared at him across the gruesome display of the bodies.

"Hey, Doc, help me out here!" the detective protested. "We just received the reports when we were called out here. Throw us a bone, here, please. Help in any way you can."

"I'm doing my best—with what I've got," Augie said. "Those reports were sent to you, too, Mr. Crow," he said. "I emailed you a copy of my findings just about an hour ago."

Jackson nodded. Jake said, "Thanks."

"So?" Mack Colby asked.

"It isn't death by drowning, and it's no damned accident, I'm certain," Colby said. "So, do we proceed with this as a dual investigation as well?" he asked.

"We would certainly appreciate continuing so, since Mr. Keaton has been a suspect in our existing joint investigation," Jackson said.

"Hey!"

They heard a shout from one of the uniformed officers who had been searching the surroundings on the Donegal side of the bayou.

"I've got a shotgun here," the officer cried.

He was down near the water and holding up the weapon with a gloved hand.

"Probably Toby's," Dan offered. His dark eyes were red-rimmed; he might have had a few arguments with his employer, but it was obvious he had cared. "How the damned hell did someone get to Toby when he always went out with his shotgun?"

"Maybe he saw someone he thought was a friend," Jackson suggested.

Dan's lips pursed.

"You don't have to stand here seeing this anymore," Jake said.

"I'm just waiting for gator season," he said gruffly.

"Can't blame a wild creature for acting like a wild creature," Augie said, standing and placing a hand on Dan's arm. "There was most certainly a human monster involved in this, and rest assured, the law will take care of him."

"We won't stop," Jake said as Dan looked at him.

"Hope you find him first," he said quietly.

Jake hoped they did, too; the man was extremely tall, but he was pure muscle. And that kind of muscle combined with pain and fury could be dangerous.

"You're a good man. Don't go trying to solve this yourself. There is no such thing as a righteous kill. You'll wind up in prison," Jake told him.

Dan lifted his hands. "Where do we go from here?" he asked quietly.

"You keep the place running for Toby's son," Jake told him.

"Close her down for a few days. We have to get to the bottom of this," barked Colby.

"I live here, too, in one of the old smokehouses," Dan said.

"That's fine. You stay on. But we'll need a few days of traipsing around here," Colby told him. He shook his head in disgust. "A bayou. A damned bayou filled with snakes and gators. Not easy to find much around here." He looked at Jake and Jackson. "Hell, boys, you are truly welcome to this mess!"

By the time they returned to Donegal Plantation, it was already late afternoon. The officer had brought the shotgun over to Beaumont, and Dan had positively identified it as belonging to Toby. Toby's little bayou-crossing aluminum boat was still on the bank on the Donegal side of the water as well; he had never made it back to his own property the night before.

Jake described his last meeting with Toby in the woods, repeating information he had already given Jackson to Mack Colby.

"Where the hell does the reporter woman fit into it all? What was she doing out there? High-heeled type out by the bayou—makes no sense!" Mack said.

"She was lured," Jake said slowly. "Someone lured her out on purpose." He paused, remembering what Ashley had told him the night before. She'd been frightened; she'd been up a tree. And she had seen someone below her. Toby—they had all assumed.

It had been the killer.

He felt an inner trembling and became anxious to return to the house and to the rest of the group.

There hadn't been much for the women to explain at the scene. They had come upon the feeding frenzy and shot at the alligators to get the creatures away from the bodies. Not even Colby had seen a reason to make them linger with the corpses.

Back at the house, he quickly sought out Ashley—even before heading to the shower.

Ashley, however, was showing her mettle. He found her sitting at the dining-room table with Angela, going over everything that had happened on the day of the reenactment. When Jake and Jackson came in, both women looked at them gravely.

"I'm sorry. I know Toby was your neighbor and a friend," Jake said.

Ashley nodded. "And I'm sorry about your friend. The reporter—I didn't know her."

"Well, I'm sorry, too, but we weren't actually friends. She was in my high school class."

Jackson and Angela were both there, and Jake held his reserve. But he asked softly, "Are you all right?"

"I'm fine. I'm angry. Someone is trying to destroy all of us," Ashley said.

Her eyes were level with his. She was just fine. She hadn't lost her cool for a minute when he had gone into the water, and though Angela was a crack shot, he had depended on Ashley; she knew the terrain and the ancient beasts better than anyone.

She was going to do all right.

Jake grimaced. "I'm going to shower," he said.

"This certainly sounds strange after…today," Ashley said. "But…it's almost dinner. We're having a vegetarian pasta dish, Beth decided."

Jake nodded and left the room, going upstairs.

He was surprised, yet not really, when Ashley appeared ten minutes later; she slipped into the shower behind him and wrapped her arms around his waist, resting her head against his back. He set his hands on hers, and they listened to the beat of the water and felt the steam around them for a minute. Then he turned and took her into his arms.

He kissed her; they touched and kissed in the hard spray for a long time.

"Is this horrible?" she whispered.

"No. It's life-affirming," he replied.

They made love quietly, and then more passionately, beginning in the heat and steam of the clear, clean water and ending up on the softness of the bed, entwined in one another's arms.

When they were done, her eyes were closed, and he leaned on an elbow looking down at her. She smiled slowly, a little wistfully, somehow feeling his gaze.

Her eyes opened.

"You used to do that all the time," she told him.

"What?"

"Watch me. It's a bit unnerving, you know."

He kissed her lips lightly. "I used to watch you and wonder that you were with me."

She was quiet, not meeting his eyes, staring up at

the ceiling. "That's crazy. It was a wonder that you were with me."

"You were the one who ended it."

"I was...scared."

"Of me?"

"Of what you seemed to know," she said.

He pulled her to him. "And are you still scared? Nothing about me has changed."

"But something about me has." She rolled away from him and rose. "It's going to be time to eat, and as awful as it seems after today, my stomach is beginning to growl fiercely."

He nodded. "It's just biology."

She reached for her jeans, closing her eyes briefly. He could clearly imagine the pictures in her mind; he had seen them, too.

She looked at him and tried to smile. "Get up! They'll all know where we are and what we're doing, but I'd just as soon they don't have to come find us."

"They know?" he said, frowning.

"Cameras, remember?"

He groaned softly; he hadn't thought of that aspect.

"Well, they'll know we're safe together, and these days, that's a good thing. I just feel a little guilty...."

"Because of me?"

"Because of Frazier."

Her grin turned real. "If we weren't in the middle

of a horrible mystery, I'd even suspect that Frazier knew exactly what you were doing and who you were working for—and called Adam just to get you back here." She paused and kissed him lightly on the lips. "Come on down, Mr. Mallory, please."

Buttoning her blouse, she headed for the door.

He watched her go, worried. Images flashed through his mind.

Charles Osgood, hanging from the statue.

Toby Keaton and Marty Dean…what was left of them.

He stared at the ceiling, trying to let the logic in his mind take over. Toxicology reports would affirm, he was certain, that both victims had received a similar cocktail to that which had been given to Charles Osgood to keep him compliant until the time of his death.

This time, though, it seemed that the killer hadn't had any intention of keeping his victims alive for long. He had probably discovered that a good shot of his drug cocktail immediately disabled his victims.

He knew, just as predatory alligators did, that he could be hurt himself in a fight. That was why alligators drowned their prey; they disabled them before they could be attacked in turn.

The killer was basically a coward. But he was changing his method, like a man with an agenda. He didn't fit the profile of a killer who sought out a certain type of victim; he didn't molest his victims.

He was there for the kill itself, and it was beginning to look like the kill itself was the goal.

Jake's head jerked up. A killer who had started with an agenda, and now had discovered how much he liked killing.

He would hunger for more and would strike again. Eventually, his need would make him careless. Eventually—but how many would have to die first?

Downstairs, Ashley found Will and Whitney speaking quietly to one another as they watched the monitors. Jackson, Angela and Jenna were holed up in the study with Frazier. Cliff hadn't come in yet, and Beth was watching her marinara sauce simmer.

"Ten minutes," Beth told her. She shivered, looking back at the stove.

Ashley decided that she'd take a walk up to the attic.

There, she looked around. They were definitely going to need all their household help back when the killer was caught, she decided. Black dust covered just about everything; all the cases that held family bibles, period weapons, jewelry, buttons and other odd objects that had been owned by the family over the years.

She walked over to the empty case, wondering whether they would get the Enfield back, and then wondering if she wanted it back.

She felt someone behind her and turned quickly, but there was no one there.

"Marshall?" she asked.

But her ancestor didn't appear. A sense of discomfort and aloneness filled her. She had never felt so in her own house. She hurried back out to the small attic hallways and made her way down the narrow wooden stairs.

As she walked toward the grand staircase that led to both parlors, she paused. She saw that her ghost was now making an appearance before her on the landing.

There was no one on the second floor then; Jake's door—the door to the Jeb Stuart room—was open, but no one was inside.

She walked up to Marshall, who looked tormented.

"Were you just in that room behind me, trying to scare me?"

"No. Why would I try to scare you?"

"Well, I don't know. You led me out last night to show me the gravestone, and I might have been killed."

"Good God, I didn't know anyone was in the woods. And what descendant of mine would fall off a horse? You should be a better rider, young woman," he said gruffly.

"Did you see anything last night?" she demanded.

"You," he said softly.

"Me?"

"I followed you when I heard the thud."

"You've heard what happened today, of course."

"Of course. I'm damned good at being a ghost. My senses are highly attuned," he informed her indignantly.

"I might have been killed!" she told him.

"Indeed. So you must cease behaving so senselessly."

"But *you* led me out! What good are you doing me?" she asked him. "Other than making me talk to myself—or my imagination, or whatever is going on."

"I will protect you—even from yourself!" he vowed valiantly.

"And you weren't behind me in the attic?" she demanded again.

He looked toward the stairs. She was startled by the look of agony that seemed to come over his misty countenance.

"No. I—I can't go in the attic," he said.

"What?"

"I can't go in the attic!" he repeated. "Leave it be, damn you. I can't go in the attic!"

He must have been really angry with her; he disappeared in a blink.

"I'm sane, and I have a ghost," she mused. "Or I'm totally insane. Or my mind is trying to make me recall something."

As she walked down the stairs, she wondered if she had ever heard a story about Emma having had an affair with an ex-slave and producing the child who would be one of Cliff's ancestors.

For the life of her, she was certain that she'd never heard such a story before.

Dinner was a solemn affair. When it was over, Jackson called Jake into the study, and they took out their list once again; they were down a suspect.

"What about Hank Trebly? He did want to buy the property when the Donegal family was down," Jackson suggested. "And, he's one rude ass."

Jake said, "Yes, but being a rude ass doesn't make a man a killer. Maybe the forensics lab will give us something."

"Alligator saliva," Jackson said.

Jake smiled tightly. "We'll know if they were drugged, the same as Charles Osgood." He leaned forward. "You know, though, I don't think that Toby was the intended victim. He was in the woods with his shotgun when we saw him, and I was pretty damned skeptical of him then. But he said he was over to check out noises he had heard. His dog had been going crazy. I believe Marty Dean was the intended victim, lured out because the killer wanted her dead for some reason in his head, and Toby stumbled on her killer."

"Sadly, that means Toby Keaton is cleared," Jackson said. "All right. So…we have Ramsay Clayton, Griffin Grant, Cliff. The one remaining 'Yankee' who hasn't been cleared, Justin Binder. Justin was

here for the reenactment, and he stayed at the plantation after." He ran his fingers through his hair. "What
the hell am I missing?" he asked.

"The doctor and the sutler," Jake reminded him.

"All right. We'll interview those two tomorrow,"
Jackson said. He shook his head. "I'm still not seeing
a clear motive. The killer went after Charles—but
was Charles the victim because he was Charles, or
because he was playing Marshall Donegal? Why go
after Marty Dean either way?"

Jake thought for a moment. "He wanted another
kill. I think that he felt compelled to create a *real*
reenactment of the death at Donegal Plantation. But
then, maybe, in his head, Marty posed a danger. He
needed that first kill associated with Donegal, but
he's smart enough to know that the grounds here are
being watched. He killed Marty Dean because she
would do anything for a story. He lured her out to
a place where he could kill her and where her body
might not have been found for ages—if ever. I've seen
what alligators can do with prey. In three months,
someone might have stumbled upon a foot bone."

Jackson nodded. "But if the body wasn't found,
how would that have hurt Donegal Plantation?"

"She was a news anchor. People would definitely
have gone insane looking for her. Somewhere nearby,
the police are going to find her car. They're checking the switchboard, so they may even be able to
trace the call that led her out here. They might have
looked forever, and it would have just added to the

sensationalism and mystery regarding Charles. But I think he killed her because he had to kill her. And I think that Toby just stumbled upon him."

"You know that this killer either called from a pay phone or from a prepaid cell that can't be traced. He would have purchased it with cash," Jackson reminded him.

"Yes, but they may be able to find a satellite locator—at least tell us where the call originated," Jake said.

"That's possible," Jackson agreed. "All right. Will and Jenna will head out and speak with the sutler and his wife, John and Matty Martin. We can't afford to wait on the reports. Tonight, you need to get going on the computer again—find out who might have access to those drugs—"

He broke off.

"Yeah, I was thinking that earlier," Jake said.

"The doctor," Jackson said. "Well, he was already on the list."

Ashley played chess with Frazier for a while, worried about how her grandfather was bearing up under the strain.

But though Frazier was grave and obviously thinking about their problems, he appeared strong—and was delighted when he beat her.

She watched the screens off and on with Whitney, Will and Jenna. Frazier tired and went to bed, and

Ashley walked over to sit with Beth as she leafed through magazines. Beth set hers down. "Ashley."

Ashley looked up at her. Beth's large dark eyes were sorrowful. "Ashley, I—forgive me. I can't stand this. I have to go. I'm not quitting, mind you. I love this place. I love you and Frazier, and I love Cliff— I don't believe for a second that he did it—and I've tried, honestly, I've tried, but…oh, God, bodies consumed by alligators? I have to leave—just for a while. There's a crash course in vegetarian entrees being taught next week at a cooking school in New York City, and I thought I'd run up and spend a week learning something that will help us in the future. You could go with me, you know. You and Frazier!" Beth added excitedly.

Ashley thought about the dwindling coffers that held the plantation together.

And she thought about Jake. She was safe here; she had a government team living at her house.

And it was her home. She just might be part of the answer, when they kept digging to find the twists and turns of the great riddle.

"I can't go, Beth."

"I knew you'd say that."

"But I want you to go, and learn well, and we'll get the restaurant back up and running. God knows, once we do, we can hire a full-time security guard. People will flock back."

Beth kissed her on the cheek. "I'll probably leave

tomorrow. I'll have to see what kind of a flight I can get out."

"Good night—and it's all right, Beth. It's really all right."

Beth left her. She hadn't realized that Angela had been curled in one of the wingback chairs near them, reading as well.

When Beth had gone, Angela walked over to Ashley. "I'm sorry," she said.

"I love Beth. I'm happy that she's going to leave and do something useful," Ashley assured her.

"What a cook we're losing," Angela said lightly.

"True."

"Don't worry—we're actually pretty good in the kitchen as a team," Angela said.

Ashley tried to smile. The effort fell flat.

Angela took Beth's chair and spoke to Ashley seriously. "Ashley, the answer here may really lie in the past."

"Really? Do you think the four dead Yanks are rising to get revenge on the South? Or are my Southern ancestors getting revenge—on themselves?" Ashley knew she sounded skeptical, but it was just too much!

Angela shook her head. "No, there's a flesh-and-blood killer out there. But he has something on his mind. Something he plotted out for years, maybe. And it just may have something to do with the past. You need to start thinking about that. Go back and trace the ancestry of everyone involved and see if we've missed anything."

"That may be easier said than done. You want me to trace the lives of nine men and their offspring through over a hundred and fifty years?" Ashley asked. "We have records on the men who fought, and Daughters of the Confederacy probably has similar records on their lineage, but you're talking about a number of offspring through the centuries!"

Angela stood. "Yes. And if anyone can do it, it's you."

She bid her good-night and started for the stairs, then paused, looking back. "I believe that both Emma and Marshall Donegal are trapped here. Their souls are trapped. For some reason, they are unable to communicate with one another. If we can find out why, perhaps we can find out the truth."

Ashley nodded, feeling a pang in her heart.

The door to the study was still closed. Will and Whitney still watched the screens, while Jenna had gone up to catch a few hours of sleep before taking over for the pair. Cliff had long ago returned to his apartment in the stables.

Ashley stood and stretched; she was about to say good-night to Will and Whitney but she saw that they were resting themselves: open-eyed, but resting. Apparently, they were accustomed to watching the screens, and after today, they weren't going to rely on tapes—they were going to watch every movement on the property by night.

She didn't make it to her room; she stopped in front of Jake's. She smiled. The hell with the screens. She waved to Will and Whitney and went into Jake's room to wait.

He arrived an hour later.

She didn't speak; neither did he. She curled into his arms, and they started to kiss.

It was definitely life-affirming.

# *Interlude*

*He watched the news. Of course, a different newscaster talked about the grisly discovery of the two bodies in the bayou separating Beaumont and Donegal Plantations.*

*Viewers would recall, of course, that police and the FBI still had an open investigation on the case of Charles Osgood, so recently murdered in the old cemetery at Donegal.*

*Ah, yes, despite the fact that the murders had occurred in plantation country, it was important that viewers take extreme care in the days to come, since police and marine biologists alike thought it unlikely that the newscaster and the plantation owner found dead in the bayou had been killed by the alligators; the alligators had more likely been attracted by the scent of the deceased.*

*An animal expert came on for a minute to talk about alligators, and the unlikelihood of viewers being attacked by one.*

*Then the anchor was back on.*

*Handsome man—as plastic as the woman. Frankly, he liked the other channel better.*

*But he couldn't take his eyes from the newscast. The anchor was now talking about the extreme loss the station was feeling, and that in their pain, they were proud, certain that Marty Dean had died in the pursuit of answers, as a good investigative reporter. Funeral ar-*

*rangements were pending the arrival of family members and the release of the remains.*

*"Good investigative reporter, my ass!" he said aloud, and it made him laugh.*

*Oh, what a lovely kill!*

*He wished he could have stayed. He hadn't even thought about the gators; he had simply left the bodies facedown in the water, caught on straggling branches from a fallen old oak. He had never really imagined that his crimes would be so delightfully...mutated, mauled—dissected!*

*More clever than he himself had known. They'd just never get it. They'd never really appreciated his amazing ability to move quickly and decisively!*

*He leaned back, swallowing down a delightful sip of hundred-year-old cognac.*

*His phone rang; regretfully, he answered it.*

*A problem at work. With his crisp voice, he quickly barked out commands, changing gears as cleanly and swiftly as the transmission of a Rolls-Royce.*

*When he hung up, he smiled. He looked at himself in the mirror.*

*Down, down, down, everybody was going down, down, down.*

*He had his next move to plan, of course. But he would do so, easily and well.*

*As he walked to his bedroom, he noted one*

*of the pictures on his wall. A picture taken nearly a decade ago after a reenactment.*

*He paused to look at it. Patrick Donegal, Ashley's father, had still been alive. He'd been playing the role of Marshall Donegal that day.*

*Too bad he hadn't been so clever back then! Taking down Patrick Donegal would have been a coup! But now...*

*There she was. Ashley. Beautiful as a teenager, not quite as refined as she was now, but beautiful, even in a quick snapshot.*

*The boy was in the picture, too. Jake. Jake Mallory. Hell, he'd heard the damned name so much he was sick. He was a savior. A tireless benefactor to the city. So damned good, the feds had wanted him, and he'd gone to them and brought down the mighty. Staring at the photo, he frowned.*

*Jake really needed to go down, too.*

*Really.*

*Pleased that he had a list of victims together, he walked on past the picture and headed to bed.*

*Tonight, he would rest.*

*Tomorrow would be his next kill.*

# 12

"Okay, look—you can see, I'm coming right back!" Beth said. She pointed to the overnight bag she had packed. "One week of clothing, and that's with doing a load of wash sometime in between. Oh, Ashley, come with me!" she pleaded, standing by the front door.

Ashley hugged her best friend tightly. "I'll be here when you come back," she promised.

"Frazier!" Beth said, and turned to hug Frazier as well. "Now, you really should come with me!" she said firmly.

He smiled. "To a vegetarian cooking class? Perish the thought. I was born right here, my dear. I'm not going anywhere else in my dotage—not until they drag me out." He kissed her forehead. "Come back soon."

"You know I will."

"We need to get moving. We have to stop by Benjamin Austin's office, and then it's a bit of a drive into New Orleans," Jackson said politely.

Beth hugged Ashley once again.

"What time is your plane?" Ashley asked her.

"I'm not sure yet which I'm taking. The boys are going to drop me in the city, and I'll stow my bags at one of the hotels while I take a look around. I love NOLA—I'm going to miss it, even if I only go away for a week..." Her voice trailed. "Take care of yourself. Ashley, damn it, I mean it. Take care of yourself!"

Ashley smiled. "Go!"

Jake turned to Ashley as Beth said a swift goodbye and good luck to the others.

"Stick close to the house today. Please?"

She nodded. "I'm delving into the past, per Angela's orders," she told him. "I'll be a good girl."

"She will!" Frazier assured him, setting his hands on Ashley's shoulders.

Beth saved her last goodbye for Cliff, giving him a big kiss right on the lips. "And you hang in, mister, you hear?"

"We'll miss you," Cliff told Beth.

Then, finally, the three were gone.

"I have some feed bills to finesse," Cliff said, shaking his head. "I'll be in my apartment if you need me."

"I'll be in the study, playing with bills myself," Frazier said.

"Grampa, I can do that!" Ashley chided.

Frazier shook his head. "No, thank you. Let me be useful. The old need to be useful, you know."

"There's no one more necessary," Ashley told him. He grinned, kissed her cheek, and disappeared.

"I'm out for a walk by the cemetery," Jenna said. "Will and I are supposed to go down the road and check out your sutler friend, John Martin, but that won't take long, I don't think. It's a formality. They don't really suspect him. We've got some time. Where was it that the three Yankees died? In front of the wall?"

"By the family tomb, actually," Ashley told her.

"You can't be out there alone," Will said. "I'll go with you. I'll keep quiet so you can commune, Jenna, but you're not going out there alone."

"A team member is always welcome," she said.

"Well, back to the monitors," Whitney said.

"What have you seen lately in the screens?" Ashley asked. Whitney looked at her, and she blushed. "I mean, besides our movements—and those shadows you've shown me."

"A great deal actually," Whitney told her. She studied Ashley for a minute and glanced at Angela. "Come on over," she said to Ashley, as if Angela had given her a silent accord.

The three women went back to the screens. On one, Ashley could see Jenna and Will walking toward the cemetery.

On other screens, she could see empty rooms.

"I'm rolling back tape," Whitney said. "This is from yesterday afternoon."

Ashley saw herself heading into the attic, walking

around thoughtfully—and making a face at the mess of black fingerprint powder that was in the room.

Then, she saw something else. Something that seemed to form out of thin air. It wasn't dark, like a shadow. It was something light—benign, in a sense. The light seemed to reach out and nearly touch her shoulder.

But then she spun around, and the vision of light faded.

"What was that?" Ashley asked, her throat tight.

"Nothing bad—certainly nothing bad or evil!" Angela assured her.

"And you know this…how?" Ashley asked her.

"I know because I've met many entities now, and even when they're hiding, keeping themselves from me, I can tell when something is there that means nothing but kindness and love," Angela said. "There are many spirits, ghosts, or whatever you want to call them here. Energy, as some believe. I haven't encountered anything *evil* here at all. Neither have the others."

"But—you were expecting something evil?" Ashley asked.

Angela was thoughtful for a minute. "Evil can remain. As I told you. Someone out there—a living someone—seems to feel that this place is calling out to them, demanding some kind of vengeance. The *good* revenants that are here are reaching out to you, trying to help you. And you've seen one of them—you just don't want to admit it. Did you meet the spirit in the attic?" Angela asked.

Ashley shook her head. But tension, fear and then trust in Angela filled her. She spilled out the truth. "No, but I have an ancestor here that I have seen. He talks to me as clearly as you do."

Whitney smiled. "Marshall Donegal?"

Ashley nodded.

"Can you talk to him now?" Angela asked. "He's here. I can feel him."

"I can't see him right now," Ashley told her. She shook her head. "I mean, did you want to have a séance or something? Would you act as a medium?"

Angela smiled. "He isn't interested in speaking with me. Just you. When did you first see him?"

"In a dream."

"Then go lie down. Let him enter your dreams. Let him walk you through the original battle," Angela told her. "And don't be afraid. We're all nearby."

"Can it really help?" Ashley whispered.

"We won't know until you try," Angela told her.

Ashley nodded. She walked up the stairs and into her own room.

That was where Marshall Donegal had found her first. In her dreams.

Dr. Benjamin Austin's office was a busy place; the receptionist looked at them as if they were crazy when they asked to speak with him. She indicated the waiting room. There were four rambunctious children running back and forth to their mother with magazines. There were several elderly patients waiting, and two young women and two young men besides.

"You have to see him now?" she asked.

"It will just take a moment," Jackson said, producing his badge.

The receptionist quickly ushered them into an office.

A few minutes later, the doctor hurried in with two of his patients' charts in his hand.

"Hello," he said, trying to juggle the charts and shake their hands. "Jake, I heard you were with the government now. Good to see you. We get all the New Orleans news out here. Your name was involved with the Holloway case. This is about Charles Osgood, isn't it? You know, the police were already here."

"We know that," Jackson told him. "And we appreciate your time. We can see that you're extremely busy."

Benjamin Austin nodded, but said, "That's all right. Anything I can do to help."

"This is confidential information right now," Jake said. "But we know what drugs the killer used to subdue Charles Osgood, and the coroner's office is testing to see if the same drugs were used on the latest victims."

"Latest victims?" His eyes widened. "Oh, God, yes, they're thinking that alligators didn't kill Marty Dean and Toby Keaton?"

"That's right. Where were you the night before last, Dr. Austin? Forgive the question—it's necessary," Jake said.

He stiffened but eased quickly; he seemed to understand. "Well, that I can tell you exactly, and you can verify the information without leaving this office. I gave a speech at eight at a meeting at the Best Western down the road, had dinner at twelve—and stayed at the hotel. I didn't sleep alone. You met my girlfriend—the receptionist who led you here."

"We will verify, of course," Jackson said.

"Please do."

"We have another question," Jake told him.

"Yes."

Jackson pulled out his organizer and said, "We're looking to find someone who might have gotten hold of these two drugs. Can you help us?" He handed the organizer to Benjamin Austin so that he could read *benzodiazepine* and *chlorzoxazone* himself.

To Jake's surprise, the man seemed stunned. His face became white.

"What is it, doctor?" Jackson asked.

"I had a robbery—but it was more than a year ago," Austin said, swallowing. "I have a nurse anesthetist on my staff, and I do some minor surgery right here in the office. Our nearest hospital is a bit of a trek," he explained. "The muscle relaxants are more common, but...this office was sacked. We were missing a lot of drugs."

He saw the way they were looking at him.

"I filed a police report—you can check on that,

too," he said. "Oh, God…this killer might be using drugs he stole from *me?*"

"So it appears, Dr. Austin. So it appears," Jackson said. On that slightly ominous note, they bid him farewell.

Beth had chosen to wait for them in the car. "Anything?" she asked.

"Maybe," Jake said. She stared at him with such concern that he sighed. "Drugs were used on the victims—you've been around everything going on; you probably know that."

"Then—oh, my God, it was him? The doctor?" Beth asked.

Jake shook his head. "He said that his office was broken into—over a year ago."

"I'm checking on that," Jackson said, and Jake knew that he was dialing Detective Colby.

Jake, driving, tried to listen, but he couldn't hear Mack.

Jackson hung up. "Good Dr. Austin seems to be telling the truth. He reported the drugs stolen, and he did give a speech at the Best Western. Mack is checking with the hotel to find out if he had room service or anything else—if he was seen. I believe the man was telling the truth."

"But someone out there is lying, that's for sure," Jake said.

Ashley didn't know if her eyes were just closed, or if she had dozed. She heard her own words from the recesses of her mind.

*Help me.*

*I'm here,* he told her.

*I need to see the battle.*

*No, you don't. Battle is ugly and horrible, and no one should see it.*

*I need to see, please.*

Somehow, in the dream, she was Emma again. Marshall Donegal was in front of her, shouting at her, telling her to get the children and get them up to the attic. His voice was rough, commanding, and she was shocked, because he didn't speak to her like that.

But then he paused. She felt his passionate kiss on her lips, and then he held her away, torment in his eyes. "The children, Emma, please—protect our children."

She turned as he'd ordered and hurried the children up the stairs. When she reached the attic, she made the little ones hunch down by the wall.

And she went to the garret window to watch.

First she saw the black powder; it exploded and filled the day. The howitzer managed to put holes in the ground, but it didn't hit the buildings.

No matter; the Yankees were coming.

She heard the squeal of the horses. Shouts came from the area of the stables; then she saw the defenders rush out and head toward the cemetery walls.

Rifles flared, and flared again. She saw Marshall retreat behind the walls, calling his men around them, but they weren't all there; they were engaged closer to the house. The men in blue began to enter the cemetery.

From her vantage point, high above the roofs of their family "city of the dead," she could see as they began to surround her husband. He brought one down with a direct hit from his rifle; then the fighting was too close. They were going after one another with bayonets. Marshall was a fighter. Two more died at his feet. And then, with one of his men shouting a warning and rushing in, Marshall was stabbed himself. She saw her husband's eyes as he returned the blow. The last of the men in the cemetery was dead. Two more rushed in but saw the three dead in their own colors. They turned and fled, and in seconds she heard the sounds of horses' hooves as they rode away. Six Yankees altogether; four dead and two running.

"Nancy, stay with the children!" she pleaded, calling to her housemaid and then rushing down the attic stairs and out to the cemetery. She pushed by her husband's men, who were at his side, and fell down beside him, taking his head onto her lap. He opened his eyes once. He mouthed the words, "I love you. I'm so sorry."

And then he died.

They came around her, her husband's men. One of them pulled her gently to her feet. "He's gone, now, Emma. We'll see to him. He's gone, please…."

She was blinded by her tears. She was barely aware as she was led into her house, led to her room.

"Drink this. Drink this, Emma—it will steady your nerves."

She had no nerves; she had nothing. Marshall was dead.

Four days later, Marshall was laid to rest in the family vault. *He* was there; he told her he'd be back; he'd help her until it was time for him to ride to war.

And then he came back again.

*To help her, so he said.*

And he was kind at first. He helped her haul in some water. He made her sit by the fire, and he poured her a whiskey, telling her that she needed whiskey. She drank it. She would have enjoyed the entire bottle. It warmed her. It numbed her. She could barely hear what he was saying, and she didn't really care.

But then he knelt by her feet and started to rub them, and she was instantly alarmed.

"Emma…"

"No, no, stop!"

"You need me here."

"My husband is barely dead!"

"It's a harsh world, Emma. It will only get worse with the war. You know you need me; you need help through this, and by God, if I'm to be a man for you, you will be a woman for me."

She was shocked.

But when she tried to stand, she began to teeter. She fell, and fell into his arms. He kept speaking, words that made no sense. The world began spinning, but it was still full of agony.

Then she felt him.

Felt him on her. Felt his hands on her, ripping at her clothing.

*No!*

But his hand fell over her mouth; he was strong and brutal, and her clothing was being ripped from her. She couldn't believe it. This was a friend….

*No…*

She was powerless.

*Help…*

The word escaped her.

And she still felt him, the bastard on top of her, felt her flesh, his flesh, but it wasn't her; no one could really touch her anymore.

Then help came at last, and he was ripped from her. She tried to stumble up, tried to call out….

Ashley jerked up.

Tears were streaming down her cheeks. Her body felt bruised—and violated.

But nothing had happened. She was in her own bedroom. Her clothing was intact. She hadn't been touched.

Not in this world, not in this time.

Marshall Donegal stood by the window. He was looking out at the cemetery where he had died.

She realized that he had led her to the battle, but

that something else had happened in her dream. She had seen what he had never seen.

One of his own men had betrayed him after his death and violated his wife.

He turned to her. "Battle is ugly. It is blood and slashed limbs and smashed brains. It's horrible, and it's ugly, and perhaps we all sin when we take up arms against one another."

"Some battles have to be fought," she whispered.

He came to her, and she thought she felt his hands on her shoulders. "Yes, battles must be fought for defense of all that is right and holy. But we need to be sure of what is right and holy before going to war." He winced. "Those men who fight demons in their own mind, or join with demons to fight, they must be stopped. Because they are the transgressors."

He pulled her against him. She was certain that she could actually feel the strength of his chest, and of his mind, and all that he had managed to learn— in his afterlife. She felt tears on her cheeks again, and she heard him whisper, "I'm here to try again to defend you. I failed my family once. I cannot do so again."

Jake was surprised at how emotional it was to drop Beth off in the French Quarter. They were on Royal Street, in front of the hotel where they had stayed after the Holloway murder, and they knew that Beth would be able to stow her luggage easily for the day.

"You go on and solve this thing so that I can come back!" Beth told them. "And don't worry about me. I'm just doing a little shopping. I'm going to indulge in a sugar-swamped beignet at Café du Monde, and then I'll be on my way. You gentlemen get busy."

And so they did, leaving the car at street parking on Decatur Street and starting off on foot. As they walked, Jackson made the necessary phone calls.

Fifteen minutes later, Justin Binder met them in front of the square as he was crawling down from a carriage ride with his family. He kissed his daughters and told them he'd meet up with them for dinner as they went off with his mother-in-law to view a Mardi Gras exhibit.

"We can go to my hotel room and talk there," Justin told them.

Jake hoped immediately that Justin was all that he seemed: a family man who respected his mother-in-law and loved his children.

His hotel room was a little suite with a bedroom area where, apparently, his mother-in-law had been sleeping with the children while Justin took the couch in the parlor area. He apologized; the housekeeping staff hadn't been up yet, and Justin closed the couch quickly so that they could sit.

"I heard about the latest," Justin said, sitting. "The newscaster and Toby Keaton. He was all right. I was so sorry to hear about him. Eaten by gators. Well, hell, that's just sad. The man grew up with the creatures, spent his life around them."

"We don't believe he was killed by the gators," Jackson said.

"Neither does the media," Justin said.

"Well, we're back to the usual question. Where were you night before last?" Jackson asked him.

"Here. I took the girls to a live theater experience at Le Petit Theatre, and we and my mother-in-law went to dinner at Muriel's. Then we were back at the hotel—and I had a stomach ache. I called down to room service for warm milk around one in the morning. I was seen by the waiter, and my mother-in-law will assure you I was with my family all night. Thank God I can prove that!"

"What can't you prove?" Jake asked.

Justin met his gaze openly. "When the battle ended, I 'skedaddled' with Ramsay Clayton. That means we rode hard to the sugar-mill fences, up to the road and then back. Ramsay was with me—he kept telling me it was okay to play a Yankee. He liked being on the winning side. We rode back in time for the singing. When it first happened, I kept thinking that Ramsay had to be involved somehow—he was supposed to have been Marshall Donegal—but he was with me, then, and I could swear that I did see him in the crowd before we finally all wound up in the parlor at the house. And I was scared as hell, too, that I would be a suspect because we were staying at the plantation. I searched high and low with the others that night and wound up on a ride all the way over to Beaumont the next day. It was a nice ride—my girls loved it. But…".

"But what?" Jake asked.

"There was something strange about Ashley that day. Once we could see Beaumont across the bayou, she kept looking up at the windows. And she seemed to be afraid of something. She pretended it was nothing, but I've been thinking about it ever since. Don't get me wrong—Ashley sure as hell isn't guilty of anything. She was just about in tears about Charles being missing the day before, and she really came on the ride to keep searching the property. But— she saw something. She saw something that day at Beaumont."

Ashley's legs wobbled as she descended the stairs. Angela ran up to her quickly, frowning and setting a supporting arm around her shoulders. Whitney came over to her as well, her face a mask of concern.

"What?" Angela asked anxiously.

"I didn't see who did it."

"Who did what?"

Ashley looked at Angela. "I saw Marshall Donegal. He didn't want to let me see the battle with him, but I insisted. Then—it was as if I lost him. I became Emma. She was raped, Angela—just days after her husband was killed."

"By the enemy? But I thought—" Whitney began.

"Not by the enemy! By one of her husband's men."

"Who? Which one?" Angela asked.

"I couldn't see, Angela. But—"

"But what?" she prompted.

"I think that Harold Boudreaux came to her rescue. I think that he pulled the rapist off of Emma, and that's when they formed their real bond. I think that we never see Marshall and Emma together because *he doesn't know.* It wasn't her fault, but she's ashamed, and she can't go to Marshall or be with him because of what happened."

Angela was thoughtful. "Maybe we can help them. First, however, we have to find out who the man was. We have to find out what happened to him and figure out why one of his descendants would be after revenge now."

"What should we do next?" Ashley asked.

"Records!" Angela turned to Ashley. "Can you get those accounts of the battle we were wondering about earlier? We'll start on one of the ancestry sites and see what we can dig up on these men by name."

"I'm on it," Whitney said.

"Look, I should be doing this," Ashley said.

"Later. Let Whitney get started," Angela said. "You come with me and find Jenna. She is in the cemetery. She's—communing." Angela looked at her and apparently decided that Ashley had figured out that Jenna did, indeed, see ghosts. "Jenna was meditating, in a way. She gets into a state, and if there are spirits around, even if they won't communicate with her, she can usually see them, and we may see more clearly through her." She took Ashley's hand.

"Are you afraid?" she asked her softly. "Everyone is afraid at first—it's having to believe the unbelievable. It's accepting that there is a greater power."

Ashley shook her head firmly. "No. I'm not afraid anymore. I want the truth."

Griffin Grant's office was in a massive building in the Central Business District, all beautiful glass and chrome. It was furnished with ultramodern pieces— but a picture of a Civil War cavalryman hung on a far wall of the reception area, with a pair of crossed swords above it. "Must be his ancestor," Jackson said.

Jake walked over to the painting. The man had one hand behind his back in the painting; he held his sword in front of him. There was something a little bit odd about him.

"Henry Hilton!" Griffin's secretary told them. "Interesting painting, isn't it? Well, it should be. It was done from a death likeness. Creepy, if you ask me, but these boys do enjoy their reenactments and their roundtables. Henry was killed at Manassas, but he was already wounded."

"Uh—he was—an admirable soldier," Jake said. As he spoke, Griffin came out of his office.

"I know, I know, it's a strange painting, but it's a family heirloom," he said dryly. "Please, come in." Griffin ushered them into his office, quickly dismissing his secretary and offering them coffee or drinks from the handsome marble wet bar set to the far left of his desk. "Soda, whiskey, water—anything?"

Jackson declined. Jake accepted a bottle of water, thanking him and taking a seat in one of the executive chairs in front of the desk.

"I heard about Toby," Griffin said gravely. "Do you know anything about funeral arrangements? Had his son been told about his death?"

"Detective Mack Colby was notifying the family," Jackson told him. "And they won't release the body until a full autopsy has been done."

Griffin nodded and frowned. "They believe that these murders were related to Charles Osgood's death? But...well, a man in a cemetery in full uniform and two people killed after a strange assignation near the bayou? Seems a stretch, doesn't it?"

"Not really. Toby Keaton took part in the reenactment. Marty Dean wanted news on it so desperately I think she would have met anyone anywhere," Jake said.

"Oh. I suppose you're right." Griffin drummed his fingers on his desk. "I wish I could help you. I don't think there's anything at all I could tell you about the newscaster. I didn't know her. I knew Toby well, of course. We've all been friends forever. But I keep thinking that I should have remembered something about the night Charles disappeared. I mean, I was right there! Right there, in the midst of those rushing forward when we heard that Marshall Donegal was being beset in the cemetery—outside the cemetery for the reenactment, of course. I think I saw…maybe it was John Ashton? Helping him to his feet. But we were all there standing around when it ended. Charles was so proud! He wore his battle wounds and fake blood with such pleasure. I kept thinking that Ramsay had done him a real favor, helping him out that day. He made something of a man out of him, if only for a few hours. I swear, I *keep* trying to remember," he said. He leaned forward. "It haunts me, you know? Thinking about it. First Charles, now Toby…"

"Who do you think might have done it? Any idea of anyone with a grudge?" Jake asked.

Griffin Grant shook his head. "We all had opinions, spats, disagreements, but they were all good guys." He grimaced. "Even the Yankees. I mean, we do seriously like to argue tactics, but that's not even a matter of sides. We've all done this so many times, with changes here and there through the years. The Yanks are good guys. I can't imagine that any one of us would have ever done such a thing."

"Well, here's the usual—where were you the night before last?" Jake asked him.

He seemed surprised. "Right here. You can ask my secretary. I worked forever—we have a new lineup coming out, and it's a bitch, making sure your shows and your sponsors are all aligned just so."

"Thank you," Jackson said, rising. He offered Griffin his hand. "Thank you for your time and your help."

"I'd do more if I could," Griffin told them.

They left his office and stopped by his secretary's desk. "Miss Tierney" read the nameplate in front of her. "Miss Tierney," Jackson said politely, "can you verify that Mr. Grant was in his office late the night before last?"

"Oh, yes!" she said. "Why, that poor man has just been working all hours."

"How late were you here?" Jake asked her.

"Late—seven," she said dryly. "So much for nine to five. And when I left, I could still hear him on the phone in there, placating a diaper company!"

Jackson thanked her.

Out on the street, Jake sighed wearily. "Time to find Ramsay Clayton," he said.

Ramsay wasn't in his hotel room. The desk clerk told them that they could probably locate him on the square, displaying his art.

Jenna sat on one of the few individual white sarcophagi in the cemetery; it belonged to the Donegal brother-in-law who had been killed during World War I.

At first, walking toward her with Angela, Ashley saw nothing. Will was leaning against her family tomb, and he spoke gently to Ashley. "She has brought them out. Sit quietly, and you will see them."

No longer hesitant, Ashley took a seat next to Jenna. Jenna took her hand and gripped it tightly.

And in a minute, they began to appear to her as well.

There were four of them there, soldiers in blue. They walked in a procession, pacing the cemetery right in front of the family tomb. She could see clearly through them, and then she could not. They began to form something that appeared of real substance.

"They are illusions," Will said quietly, "but illusions of the mind. That is the place where we know another sense: of the living, and of the dead."

As she sat there, Marshall Donegal appeared as well. She tensed, thinking that there would be some kind of a confrontation.

But though they recognized one another, acknowledged one another, it was merely with sorrow.

"Talk to them," Jenna said. "They will hear you."

"I need help," she said. "Please."

Marshall walked to one. "We were sad enemies. No more. We are united in death, and the country is united now, through our deaths. We have made peace. Help my girl, please. Help her."

The one who seemed to be a captain turned from Marshall to Ashley.

"I would help you, if I could. What do you need?"

"I need to know…Emma came to her husband as he lay dying. She was dragged away, taken to the house. Who took her? Which soldier? Please, it's so important to know."

"I was dying then," he said. "I was dying then myself. But, I saw her. I saw her tears. I saw the uniform. I saw…the man was blond. He had blond curls. I didn't know his name."

"Can anyone help?" Marshall called out.

One of them stopped by him, setting a hand on his shoulder. "I was gone, Marshall. I was gone when she came to the cemetery. We were hotheaded as were you—we'd never have hurt your wife or your children. What man would do so?"

*Not a man, a monster,* Ashley thought. She wasn't afraid of ghosts, she realized. She had learned to fear monsters instead.

The captain spoke softly. "One will know," he said.

"Who?" Marshall asked.

"Emma," the captain said.

Marshall shook his head. "She is gone," he said softly.

"No," the captain said. "I see her at the attic window."

The ghost of Marshall Donegal fell to his knees in the cemetery and wept.

"Why, hey, you!" Beth said, surprised to see the man who was looking into the shop window along with her.

"Beth!" he said, equally surprised. "What are you doing here?"

"Leaving," she admitted. "I've got to get away for a while."

"Donegal Plantation will be missing the world's finest chef," he said gallantly.

"I'll be back," she said.

"I'm sure you will."

"So…"

"So, I've got some time. Do you need a ride to the airport?"

"Well, that would be great. But I can just take a cab—"

"Don't be silly. I've got a car."

"My things are at the hotel—"

"We'll stop and get them. Come on, no big deal, I promise."

"It's a half hour drive there, and back."

"Worth it, if I can imagine you'll return and cook again!"

As the breeze moved her hair and she pulled a strand from her face, she remembered that he had been on the original suspect list. But that had been before.

"Sure, thanks."

They were going to get in a car; they were going to get coffee. No danger in that. Besides, she didn't believe it. She just didn't believe it.

They walked to his car. She noted, as she started to get in, that he had a little case, like the kind kept by a diabetic. Was he diabetic? She couldn't remember.

He shut the door as she sat.

He came around and got in beside her.

And then, of course, she realized.

She put her hand on the door; she opened her mouth to scream.

He slammed her head against the car window as he picked up a needle; she felt it piercing through her skin, and then she felt no more.

# 13

---

Jackson and Jake walked the square over and over looking for Ramsay Clayton.

He wasn't to be found.

"Strange. The bastard answered me this morning when I called him and said we'd find him at his hotel," Jackson said.

Jake stopped to ask a young woman selling paintings of the square if she had seen Ramsay Clayton that morning.

"Oh, yes, he was here for a while," she said. "He said that he had to get back to his hotel room to meet some friends. I haven't seen him since, but he is usually right here. Says lately he likes to be where there are lots and lots of people! The guy is as nice as can be, and darned good-looking, too, but he's sure gotten strange, always looking as if he's about to run! Such a scaredy-cat."

Jake thanked her for the information.

"He's either scared—or guilty," Jake said.

"We'll head to the hotel again," Jackson said. "But

first I'm going to buy a couple of Lucky Dogs and some sodas. I'm starving. We'll get the car and head to the hotel. I have a feeling we're not going to find Ramsay, though. Where the hell did he go? If he's such a damned scaredy-cat?"

"Maybe he's not—maybe it's all an act, down to his kindness," Jake suggested.

"Justin said that Ramsay was with him, and that Ramsay said that he had fun playing a Yankee," Jackson reminded him.

"But he's not here," Jake said. He walked back to the woman. "I'm sorry to bother you again," he told her. "Did you see Ramsay Clayton here the day before yesterday?"

She frowned, going into deep thought. He thought she might have smoked a little bit too much weed in her teen years. Her mind seemed a little misty.

"The day before yesterday... Oh, yes! He was here. He was here. In fact, we were both here until dusk."

"And then you both left?"

"Well, I left. I think he left soon after."

"Why do you think that?"

She smiled. "Because I was gone. I told you—he likes to be around people. Some of the artists stay out late in the night, but by then people really want music and tarot readings. So he must have left. He's not like you."

"Pardon?"

He hadn't realized that his Glock, a standard FBI

issue—he knew how to shoot, but he wasn't fond of guns—was visible since his hand was on his hip, pushing his jacket back and exposing the belt holster.

"Maybe he should carry a gun, too. Are you a cop? Is he in trouble?"

He smiled. "I just need to speak with him, that's all."

"Maybe you can give him some courage!" she said cheerfully.

"Well, thank you," Jake said, striding back to Jackson, frustrated. "He was here until dusk the day that Marty and Toby died. I think."

"You think?"

"I'm not sure she knows what day it is today," Jake said.

Jackson nodded. "Okay, let's get food and try the hotel. Then we can head back. I'll get the dogs, you get the car."

Jackson stopped at a cart and bought them both a soda and a couple of hot dogs while Jake walked down to the car. He had just eased it out of their parking spot when Jackson caught up with him. He reached for the food; Jackson slid into his seat, a Lucky Dog halfway in his mouth. "Sorry—I'm really hungry. We're all going to miss Beth."

"Yes, but she wanted to be away—maybe *needed* to be away," Jake said. He found that he felt oddly uncomfortable once he had spoken.

"What's wrong?" Jackson asked him.

"I don't know. I think we should have taken her straight to the airport in the morning."

"Call her."

Jake did. He got her voice mail right away.

"She's probably on an airplane," Jackson said.

"Probably," Jake agreed.

A feeling of unease had begun in him; it wasn't lessened any when they reached the hotel and found no sign of Ramsay Clayton.

They sat around in the roadside parlor. Ashley was on the registration-desk computer, and Will was working with her. Angela and Whitney were poring through content files on Whitney's laptop.

Jenna was in the attic, hoping that she could reach Emma Donegal.

"Okay, Confederates," Ashley said. "Marshall Donegal, of course. O'Reilly, Charles's stepfather's ancestor. We know that he survived the war—he came back and saw Emma. He probably had a guilt complex about causing the whole skirmish."

"That's two down. Now the rest?"

"One was actually a Clayton; I know that," Ashley said. "Ramsay is a direct descendant."

"Find out what happened to his ancestor," Angela said, looking up. "We're trying to trace a fellow named Pierre Lamont—one of the Confederates."

"He was Toby Keaton's great-great-whatever," Ashley said. "Toby comes down through the mater-nal line. It's a good thing they named it Beaumont,

Beaumont—beautiful mountain," she said with a grimace. "Not that it's exactly on a mountain, but there is a little rise in the terrain. The family name changed many times."

"Yes, but we can let Toby go on this one," Angela said softly. "He's dead."

"I guess so," Ashley agreed.

"What about Griffin Grant?" Whitney asked.

"Family name change, too. His ancestor was… Hilton. Henry James Hilton. And he was killed in the war—1862, the Second Battle of Bull Run, or Manassas. We can do more research on Hilton."

Ashley stared at the screen, searching site after site for the Ramsay Clayton who had fought in the Confederate cavalry during the Civil War. She found him at last and turned to look at the two of them. "Ramsay Clayton—the one our Ramsay is named for—was killed at Gettysburg," she said. "Obviously, he was already a father."

"Okay, so…nothing dastardly happened to him?" Whitney said.

"Not other than a grisly death on a battlefield," Ashley said. "And that would mean a half a million men who died might be vengeful."

"That doesn't seem like something that would bring about revenge or a sick sense that you needed revenge in a future generation," Will said. "We're looking for something that might have come about because of what happened at Donegal that day."

"What about Hank Trebly?" Angela asked.

"Trebly—that was his ancestor's name, too."

"See what you can find on him."

They all worked in silence for a while.

Whitney sighed as one site after another came up blank. "Not found," she said. "Sorry. We need Jake. He's the one who can find anything on a computer."

"Could you take over for a few minutes, Will? My back is killing me!" Ashley pushed away from the desk. Will stepped back, looking at her.

He nodded. "Sure. Why don't you go and try the attic with Jenna? See if you can sense, or even find, anything there?"

She nodded. "I'm just going to grab some water first. And a cheese stick."

"Food!" Will said. "We haven't eaten since breakfast."

"All right, everybody, meal break," Angela said. "Every man for himself. There's no Beth to feed us delicious delicacies today."

"We'll make a real dinner," Whitney said, yawning. Then she leapt up. "Angela is right! Every man—and woman—for themselves! And dibs on the crab cakes!"

As they started for the kitchen in a sudden mad hurry, they nearly collided with Jenna, who was coming down the stairs.

"Anything?" Angela asked her.

Jenna shook her head, frustrated. "I can feel her,

and I've talked myself blue. But she won't appear for me, or she can't appear for me."

"I can try," Angela said.

"I know who can reach her. She's been trying to reach him," Whitney said.

They all stared at her.

"Jake," Whitney said. "Before we even knew about Charles being missing, I think he saw her. I was kind of ignoring him, because he was just talking about someone he thought was about to lead a tour. But then we couldn't find her. The way he described her, she was a Southern white woman. He saw her coming through a crowd when we were at Café du Monde. He told me that she had been trying to talk to him, and I said that was rather ridiculous, because she was across Decatur Street, and there was a lot going on, and unless she had been shouting, he couldn't have possibly heard her. But now, I think it all makes sense. It's Emma, and she's decided that if she's going to communicate with the living, it's going to be Jake."

Angela was thoughtful for a minute. "All right, then. We'll all get back on the computers after our very late lunch, and when Jake gets back, we'll just lock him in the attic."

"It's a plan," Ashley agreed. "I'm going to get my grandfather out of the study; he's been poring over bills long enough."

Frazier wasn't sorting through their bills. He

was seated there thoughtfully, staring down at his hands.

"Grampa?" Ashley asked him.

"Ashley," he said, looking up and giving her a brilliant smile.

"I'm going to get some lunch. Would you like to eat here, or in the dining room?"

He didn't answer her right away.

"Grampa?"

"I'm sorry, my dear." He let out a soft sigh. "Ashley, I can't help being afraid that if this drags on, we're going to lose the place."

"I won't let that happen!" she promised him. "I swear, I won't let that happen."

He lifted his hands. "It's a house, Ashley. It is built of brick and mortar and stone. Life is what's important. I'm thinking that Beth was right, that we should just leave. People are important, Ashley. You and I are important."

"I agree," she told him. "But we have the best of the best on this. They will find the killer. They will find him."

"I'll eat right here, Ashley. Then I'll drag my old bones up for a nap. Heaven knows, maybe we can get one of those reality programs to pay us the big bucks to come in and do a ghost documentary!"

"Maybe," she said. "Though I shudder! But I'll shudder away, if it helps us keep Donegal Plantation."

Grinning, she headed into the kitchen. Even with

Beth gone, it didn't have to be every man for himself. There was plenty of food for everyone; Beth kept her leftovers well-packaged and dated.

Ashley found gumbo and heated it up for whoever might want it when they came down. She brought Frazier lunch on a tray, and then realized that it was late afternoon. It would be late when they were hungry again; they'd call out for pizza, maybe.

"Angela," she said.

"Yes?

"What happened to the cops who were always outside?" Her grandfather's concern remained in her mind.

"They're doing patrols now, since they found the new bodies in the bayou. The logic is that this house is filled with agents—and since others were killed at the bayou, the cops are more useful elsewhere. And we do have cameras going all over the property. Are you all right with that?"

"Sure. I'd rather have a houseful of agents anytime," she assured her.

When she had finished her own bowl, she walked out to the back porch. She shouldn't call Jake; he was busy, but she decided to call him anyway; she could just let him know that they were all fine.

He answered on the first ring. "Ashley? Everything is all right?"

"Everything is fine. I just thought that I would call and tell you so. Is, uh, is everything all right with you?"

"We can't find Ramsay Clayton, and I'm sitting in front of a hotel, waiting for Jackson to see if anyone can tell us where he might have gone," Jake said. "Is there anything new?" he asked her.

"Actually, yes," she told him.

"What?"

"Well, we've been on the computer all day and tearing through the household records and accounts of the battle," she said.

"And?"

"Jake, I think that, after the battle, Emma was raped."

"What—by whom? The enemy didn't take the house. Four were killed and two disappeared."

"By one of her husband's supposed friends. One of the Confederate soldiers. And…and I think that he was attacked by someone else while he was raping her, and I think that person might have been Cliff's ancestor."

"This was in the household records? That's surprising," he said.

She was silent a second.

"Ashley?"

"No. I know this, Jake." She was silent again for a minute; then words rushed from her. "I pushed you away once, Jake. I thought I was afraid of you, but I was afraid because I was terrified my father would appear before me, too, or that there was always something there that I didn't see and didn't want to see, but I *do* see. My ancestor *is* here. I can reach him, Jake, I can reach Marshall Donegal. He's trying to help. We need you here, when you can come. I think—and the others agree—that whoever attacked Emma Donegal was the ancestor of the man who attacked Charles Osgood, and then Toby Keaton and Marty Dean."

He was silent.

"Jake?"

"Ashley," he said huskily.

"Forgive me?"

"Always." He cleared his throat. "I guess it falls in. We've known it was someone close who had to be the murderer. I didn't know that Emma had been attacked—until you told me. Are you certain about that? Wouldn't it have shown up in the records somewhere?"

"Jake, only a small percentage of women report a rape now. Back then, Emma Donegal would have never breathed a word of it—any more than she would have mentioned she'd taken on an ex-slave as a lover and borne a child of his. He brought me—he brought me back there. In a dream, Jake. I—I saw it. I saw it all. And it was real."

"I believe you. You know I believe you."

"Jake," she said softly. "Only Emma can tell us. And Whitney says that you're the one who can reach her."

"I've seen her," he admitted. "She brought me to you when you were out riding. But…I can't seem to get her to talk, to stay. Maybe she's ashamed, even though nothing was her fault."

"Jake, she trusts you. She at least shows herself to you."

"We'll be back soon. Take care until then, huh? Wait, hold on a minute!" The line fell silent and she frowned with concern. "Jake?"

"I'm here—Jackson just had a conversation with Detective Mack Colby. Seems that the remains of Toby and Marty yielded the same drugs—they were able to push the toxicology reports to the top level. You all be careful there, swear it!"

"Absolutely," she promised him. "We're here, we're together, and we don't intend to let anything happen."

"The best intentions," Jake murmured.

"Pardon?"

"Stick together. I think that this killer is basically a coward—that's why he has to attack with a drug cocktail that's so potent it immediately renders his victims powerless. If you remain en masse, you'll be fine. We'll be there soon."

"I'm glad," she said softly. "Jake."

"Yes?"

"You know, I was only afraid of you. I never stopped loving you."

He was quiet for a minute; she wondered if she had spoken those words aloud.

"I've loved you forever," he said and hung up.

Ashley looked at the phone and smiled. Walking back in, she found that Angela was washing dishes at the sink. "Hey," Angela said. "I was going to bring some tea up to Frazier, but I thought that you might want to."

"Yes, thank you. I should sit with him for a few minutes. This has to be taking a terrible toll on him. Not because he isn't strong at heart, but just because—"

"He's in his eighties. The body wears down, and that's the way it is," Angela said. "The water is just whistling now. You go on up. We'll keep at it on the computer."

Ashley poured hot water over the leaves in the pot, turned off the stove and added a cup, sugar and milk to her tray. She started through the parlor; Whitney was sitting at the screens again, watching to see if there was any activity in the key areas.

"Hey, you know anything about this?" she called to Ashley.

Ashley walked over to her.

"Amundsen's Hay—Finest Feed. That's what that truck says," Whitney said. "Is that a usual delivery?"

Ashley shrugged. "Yes, that's our feed store. When were they here?"

"Just a few minutes ago. I think the trunk—yep, there it goes, out the drive now."

Ashley balanced the tray in one hand and dug her phone from her jeans pocket with the other. She speed-dialed Cliff's apartment.

"Hey," she said, relieved when he answered.

"Hey, yourself."

"And hey—as in hay for horses. We just got a delivery? I thought it was due yesterday," Ashley said.

"It was, and it came. Seemed we had some kind of a double order. Amundsen's kid was driving the truck, and somehow it wound up on his books two days in a row. Rather than take back the order, they gave me a fifty-percent discount. I took it. Seemed like the thing to do right now," Cliff said to her. "That all right?"

"Of course. That's always your decision. Those poor creatures would probably die if they had to depend on me."

"Ah, Ashley. Our four-legged creatures love you."

"Just checking that everything is fine," Ashley said.

"Yep. And I'm a big old dude, Ashley. Don't be worrying about me."

She laughed. "You're not old, and every female who comes out this way winds up with a crush on you. Don't go fishing for compliments."

"Guess I'm just not feeling as if the love is going to come pouring in right now," he said. "Seriously, all is good. I'm working in the stables. My eyes are open. I'll holler if I need anything."

She hung up. The tea tray was starting to get heavy in her one hand. She shoved her phone back into her pocket and grasped the tray with both hands. "It's all good," she told Whitney.

Whitney nodded and gave her attention back to the screens.

Ashley walked up the stairs to her grandfather's room.

"Hey, Ashley," he said, opening his eyes when she entered. He'd been lying back on his pillow with his eyes closed. "I told Angela you all didn't have to bother."

"Only so many names for so many of us to try to track," Ashley said cheerfully.

He frowned.

"We think that it all stretches back to something that might have happened with one of the soldiers here linked to the original fight. Something that this latter-day idiot may see as a perceived slight that needs to be rectified."

Frazier closed his eyes again. "I didn't think that anyone would actually be after Charles Osgood," he said.

"Poor Charles."

"Well," Frazier told her, opening his eyes and plumping his pillow to rise against it for his tea, "I can say this. Charles was happy. We can be glad we gave him his moment in the sun, brief though it was."

"Well, actually, Ramsay gave him his moment in the sun," Ashley said.

Frazier smiled and nodded. "I never saw him happy, though. Never until that day."

"True," Ashley said. She was silent for a minute.

"Grampa, have you ever managed to talk with a ghost?" she asked him.

His lashes flickered over his eyes, and he was silent for a minute. "Ghosts—are they memories? My life is now filled them, and when we are accustomed to sorrow or loss, we learn to appreciate what shining moments we had. Your father! God, how he loved your mother. Well, you knew that. He'd have never have left you on purpose, but...I try to think that death for him was being with her. And that's how I find my peace."

"That's beautiful, Grampa."

He glanced at her wryly. "Well, it's all right. In all actuality, I wish we'd known that she was allergic to bees, and that it hadn't taken such a toll on your dad, and that they were still here with us. I ache a little every day. But I watch you—and I thank God for what I have."

She leaned over and kissed his forehead. "You're the best."

"I like that," he told her.

He sipped his tea. "Grampa."

He set the cup down on his bedside table and closed his eyes.

"Grampa?"

He waved a hand in the air. "Ghosts exist. There. If they can reach you, you are among the lucky. I want there to be ghosts. I want to talk to my son again. I'd love a chance to tell my own father what a good man he was and what a rebellious rotten kid I was.

But they're gone. And if they're not, they don't reach out to me. So, I carry on conversations daily in my head. I tell your mother how beautiful you are and how good you are to your old grandfather. I tell your dad how proud he'd be of you. Do they hear me? God knows.

"Cherish your ghosts, child. Real or in your head. Cherish them. Now, go work with those young people below, and let me get some sleep."

She smiled, and sat in the chair at his bedside.

He opened his eyes again. "What?"

She laughed. "I just want to be near you for a few minutes."

He reached for her hand. She grasped his.

She sat with him in silence, and in time, she heard his even breathing. He was napping.

She almost dozed with him herself. Then her cell phone buzzed, and she jumped up quickly, hurrying out to the hall to answer it.

When she answered it, there was no one there.

She looked at the caller ID. Beth.

She dialed back, feeling a sense of relief. Beth had already made it to New York.

Once again, she got nothing but voice mail.

She left a message. "Beth! It's Ashley. I think you're there, because you called me. But now you're not answering. Call me. Now you got me worried."

She hung up. She found herself looking at the attic stairs. Tempted, she walked up and stood in the room again.

"You were with me this morning!" she said. "Marshall started my dream, but you were with me this morning. You made me see—but not clearly enough. Please, help me."

She realized that dusk was coming, falling softly and surely beyond the garret window, the window from which Emma had watched her beloved Marshall fall in a bayonet attack.

But Emma was not going to appear for her, or so it seemed. Sighing, she flicked on one of the small lights over a display cabinet containing family letters and other artifacts. She slid open the case, thankful now that the cases were never locked—which, of course, had made it easy for the killer to take the Enfield and the bayonet.

She picked up a letter and began to read it. She couldn't make out who it had been written to; the script was all but illegible. She'd catalogued everything in the room, and had reviewed them recently for the team, but she'd never read this one in depth. It was too difficult to decipher. She narrowed her eyes, hoping that swirly cursive would become easier to read, but she couldn't really tell. She saw that it was signed on the bottom—twice. Ramsay Clayton... and there was another name. The letter, she finally realized, had been written to Ginnie. Ginnie H. And it had been signed by Ramsay Clayton—and someone else. Either someone had written the letter for Ramsay Clayton, or Ramsay Clayton had written it for someone else. She thought that she saw an oddly shaped *4* beneath the name Ramsay Clayton. "My dear wife," she read aloud. "Forgive that this is not my hand; it has been broken in a ski…ski accident?" she said, and almost laughed at herself. "Skirmish! It says skirmish."

The sound of her own words faded away. She turned and saw her.

Emma was pale and almost a shadow against the far wall, where she had once urged her children to gather.

"Help me," Ashley whispered. "Please, only you know!"

The phantom figure of Emma started to move toward her. She was going to speak. She seemed to be pointing toward the letter.

Ashley's phone began to ring again. She cursed the sound; the phantom figure coming toward her evaporated into thin air. She set the letter down in the case as she answered the phone.

She answered tersely. "Hello?"

The line went dead again. She muted the phone and tried calling back quickly, but she got her friend's voice mail again. At least she was able to call. She looked around, but saw nothing but the shadows of the darkening day fill the room. "Please," she said softly, "Please, come back."


Cliff stopped raking hay off the main floor and looked up. Varina was whinnying loudly, as if she was in distress.

Once Varina started up, Jeff decided he was going to make some noise, too.

"Hey, girl, what's the problem?" he asked. He walked over to pat the horse, gentle as he stroked the softness of her nose. "It's all right, girl, it's all right."

She tossed her head back, unappeased by his words.

"Calm down, girl. You're the one they all look to here, just like your mistress, you know. Calm down."

The horse let him soothe her. Then the mare gave another toss of her head again, letting out another loud whinny.

On the other side of the stables, Tigger grew restless. Cliff heard something like a bang from his stall, and he walked over to soothe the young gelding. "Tigger, don't you go getting feisty on me, now. These are tiring days, boy."

He hoped that kick hadn't broken off part of the stall's side. He couldn't see. It was getting dark. He cursed and went to flick on the overhead bulb that would light up the entire stables.

Though the light banished the shadows, he was still uneasy. He stepped back into his apartment for his shotgun and came out again, looking around.

The horses were still restless.

Ashley stood in the near darkness when she felt the tremor of her phone. She had just about thought that she had seen a figure growing from the shadows.

"Damn it!" she swore. She glanced at the caller ID. "Beth!"

"What is it, where the hell are you that this number keeps going dead?" she said aloud. She punched the return key.

This time, there was a click.

"Beth, damn! This has been driving me crazy. Where are you? Are you having fun in the city?" she said, realizing she was speaking in a rush.

There was silence at the other end, and then the sound of breathing.

"Beth?"

A throaty, masculine voice came to her—not Beth's.

"Ashley."

"Who is this? Where is Beth?"

The chuckle that sounded in her ears seemed barely human. She shook her head. There was no devil on the other end of the line. There was a human monster, and she had to be very careful now.

"What do you want? Who is this? Where is Beth?" she asked again.

"Beth is still alive."

"What do you want?" she demanded.

"I can see you," the voice said.

She froze. "If you can see me, where am I?" she demanded.

Her heart was racing; she wanted to find Angela and the others, but she was afraid that he really did see her.

And that he really had Beth.

The chuckle came to her again; the chuckle that seemed to make her heart stop and her blood turn to ice.

"You're in the attic," he said.

It was dark here; he couldn't possibly see her now.

"No, I'm not. Actually, I'm in the parlor, and everyone around me can hear the call," she said.

The laugh—more irritated now. "You're in the attic, and if you talk to any of the people in that house with you, Beth is going to die. You know that I'll do it. And you know that I don't care how. I can cut her, I can shoot her…drown her. She's going to die, and it will be all your fault."

She tried to control her sense of raw panic and fear. She had to be sensible. There was a chance that Beth was already dead.

"You know that I have her. I have her phone," he said.

"I still don't know what you want."

"What I want? Well, at this point, that should be obvious, Ashley. I want you. So listen to me, and listen to me good. Do exactly as I say. If you come out, I'll let Beth go. Even trade. You for her."

"How do I know that you'll let her live?"

"I can't exactly sign a contract, can I? What if I were to swear to God? Hmm, I don't believe in any God, other than myself, really. So, here it is. You meet me in the cemetery, or I kill Beth. I'll string her up on a tomb, just like good old Charles Osgood."

"The cemetery?" she said. "You know that the group inside is watching screens. They'll see what I'm doing."

"They will, but they won't think anything of it, because you're going to bring a dish of food out to Cliff." He started to laugh. "Oh, yeah, you're going to bring a bowl of food out to Cliff! And then, Ashley, I'll take it from there. I see you heading across the yard to the stables in three minutes precisely, or Beth dies."

The phone line died in her hand.

# Interlude

Good God, who had ever expected such a windfall to come directly into his hands?

This was it—the pinnacle!

He frowned for a minute; it had actually come so quickly and so easily.

To really savor this, he had to take his time.

How much time did he have? He had to make sure that they all wound up shooting one another when the going got rough. But he knew how to do that; he knew how to accomplish exactly what he wanted. Ashley wasn't stupid; she would know that he meant to kill her.

But she was too good a person to risk the life of a friend when she just might save it.

She would come; she would come.

And when she did, he was prepared.

Truly, tonight could be a wonderful bloodbath.

# 14

Jake chafed, growing restless. They'd had to make a detour to the coroner's office; Augie had called Jackson.

The facilities here were state-of-the-art. He'd been to the morgues plenty of times before—just the way that his life had gone—and he was impressed with the shiny steel gurneys and sinks and equipment, and the sterility of the place.

Too many times when he had been involved with death, the morgue had been an empty building somewhere, and the rats had already become kings.

Bright lights were now on over the bodies of Marty Dean and Toby Keaton; they had been cleaned up, and with the sheets partially covering their torsos, they looked far better than they had when he had last seen them.

Augie, in green scrubs, a cap and mask, held a chart in front of him and rattled off the amount of drugs that had been found in both bodies.

Jake wanted to grab the chart; it didn't matter

how much—the drugs had been present. And the two on the tables, though looking better, were still corpses.

"Here's what's interesting," Augie said, using a gloved finger to point out Marty Dean's lips. "Marty was drowned. Her lungs were full of water, and you can see the blue coloration around her neck. Toby Keaton, on the other hand, was strangled." He looked at them over his mask. "Despite the fact that they were drugged, I think you'll realize what this means."

"He had to change tactics?" Jake asked. "What do you think happened?"

"It looks as if the two struggled. There were tufts of some kind of black material, which I've sent to the lab, caught up in Toby Keaton's clothing—hard to find, I assure you, when everything is the color black," Augie told him. He smiled grimly. "Our lab is good. The tufts are not the same fabric as the jacket Toby was wearing."

"Ashley did see someone else that night. She climbed up that tree to escape him," Jake said.

His feeling of urgency and restlessness was growing. He needed to escape the morgue. He didn't give a damn how many times he had been in one. There was still the smell. The smell of chemicals. And death.

"We believe we've narrowed the field to three suspects," Jake said. "Ramsay Clayton, Griffin Grant and Hank Trebly."

"And Cliff Boudreaux," Jackson said. "We can't

eliminate him yet. He's had access, he's on the property—"

"He was at the stables when I rushed out to find Ashley," Jake reminded him.

"Yes, and he could have circled those woods around just about anyone. He has lived on that property all his life," Jackson said.

"The police searched his apartment with his full cooperation," Jake said, stating the fact.

"We still can't eliminate him—he knows the property like the back of his hand," Jackson reminded him.

Jake didn't argue.

"Well, gentlemen, here's why I brought you in here," Augie said. "Look at Toby's neck there."

They both studied the neck. There was heavy bruising and signs of fingers having pressed in.

"He was strangled by hand, wouldn't you agree? There are no ligature marks," Augie said.

They both looked at him.

"Well," he said, exasperated. "I can guarantee you, you're down one suspect. Hank Trebly didn't do this."

"How do you know?"

"He had surgery in his left wrist about six months ago. I know, because we discussed it at an Elks meeting the other month. He wouldn't have been able to use both hands as they were used on this victim. So, you see, if you're right, you are down to three men—Ramsay Clayton, Griffin Grant, or Cliff Boudreaux."

When they left the morgue, they were no more than a twenty-minute ride away from the house, but the compulsion Jake felt—the mounting pressure—did not let up. He called Ashley; when he got her voice mail, he nearly drove off the road.

"She's not answering!" he told Jackson.

"I'll call Angela," Jackson said calmly.

He smiled at Jake when Angela answered her phone. "Jake is in a dither. He just called Ashley, and she didn't answer."

"I see. No, we're almost there," he said. "Fifteen minutes or so."

He hung up.

"So, where's Ashley?" Jake demanded.

"It's all right. Angela said that she's up with Frazier. She just brought him some tea, and she was sitting with him. She said that they've been following computer trails all day, but that going from site to site is about to make them all buggy. They're anxious to see you."

"I'm anxious to see them," Jake said.

He stepped on the gas.

"Hey, let's arrive alive!" Jackson said.

"Call Angela back," he said. "Please, have her get Ashley to her phone."

Jackson sighed, and called back.

This time, there was no answer on Angela's phone.

* * *

Ashley carried a big bowl of gumbo in her hand. She looked up to see that Angela had followed her into the kitchen.

"What's up?" Angela asked.

"Cliff just called. He's hungry."

"He should come to the house."

"It's no bother, and he knows you all are watching the grounds," Ashley said.

"Jake called a few minutes ago. Hon, where did I leave my phone after that? Oh, hell, I have no idea. Anyway, they're almost back."

"Thank God!" Ashley said.

"I'll reserve one camera to watch you walk over."

"It's all right. Really, please."

Angela wasn't stupid. She could see something in Ashley's eyes.

"All right." Ashley let out a sigh. She wasn't alone; Ashley knew that she didn't dare do anything other than what she was doing.

She walked out of the house, relieved, knowing that someone would follow, someone would carefully follow, and stop whatever terrible thing was being planned.

She felt ill; now her stomach was churning, too.

*Cliff!*

She couldn't believe it.

But she couldn't forget the voice. *Cliff is hungry. Cliff wants food.*

And then the laughter.

She walked toward the stables; she hadn't come unprepared.

She didn't know what she expected. She saw Cliff standing in front of Tigger's stall, his shotgun in his hand.

Where had he stashed Beth?

He turned to look at her and frowned. She hurried toward him, pretty certain that she was going to have only one chance.

"Here. Take it," she said, thrusting the bowl of cold gumbo toward him.

Human instinct. He went to grasp the bowl; his shotgun was loose in his hand.

She dropped the bowl into his hands and grabbed the shotgun from him; before he could utter a word, she slammed the butt of it against his head as hard as she could.

He looked at her in disbelief as he fell back against the gate to Tigger's stall and slumped to the ground.

"Ashley," he said.

And then the lights on the property went out. Someone had hit the breaker.

Jake drove the car down the long, oak-lined path to the house. Just when he reached the drive in front, the lights went out. All of them.

The world became a misty shade of gray; dusk was upon them.

Jackson swore; Jake set a hand on his arm. "The generators will kick in!" he said.

But the generators didn't kick in.

Jackson took off for the house; Jake started to follow him, but he stopped.

She was there.

Emma Donegal was there, and she was standing on the path by the side of the house. She beckoned to him.

He followed her. She led him around to the stables. He could barely see in the near dark. The moon was rising, not quite full, but it lent an eerie glow to his surroundings.

"Where, Emma, where?" he demanded.

He heard a groan. He hurried over to the sound. Cliff Boudreaux was down on the ground, holding the side of his head.

"Cliff, what the hell happened?" Jake demanded.

"Ashley…"

"Ashley did this to you?" Jake demanded.

"Behind her…someone behind her." Cliff grasped his arm. "I couldn't see…couldn't tell…it went dark so fast. But I saw her face. He had to have called her out here. I didn't know what the hell was going on… the horses…I'll help you.…"

Cliff caught his arm and tried to struggle to his feet.

He didn't make it. He slipped back down to the ground. His head slumped to the side.

Ashley was out there. The killer had her.

*Where?*

Ashley didn't know what in the hell had hit her; she'd felt a sting, and then nothing more.

And now, she didn't know where she was.

Her eyes were open, she thought. But the world was still dark.

She tried to blink; even blinking seemed an incredible effort.

Then she felt…something. She realized that she was being carried. Her head bobbed and smacked against a man's shoulders, and she had absolutely no control over it. She tried to focus, and she realized that she couldn't see because there were no lights. Struggling to regain some clarity, she decided that he must be carrying her away from the stables.

She blinked and she could begin to see shapes around her; the moon was rising against the swiftly falling twilight. Her focus was bad, but she could try to see. She felt the man's exertion as she was hefted over some obstacle in his path.

*Cliff!*

She had practically shattered his skull, thinking that he was the one who had called. That he was the one who had somehow managed to kidnap Beth.

But it wasn't Cliff; she had just left him behind, staring at her as if she were the worst traitor known to man, which, of course, she was….

*I'm so sorry, Cliff!* she thought. But what was that going to matter now?

*Thump, thump, grind...*

Her chin fell against the man's back. He was a big man. Strong, powerful in the chest and shoulders.

She heard a creaking sound. They were back in the cemetery, she realized. She was surrounded by the towering white architecture of her ancestral city of the dead. The tombs seemed to glisten a silvery white against the dusky sky.

She'd always been meant for the Donegal tomb eventually.

It seemed that time was now.

She could barely see; barely think, barely function. But she was aware! Was this how it had been for Charles Osgood, Marty Dean and Toby Keaton?

Had they known they were about to die but been unable to respond, to react in any way? Maybe not. Maybe the dosage of the drugs they had received had been stronger. Maybe...

Hope swelled, just the tiniest bit. She needed to do something, or she was going to die.

No, Angela thought that she was with Cliff.

And Angela was trapped in the dark. Angela wouldn't know until...

Suddenly, she saw Marshall Donegal at her side. He drew his phantom sword and swiped at her carrier's neck. The sword slashed right through it. Ashley tried to smile. She felt her lips move. She did have some…some…no… She tried to lift her head, but she could not.

But a real-life rock in front of the man nearly tripped him; he stumbled. She was a deadweight, she remembered, even if she wasn't near the weight he must have struggled with when he attacked Charles Osgood.

She heard the faint sound of a creaking once again, and she realized that she was being brought into her family tomb; the temple tomb.

She felt it! She felt pain when her body was slammed down on the central altar in the tomb. Pain meant life. The still rising moon shed an eerie yellow illumination into the tomb through the grate in the far wall.

She heard her attacker working quickly, lifting the heavy marble siding from one of the shelf tombs nearby.

Marshall Donegal's tomb.

He turned to her, smiling.

She knew him before she saw his face. HJH. His wife had been Ginnie. Ginnie Hilton. And Ramsay Clayton had written a letter to her for her husband, Henry James Hilton, because Hilton's hand had been broken. It hadn't been broken in the skirmish; it had been broken when he had attacked Emma Donegal and Harold Boudreaux had set upon him, dragging him off the woman he had so brutally attacked.

"Ashley, you see me! I should have known that

you would see me. You were always so special. So precious. And now..."

He paused, listening. There was commotion going on; people shouting. She couldn't understand them, but she knew that they were searching the grounds. Angela had known where she was going, and by now they had surely found Cliff, and they would be looking for her.

She twitched her lips and managed to smile at him in return. She couldn't speak. She willed him to understand her thoughts.

*They'll know that it was you. Angela will be reading those old letters, and they'll figure it out faster than I did. They'll know. They already know that it's a sick grudge you have against my family. So, your ancestor died in the war—because his hand was broken. No one blamed Harold Boudreaux for what he did to your ancestor, because his fellow rebels knew what had happened when they saw Henry's broken hand; they were appalled that he'd attacked Emma. They didn't string up Harold Boudreaux, but they didn't speak about any of it, either. All for honor! Well, the honor here died with Marshall Donegal, didn't it? And you can't stand that. Well, I may die, but you will, too. They'll catch you, and you'll rot in prison until they stick a needle in your arm, and that will be fitting, won't it?*

He stared at her, his face growing mottled, as if he could hear her thoughts. Of course, he couldn't—he just saw that she had figured out the truth.

He slapped her, and she felt the sting again. Had he attacked so many people now that he was running out of his drug cocktail?

Perhaps she shouldn't be so happy to *feel*. She didn't know how he intended for her to die. And they were in the vault now with the gate locked. Even if they searched the cemetery, they wouldn't think to look *in* the vault. The gates hadn't been opened since her father had died; the tomb was sealed after every interment.

Yes, they had. Sometime while he'd been on the property, Griffin Grant had unlocked the iron gates and unsealed the tomb entrance. He had planned for a very long time to see that she came here.

The iron gates were closed, as if they'd never been open. The concrete sliding door behind the ornamental iron gates was barely ajar.

"I'll come back and see you, my dear Ashley," he promised. "And you won't try to enter my mind, then. You'll be dead. Everyone pays, Ashley. It's your turn to pay for the sins of your fathers. *You* have it all wrong. I know, because Henry talks to me. He told me that he needed to be avenged. He died at Manassas, but he died because he couldn't shoot. He died— because of Emma, and she was a filthy whore who teased and tormented him. Ashley, I saw the letter years ago, and then I could hear him—I could hear him crying out to me. Someone had to avenge what had happened."

She tried to move her lips. *Emma was not a whore. She was a grieving widow.*

"He came to see her, to take care of her. She led him on, Ashley. I've seen you do it, too. So many of your kind do it. You're like her. Everyone just thinks that you're honest and caring. But, you see, she didn't pay. You will. I thought it might be hard, Ashley. Do you realize that? I thought it might be hard to kill. Ramsay would have done just as well as Charles. That didn't matter. The newswoman, well, she was like a rabid dog. And that ridiculous Toby huffing on over…he wasn't quite so easy. But you know what, Ashley?"

His face came close to hers, and he smiled. She loathed him; she wanted to back away from him. She couldn't move.

"Killing is fun. I found out I like it. But this may be the finale. Ashley, beautiful blonde Ashley, the last of the true Donegals—dead with her ancestors. Oh, watching you, Ashley. My ancestor never told me it would feel so good!"

He lifted her again. To her horror, she realized that one of the heavy slabs had been removed from the shelves on each side of the tomb.

He rolled her into one of them.

It was dark in the burial ledge within the tomb, and she couldn't see. Somehow, she knew that she was nestled against the disintegrating fragments of Marshall Donegal's skull.

"And so it is done!"

She heard the faint sound of scraping as the side slab was lifted and slid back into place. And the world, with or without the remnants of her ancestors, was pitch-black.

The generator lights had finally kicked on, but they didn't offer that much illumination. Still, it was better than the murky gray they'd had before, eased only by the glow of the moon.

He'd shouted for the others, but he hadn't needed to do so. They'd heard the commotion and come running, and quickly understood that Cliff had been attacked, and Ashley was missing.

Jake was beside himself; he knew that he needed to think. Running in a thousand different directions wouldn't serve him well.

Where could the killer have taken her so quickly?

"Whitney, mount up with Will—take the woods toward the bayou, look around for freshly disturbed dirt or a stone in the ground, a grave site. Angela, I'm going into the cemetery—"

"I just ran through the cemetery. There's no one there," Angela said, disheartened. "I ran through every row of tombs, Jake, I swear!"

"We need an ambulance for Cliff—"

"Called already," Angela assured him.

"Is she in the house? Could she have gone back into the house?" Jake demanded.

"I don't know—I'll check."

"I'll go—stick with Jackson!" he shouted.

Jake tore through the back door. He sped through the ground floor, shouting her name. He hurried to the second floor, nearly wrenching doors from their handles.

He burst in on Frazier, who was just rising. Apparently, he hadn't heard the commotion, and, sleeping, hadn't realized that they'd lost power.

"Jake? What is it?" he demanded. Then with some innate instinct, he cried out, "Ashley—something has happened to Ashley!"

"She's missing, but I'll find her—I swear, I'll find her," Jake said and tore out of the room. He looked at the attic stairs, and he raced up to the attic.

She wasn't there. He started to turn. But then he stopped, seeing someone else.

Emma Donegal. She was pointing at an open cabinet. He stared at her, not understanding. She pointed straight to a letter in the cabinet. "There's no time," he whispered desperately. But he picked up the paper, and heard her voice. "Read it!" So he did, squinting.

And as he read, he saw the painting in the office-reception area of the Southern cavalry man—who had died at Manassas. Who had been injured before he'd gotten to Manassas.

They'd been so close…

And now it was so clear. Ramsay was just afraid.

And Griffin was a practiced liar, a totally functioning sociopath.

He dropped the letter, and went racing out of the house.

"It's Grant!" he roared as he hurried out. "Griffin Grant! He's out there, and he's got Ashley!"

Jackson gripped his arm. "We'll find her. How do you know—"

"His ancestor was a Hilton. Hilton died at Manassas. He died because his hand never healed correctly—at least that's what Grant must think… He's got Ashley out there somewhere. We have to find her."

"How the hell did he get on the property unseen?" Jackson demanded.

"The hay truck! He must have sent that extra delivery of hay. He got on the hay truck," Whitney said.

Jake saw that Cliff was on the ground, but Jenna, always the caregiver, was down at his side taking his pulse. She looked up at Jake. "His pulse is steady, and his breathing isn't affected. He's going to be okay."

Cliff lifted a hand. He was trying to indicate something. *The stall!* Jake realized. Tigger's stall.

He burst into the stall. The horse was nervous. He soothed it, quickly casting his gaze around the floor.

He saw the body bundled beneath hay in the corner and ran to it. He dug away the hay like a maddened dog.

He let out a cry. It wasn't Ashley.

It was Beth.

He lifted her quickly. Her head lolled. "Jenna!"

he shouted, bringing Beth's limp body from the stall.
"Jenna!"

Jenna left Cliff's side. She flashed a light in Beth's
eyes; he noted that the pupils dilated.

"She's alive. There's an ambulance on the way. He
might have overdosed her badly—thank God help is
nearly here. The detective has been called as well."

Help was nearly there. But there was no sign of
Ashley.

Jake started. This time, he saw a man.

A man in full Confederate dress; his sword in a
hilt at his side, secured by a butternut-colored sash.
The man beckoned to him with hands encased in
cavalry gloves.

Jake started walking.

A frown knit his brow. Angela had just said that
she'd searched the cemetery. Angela was thorough,
and she didn't lie.

But the ghost wanted him to follow.

The ghost of Marshall Donegal.

And so he did.

He was dimly aware of the sounds behind him
as he walked forward. Jenna was dealing with both
her patients; Whitney and Will were mounting up
to search the woods before the bayou; Jackson and
Angela were hurrying out to search the guest building, empty now for days.

He walked to the gate, and it swung out slightly
as if to invite him. He walked through the gate, and
he drew the gun that he wore in his belt holster when

he was on official business. He moved through the cemetery; like Angela, he saw nothing.

He started to hurry, making his way to the chapel in the back, and he nearly tore the door from its hinges there; he shined his light into every corner, but there was no sign of Ashley.

He turned around, and the ghost was there again, beckoning him—and showing him the way.

He ran through the trails of the small city of the dead, through temple tombs, through step tombs, pyramid tombs and every manner of tomb that had been built through the centuries.

He knew where he would end.

The ghost stood before the Donegal vault. The slab was in place; the wrought-iron gate was closed. The ghost stared at him with aggravation and turned and tugged at the gate.

Jake burst forward and tugged at the wrought iron himself; it swung open far too easily. He pushed at the concrete barrier that was usually resealed after every interment.

And it, too, gave.

The ghost was trying to speak to him; he had no time to listen. He shoved at the thin sealing slab again, and it fell backward, bursting into a million pieces in a cloud of concrete dust.

"Ashley!" He screamed her name.

Nothing.

The moon cast a yellow glow through the grating, and he blinked, adjusting his eyes to the more muted light. He moved to the altar and saw that something had lain there. The dust was disturbed. He turned...

Not quickly enough. Someone slammed into him hard; his gun went flying from his hand as he staggered for balance.

*Griffin!*

The man was using himself as a ram against Jake and trying to stab him at the same time. Jake saw his arm rise, and he saw the needle coming at him, and he, in turn, used his body and slammed back against his attacker with all his weight.

Griffin fell back a foot.

Jake caught his attacker's wrist, squeezed with all of his strength, and the needle went flying across the tomb.

But his attacker made a dive for Jake's gun. In the murky light of the tomb, he struggled desperately to keep his attacker from twisting the barrel of the gun toward his head or chest. He roundhouse-kicked his opponent, keeping a desperate and rigid hold on the gun, and the man grunted and gave slightly, but when Jake tried to use the advantage to wrest the gun fully from him, the fellow came at him, biting like a dog.

Jake shoved him off when he came straight for his throat. The gun went flying across the room.

He set at his attacker with his bare hands, but Griffin Grant had now pulled a knife from a sheath at his ankle. They were fighting blindly, but he still felt the man, felt the movement in the air, and he ducked the man's wild swing.

"You can't fight any better than your scumbag rapist of an ancestor, Grant!" Jake taunted him. He needed to get the knife; he'd never find the gun in the darkness.

Provoking him worked. Grant let out a roar and came crashing across the tomb.

That time, he nicked Jake's arm. But Jake heard the knife slide against marble and concrete and made a dash across the tomb, pinning the man there.

The knife went clattering to the floor, and the two of them fell along with it, engaged in a wrestling match that would surely leave one dead. Jake struggled for the top spot; Grant locked his legs around him in a vise, twisting him beneath. His hands came around Jake's throat, but Jake caught him with a double-fisted slam against the head.

Grant teetered.

And then the side of the one of the tombs slammed against him, throwing him off. Ashley, covered in bone and ash, emerged. Jake leapt to his feet, reaching for her swiftly and drawing her to her feet.

Grant came at his back, slamming his fists hard against him, sending Jake staggering forward, his arms enveloping Ashley lest she crash against something again. She was slipping and falling; she had no strength in her legs. He had to help her, had to protect her...

He turned his back to her, ready to withstand

Grant's next massive lunge. Grant was ready to make another ram against Jake, but suddenly an ear-splitting roar seemed to echo through the tomb, and Grant dropped to the ground; his body shuddered mightily once and then didn't move again.

Jake blinked.

Frazier was standing at the entrance to the tomb, the lost gun still smoking in his hands.

"Grampa!" Ashley said. "You go, Grampa!"

Then she collapsed in Jake's arms.

# Epilogue

"I still don't really fathom how a mind can become so unhinged. I mean, seriously, how do you carry hatred through this many generations?" Ashley asked Jake. "He told me that he heard his ancestor, Henry Hilton, telling him that he had to avenge his family against the Donegal family. His ancestor told him to do it! And I don't know what to believe because… my own ancestor saved me."

They were in the backyard, five days after the event in which Ashley had briefly joined her ancestors in death, convalescing in one of the giant swinging hammocks Cliff had just erected in the back. They could look out on the river as the cool breezes soothed them. It was a pleasant place to let the days go by while they were both "in recovery."

"The very sad truth about humanity is that we've always known how to carry hatred through time immortal, so it seems," Jake said. He gnawed on a piece of grass, just as he had when they were teens. "In Griffin's case, I don't believe that he really had any kind of gift. He would have grown up knowing more about his family's history than anyone else—we all know the little secrets of our own lives better than others. I think he was crazy, that he did just hear voices in his head. He may well have been schizophrenic. He probably showed all the signs when he was younger. It's just that he was so functional, no one saw it. He learned all the tricks." He rolled slightly to look at her. "His secretary said that she heard him in his office talking the day that Marty and Toby were killed. She did, too. When the police went into his office, they found out that he had a recording to play that went on for various lengths of time. That way, people would always swear that he'd been in his office because they'd heard him."

"He was a CEO of a major company."

"Highly functioning. Ashley, the past didn't make him bad. The past made him self-righteous. He did believe that he was like a god, or an avenging angel, to take what he wanted because of the perceived ill that had been done to him." Jake smoothed back a piece of her hair.

"I walloped Cliff," she said.

"He's forgiven you."

"But—I really love him. He's family. How could I have been so easily fooled?"

"Fear—for someone else you love. That's a pretty strong motive, Ashley. Honestly, I'm getting to know Cliff really well again, and he has forgiven you."

She smiled. "So has Beth."

"Beth didn't need to forgive you. She knew that what happened wasn't your fault."

"It wouldn't have happened if she hadn't been here."

"But that's life. The good with the bad," he told her quietly. "And, hey! You know, of course, that the cops found Ramsay. He wasn't doing anything evil—he was just trying to find courage in a bottle down on Bourbon Street."

"Poor Ramsay. He might have been the victim."

"He might have been. But, sadly, what happened worked well into Griffin's hands. Ramsay he'd have had to have coaxed. He knew that Charles would be lured by the promise of a beautiful woman. Ramsay—well, until he went through this period of trauma—Ramsay was a good-looking fellow. I'm glad you turned him down."

"The feeling just wasn't there," she said. She shuddered. "I turned Griffin down once, years ago. He'd asked me to be his escort to some kind of advertisers' function."

"Thank God you turned them both down," he said, his tone husky. He pulled her closer and faced her. "Beth is well, and Cliff is well, and I'm the one in the worst shape—feel sorry for me!" he commanded.

She laughed. He didn't mean it. He was full of bruises and cuts, but he didn't seem to mind them.

Nor did he seem to mind that others were handling the press, the paperwork and all other pieces of business that had to do with the case being over. He didn't seem to hurt too badly when they were alone at night making love, and he didn't wince at all when she kissed his bruises.

"You're thoughtful," she said.

"We still have one more piece of business," he told her. He rolled off the hammock, drawing her with him.

"Where are we going?"

"The cemetery," he told her.

She pulled back at that, but just for a minute.

"And we're going to... Oh! I see!"

They followed the path to the Donegal tomb, but they didn't stand in front of it. Jake led Ashley to the tomb of the long-dead World War I hero, and he and Ashley sat.

"Emma, your husband loves you," he said. "He loves you desperately. He loved Harold as well, and he's grateful that Harold was there to rescue you. He knows that you held your love for him in your heart all of your life, and he knows that you were treated cruelly. He just wants to love you."

"Your turn," he told Ashley.

"Marshall Donegal, you get your little ethereal backside out here! You're afraid to face your wife. You're afraid that she grew beyond her love for you, because life became so hard once you were gone. Come on, you two kids—I think this is it. Your chance at...your chance at eternal happiness," she added softly.

At first, nothing.

And then slowly, very slowly, and like pale illusions in the bright daylight, they both began to appear. She walked slowly from the path; he emerged from the side of the tomb.

She eased out to him.

He took a step.

They ran into one another's arms.

In the daylight, so locked together, they faded into the sunlight.

There were tears on Ashley's cheeks.

Jake smoothed them away. "Hey, they've found their eternal happiness," he told her, lifting her chin and dusting her lips with a gentle kiss.

She smiled.

"And I've found mine," she told him.

Yet, as the kiss grew passionate, it was suddenly disrupted.

"Jake!" Jackson called from the house. The tone of his voice was urgent.

Jake sighed. "Well, that's my world now, I'm afraid."

She didn't release him; she held him close for another minute.

"Jake, your world is now my world, in so many ways."

They kissed again.

Jackson shouted again.

But…

Jackson was a decent fellow. He'd just have to wait.

\* \* \* \* \*

One of my favorite meals in Louisiana is crawfish étouffée—I had it first in plantation country, and I've been hooked ever since! Shrimp can be substituted for crawfish. The major trick with this dish is to follow the part that says *slowly brown*....

# Crawfish Étouffée

*Ingredients*

- ½ cup roux (brown ¼ cup oil and ¼ flour, adding a pat of butter—slowly so that it does not burn!)
- ½ cup finely chopped onion
- ½ cup finely chopped bell pepper
- 1 small can diced tomatoes
- 3 cloves finely chopped garlic
- 2 cups water
- 3 lbs of cleaned crawfish meat
- 1 tsp. salt
- 1 tsp. pepper
- dash of cayenne

*Directions*

Simmer, adding chopped white onions and bell pepper. When a nice soft consistency has been reached, add in the diced tomatoes, garlic, water and seasoning. Stir this mixture constantly over medium-high heat until all ingredients are evenly combined. Cover the pan, reduce to a low heat and allow it all to simmer for 15 to 20 minutes. Next, add the crawfish (or shrimp) and bring the mixture to a boil, bring to a low boil for about five minutes or so, and then bring back to low heat. Serve over fluffy white rice.

*Mix up a green salad,*
*cut some French bread and enjoy!*

This Southern favorite is as easy as...mint!

# Mint Julep

## Ingredients

4 or 5 fresh mint leaves

Jigger bourbon whiskey

Powdered sugar (or cane sugar, or even substitute)

Water

## Directions

Mix mint and sugar in a tall glass. Add a jigger of water and stir lightly, top with bourbon whiskey and serve with a straw and topping sprig of mint!

# REQUEST YOUR FREE BOOKS!

## 2 FREE NOVELS FROM THE PARANORMAL ROMANCE COLLECTION PLUS 2 FREE GIFTS!

PARA11

# HEATHER GRAHAM

| | | | |
|---|---|---|---|
| 77486 | NIGHT OF THE VAMPIRES | ___ $7.99 U.S. | ___ $9.99 CAN. |
| 77404 | NIGHT OF THE WOLVES | ___ $7.99 U.S. | ___ $9.99 CAN. |
| 61844 | THE KEEPERS | ___ $5.25 U.S. | ___ $6.25 CAN. |
| 32998 | HEART OF EVIL | ___ $7.99 U.S. | ___ $9.99 CAN. |
| 32956 | PHANTOM EVIL | ___ $24.95 U.S. | ___ $27.95 CAN. |
| 32939 | THE KILLING EDGE | ___ $7.99 U.S. | ___ $9.99 CAN. |
| 32928 | THE PRESENCE | ___ $7.99 U.S. | ___ $9.99 CAN. |
| 32916 | THE SÉANCE | ___ $7.99 U.S. | ___ $9.99 CAN. |
| 32915 | THE VISION | ___ $7.99 U.S. | ___ $9.99 CAN. |
| 32900 | GHOST WALK | ___ $7.99 U.S. | ___ $9.99 CAN. |
| 32823 | HOME IN TIME FOR CHRISTMAS | ___ $7.99 U.S. | ___ $9.99 CAN. |
| 32815 | GHOST NIGHT | ___ $7.99 U.S. | ___ $9.99 CAN. |
| 32796 | GHOST MOON | ___ $7.99 U.S. | ___ $9.99 CAN. |
| 32791 | GHOST SHADOW | ___ $7.99 U.S. | ___ $9.99 CAN. |
| 32758 | NIGHTWALKER | ___ $7.99 U.S. | ___ $9.99 CAN. |
| 32676 | UNHALLOWED GROUND | ___ $7.99 U.S. | ___ $9.99 CAN. |
| 32654 | DUST TO DUST | ___ $7.99 U.S. | ___ $8.99 CAN. |
| 32625 | THE DEATH DEALER | ___ $7.99 U.S. | ___ $7.99 CAN. |
| 32585 | DEADLY NIGHT | ___ $7.99 U.S. | ___ $9.99 CAN. |

*(limited quantities available)*

| | |
|---|---|
| TOTAL AMOUNT | $ _____ |
| POSTAGE & HANDLING | $ _____ |
| ($1.00 for 1 book, 50¢ for each additional) | |
| APPLICABLE TAXES* | $ _____ |
| TOTAL PAYABLE | $ _____ |

*(check or money order—please do not send cash)*

To order, complete this form and send it, along with a check or money order for the total above, payable to MIRA Books, to: **In the U.S.:** 3010 Walden Avenue, P.O. Box 9077, Buffalo, NY 14269-9077; **In Canada:** P.O. Box 636, Fort Erie, Ontario, L2A 5X3.

Name: _____

Address: _____ City: _____

State/Prov.: _____ Zip/Postal Code: _____

Account Number (if applicable): _____

075 CSAS

\*New York residents remit applicable sales taxes.
\*Canadian residents remit applicable GST and provincial taxes.

31901050674672